AF147786

Hans of Iceland
Vol. 2
The Last Day of a Condemned

by

Victor Hugo

Hans of Iceland
Vol. 2
The Last Day of a Condemned
by Victor Hugo

Copyright © 2024

All Rights reserved.

No part of this publication may be reproduced, stored in a retrieval system, or transmitted in any form or by any means, electronic, mechanical, photocopying or Otherwise, without the written permission of the publisher.
The author/editor asserts the moral right to be identified as the author/editor of this work.

ISBN: 978-93-62205-01-8

Published by

DOUBLE 9 BOOKS
2/13-B, Ansari Road
Daryaganj, New Delhi – 110002
info@double9books.com
www.double9books.com
Tel. 011-40042856

This book is under public domain

ABOUT THE AUTHOR

A politician and writer of the French Romantic movement, Victor-Marie Hugo. He is acknowledged as one of France's greatest writers of all time. The Hunchback of Notre-Dame (1831) and Les Misérables are two of his most well-known compositions (1862). In his lifetime, he created more than 4,000 drawings and advocated for social concerns including the repeal of the death penalty. On February 26, 1802, Victor-Marie Hugo was born in Besançon. He was the youngest child of Sophie Trébuchet and Joseph Léopold Sigisbert Hugo. Against the desires of his mother, he fell in love with Adèle Foucher, and in 1816 they secretly were married. François-René de Chateaubriand had a significant impact on him. At the age of 20, Hugo's first book of poetry, Odes et poésies diverses, was released. With the dramas Cromwell (1827) and Hernani (1830), Hugo rose to prominence as the representative of the Romantic literary movement (1830). After being published in 1831, his book Notre-Dame de Paris (The Hunchback of Notre Dame) was swiftly translated into various languages throughout Europe. Hugo's best-known work, Les Misérables, was released in 1862. Hugo's pneumonia-related death on May 22, 1885, at the age of 83, sparked protracted national sorrow. In addition to being admired as a literary giant, he was a statesman who helped establish the Third Republic and democracy in France.

CONTENTS

HANS OF ICELAND

THE LAST DAY OF A CONDEMNED

HANS OF ICELAND

XXX

Peter, good fellow, has lost his all at dice.—Régnier.

THE regiment of musketeers from Munkholm was on the march through the narrow passes lying between Throndhjem and Skongen. Sometimes it moved along the brink of a torrent, and the long line of bayonets crept through the ravine like a huge serpent with glittering scales; sometimes it wound around a mountain, making it look like one of those triumphal columns about which curves an army of heroes in bronze.

The soldiers marched with trailing weapons and cloaks dragging in the dust, looking surly and tired, for these noble fellows are averse to anything but battle or inaction. The coarse banter and threadbare jests which delighted them but yesterday had lost their savor. The air was chill, the sky clouded. Nothing would raise a laugh in the ranks, unless one of the sutler-women should get an awkward tumble from her little Barbary horse, or a tin saucepan should happen to roll over the precipice and rebound from rock to rock.

To while away the monotony of the journey, Lieutenant Randmer, a young Danish baron, accosted old Captain Lory, who had risen from the ranks. The captain, moody and silent, moved with a heavy but confident step; the lieutenant, light and agile, played with a twig which he had plucked from the bushes that lined the read.

"Well, Captain, what ails you? You seem depressed."

"And I should say I had good cause," replied the old officer, without raising his eyes.

"Come, come, no regrets! Look at me. Am I depressed? And yet I would wager that I have quite as much cause as you."

"I doubt it, Baron Randmer; I have lost all I possessed; I have lost everything I loved."

"Captain Lory, our misfortunes are precisely the same. It is not a fortnight since Lieutenant Alberick won my castle and estate at a single deal of the cards. I am ruined; but am I the less gay?"

The captain answered in a very melancholy tone: "Lieutenant, you have only lost your castle; but I have lost my dog."

At this answer the light-minded baron seemed uncertain whether to laugh or sympathize; but he said: "Be comforted, Captain. Only think, I, who have lost my castle—"

The captain broke in upon his words:—

"What of that? Besides, you may win back another castle."

"And you may find another dog."

The old man shook his head.

"I may find another dog, but I shall never find my poor Drake."

He paused; great tears gathered in his eyes and rolled one by one down his hard, stern face.

"He was all I ever had to love," he added; "I never knew my parents. God grant them peace, and my poor Drake too! Lieutenant Randmer, he saved my life in the Pomeranian war. I called him Drake in honor of the famous admiral. My good dog! He never changed, as did my fortunes. After the battle of Oholfen, the great General Schack patted him, and said: 'You've a fine dog there, Sergeant Lory!'—for I was only a sergeant then."

"Ah!" interrupted the young baron, slashing his switch, "how queer it must seem to be a sergeant."

The old soldier of fortune did not hear him; he appeared to be talking to himself, and Randmer could only catch a word here and there.

"Poor Drake! After surviving so many breaches and trenches, to be drowned like a blind kitten in that confounded Throndhjem fjord! My poor dog! my trusty friend! You deserved to die on the field of battle, as I hope to do."

"Come, come, Captain!" cried the lieutenant, "how can you be so despondent? We may get a chance to fight to-morrow."

"Yes," contemptuously answered the old captain, "with a pretty enemy!"

"What! do you despise those rascally miners, those devilish mountaineers?"

"Stone-cutters, highwaymen, fellows who don't know the first rudiments of warfare! A fine set of blackguards to face a man like me, who has served in all the wars in Pomerania and Holstein, in the campaigns of Scania and Dalecarlia; who fought under the glorious General Schack and the brave Count Guldenlew!"

"But don't you know," interrupted Randmer, "that these fellows are led by a formidable chief,—a giant as big and as brutal as Goliath, a rascal who drinks nothing but human blood, a very Satan incarnate?"

"And who may he be?" asked the captain.

"Why, the famous Hans of Iceland!"

"Pooh! I'll wager that this great general does not know how to shoulder a musket or handle a carbine properly."

Randmer laughed.

"Yes, you may laugh," continued the captain. "It will be very funny, no doubt, to cross swords with scurvy pickaxes, and pikes with pitchforks! Here are worthy foes indeed! My brave Drake would have scorned to snap at their heels!"

The captain was still giving free vent to his indignation, when he was interrupted by the arrival of an officer, who ran up to them all out of breath,—

"Captain Lory! my dear Randmer!"

"Well?" asked both at once.

"My friends, I am faint with horror! D'Ahlefeld, Lieutenant d'Ahlefeld, the lord chancellor's son! You know, my dear Randmer, that Frederic—such a dandy! such a fop!"

"Yes," replied the young baron, "a great dandy! Still, at the last ball at Charlottenburg my costume was in much better taste than his. But what has happened to him?"

"I know whom you mean," said Lory; "you mean Frederic d'Ahlefeld, lieutenant of Company Three. The men wear blue facings. He neglects his duty sadly."

"You will not have to complain of him again, Captain Lory."

"Why not?" said Randmer.

"He is garrisoned at Wahlstrom," coldly added the old officer.

"Exactly," said the new-comer; "the colonel has just received a message. Poor Frederic!"

"But what has happened? Captain Bollar, you alarm me."

Old Lory added: "Nonsense! The popinjay was absent from roll-call, I suppose, and the captain has sent the lord chancellor's son to prison: that is the misfortune which distresses you so sadly; I am sure it is."

Bollar clapped him on the shoulder.

"Captain Lory, Lieutenant d'Ahlefeld has been devoured alive."

The two captains looked each other in the face; and Randmer, startled for an instant, suddenly burst out laughing.

"Oh, Captain Bollar, I see you are as fond of a joke as ever! But you can't fool me in that way, I warn you."

And the lieutenant, folding his arms, gave way to mirth, swearing that what amused him the most was to see how readily Lory swallowed all Bollar's ridiculous stories. As for the story, he said it was a capital one; and it was a most clever idea to pretend that Frederic, who took such dainty, such absurd care of his complexion, had been swallowed raw.

"Randmer," said Bollar, seriously, "you act like a fool. I tell you d'Ahlefeld is dead; I have it from the colonel,—dead!"

"Oh, how well you play your part!" rejoined the baron, still laughing; "what a funny fellow you are!"

Bollar shrugged his shoulders, and turned to old Lory, who quietly asked the particulars.

"Oh, yes, my dear Captain Bollar," added the irrepressible mocker; "tell us who ate the poor devil. Did he serve as breakfast for a wolf, or supper for a bear?"

"The colonel," said Bollar, "received a despatch just now, informing him, in the first place, that the Wahlstrom garrison is retreating toward us, driven back by a large party of rebels."

Old Lory frowned.

"In the second place," resumed Bollar, "that Lieutenant Frederic d'Ahlefeld, having gone into the mountains three days since to hunt, was captured near Arbar ruins by a monster, who carried him to his lair and there devoured him."

At this, Lieutenant Randmer's merriment increased.

"Oh, how our good Lory swallows your stories! That's right; keep up a sober face, Bollar. You are wonderfully amusing; but you don't tell us what this monster, this ogre, this vampire was, that carried off and ate up the lieutenant like a week-old kid!"

"I will not tell you," impatiently answered Bollar; "but I will tell Lory, who is not such an incredulous fool. Lory, my dear fellow, the monster who drank Frederic's blood was Hans of Iceland."

"The leader of the rebels!" exclaimed the old officer.

"Well, Lory," rejoined the scoffer, "do you think a man who handles his jaw so ably needs to know how to shoulder a musket?"

"Baron Randmer," said Bollar, "you are very like d'Ahlefeld in character; beware lest you meet with the same fate."

"I declare," cried Randmer, "that Captain Bollar's immovable gravity amuses me beyond expression."

"And Lieutenant Randmer's inexhaustible laughter alarms me more than I can say."

At this moment a group of officers, engaged in eager conversation, approached our three speakers.

"Zounds!" cried Randmer, "I must amuse them with Bollar's story."

"Comrades," he added, advancing to meet them; "have you heard the news? Poor Frederic d'Ahlefeld has been eaten alive by the barbarous Hans of Iceland."

As he said these words, he could not repress a burst of laughter, which, to his great surprise, was received by the new-comers almost with shouts of indignation.

"What! can you laugh? I did not think, Randmer, that you would repeat such a dreadful piece of news so lightly. How can you laugh at such a misfortune?"

"What!" said Randmer, much confused, "is it really true?"

"Why, you just told us of it yourself!" was the general cry. "Don't you believe your own words?"

"But I thought it was one of Bollar's jokes."

An old officer interposed.

"Such a joke would be in very bad taste; but unfortunately it is no joke. Baron Vœthaün, our colonel, has just received the sad news."

"A fearful affair! It is really awful!" repeated a dozen voices.

"So we are to fight wolves and bears with human faces," said one.

"We are to be shot down," said another, "without knowing whence the bullet comes; we are to be picked off one by one, like birds in a cage."

"D'Ahlefeld's death," said Bollar, in a solemn tone, "makes me shudder. Our regiment is unlucky. Dispolsen's murder, that of those poor soldiers found dead at Cascadthymore, d'Ahlefeld's awful fate,—here are three tragic events in a very short space of time."

Young Baron Randmer, who had been silent, looked up.

"It is incredible," said he; "Frederic, who danced so well!"

And after this weighty remark he relapsed into silence, while Captain Lory declared that he was greatly distressed at the young lieutenant's death, and drew the attention of private Toric-Belfast to the fact that the brass clasp of his shoulder-belt was not so bright as usual.

XXXI

"Hush, hush! here comes a man climbing down a ladder."

"Oh, yes; he is a spy."

"Heaven could grant me no greater favor than to let me offer you—my life. I am yours; but tell me, for mercy's sake, to whom does this army belong?"

"To a count from Barcelona."

"What count?"

"What is it?"

"General, one of the enemy's spies."

"Whence come you?"

"I came here, little dreaming what I should find; little thinking what I should see."—Lope de Vega: *La Fuerza Lastimosa.*

THERE is something desolate and forbidding in the aspect of a bare, flat region when the sun has set, when one is alone; when, as he walks, he tramples the dry grass beneath his feet, the dead brown leaves drop rustling from the trees, he hears the monotonous cry of the cricket, and sees huge, shapeless clouds sink slowly on the horizon like dead ghosts.

Such were Ordener's gloomy reflections on the night of his vain encounter with the Iceland robber. Startled by his abrupt disappearance, he at first tried to pursue him; but he lost his way in the heather, and wandered all day through a wild and uncultivated country, where he found no trace of man. At nightfall he was in a vast plain stretching to the horizon on every side, where there seemed no hope of shelter for the young traveller exhausted by fatigue and hunger.

It would have been a slight relief if his bodily suffering had not been aggravated by mental distress; but all was over. He had reached his journey's end without accomplishing his purpose. He could not even cherish those foolish illusions of hope which had urged him to pursue the monster; and now that nothing was left to sustain his courage, countless discouraging thoughts, for which he had hitherto had no room, assailed him. What could he do? How could he return to Schumacker unless he could take with him Ethel's salvation? What was the frightful nature of the misfortune which the possession of the fatal casket would prevent, and what of his marriage to Ulrica d'Ahlefeld? If he could only free his Ethel from her undeserved captivity; if he could fly with her, and enjoy uninterrupted happiness in some distant exile!

He wrapped himself in his mantle, and threw himself upon the ground. The sky was dark; a tempestuous light ever and anon appeared in the clouds as if through a veil of crape and then vanished; a cold wind swept across the plain. The young man scarcely heeded these signs of an immediate and violent storm; and besides, even could he have found shelter from the tempest and a place to rest from his fatigues, could he have found a spot where he might avoid his misery or rest from thought?

All at once confused sounds of men's voices fell upon his ear. In surprise, he rose upon his elbow, and perceived at some distance a number of shadowy forms moving through the darkness. He looked again; a light shone in the midst of the mysterious group, and Ordener, with astonishment which may easily be imagined, saw the weird forms sink one after the other into the centre of the earth, until all had disappeared.

Ordener was above the superstitions of his age and country. His serious and mature mind knew none of those vain beliefs, those strange terrors, which torture the childhood of a race as well as the childhood of a man. And yet there was something supernatural about this singular vision which filled him with devout distrust against his better judgment; for who can tell whether the spirits of the dead may not sometimes return to earth?

He rose, made the sign of the cross, and walked toward the spot where the apparition vanished.

Big drops of rain now began to fall; his cloak filled like a sail, and the feather in his cap, beaten by the wind, flapped in his face.

He stopped suddenly. A flash of lightning revealed just at his feet a large, round well, into which he must inevitably have fallen headlong had it not have been for this friendly warning. He approached the abyss. A faint light was visible at a fearful depth, and cast a red glow over the bottom of this huge opening in the bowels of the earth. The light, which seemed like a magic fire kindled by elves, only increased the immeasurable darkness which the eye was forced to pierce before reaching it.

The dauntless youth leaned over the abyss and listened. A distant murmur of voices rose to his ear. He no longer doubted that the beings who had so strangely appeared and disappeared before his very eyes had plunged into this gulf, and he felt an unconquerable desire, doubtless because it was so fated, to follow them, even should he pursue spectres to the mouth of hell. Moreover, the tempest now burst with fury, and this hole would afford him a shelter; but how was he to descend? What road had those he longed to follow taken, if indeed they were not phantoms? A second flash came to his aid, and showed him at his feet a ladder leading into the depths of the well. It consisted of a strong upright beam, crossed at regular intervals by short iron bars for the hands and feet of those who might venture into the gulf below.

Ordener did not hesitate. He swung himself boldly down upon the dreadful ladder, and plunged into the abyss without knowing whether it reached the bottom or not,—without reflecting that he might never again see the sun. Soon he could only distinguish the sky from the darkness overhead by the bluish flashes which lit it up at brief intervals; soon the rain pouring in torrents upon the surface of the earth, reached him merely as a fine, vaporous mist. Then the whirlwind, rushing violently into the well, was lost above him in a prolonged moan. He went down and down, and yet seemed scarcely nearer to the subterranean light. He went on without losing heart, never looking below lest he should become dizzy and fall.

However, the air becoming more and more stifling, the sound of voices more and more distinct, and the purplish glow which began to tinge the walls of the pit, warned him that he was not far from the bottom. He descended a few more rounds, and saw plainly at the foot of the ladder the entrance to an underground passage lighted by a flickering red flame, while his ear caught words which won his entire attention.

"Kennybol does not come," said an impatient voice.

"What can detain him?" repeated the same voice, after a brief pause.

"No one knows, Mr. Hacket," was the reply.

"He intended to spend the night with his sister, Maase Braal, in the village of Surb," added a different voice.

"You see," rejoined the first speaker, "I keep my promises. I agreed to bring Hans of Iceland for your leader. I have brought him."

An indistinct murmur followed these words. Ordener's curiosity, already aroused by the name of Kennybol, who had so astonished him the night before, was redoubled at the name of Hans of Iceland.

The same voice continued:—

"My friends, Jonas, Norbith, what matters it if Kennybol is late? There are enough of us; we need fear nothing. Did you find your standards at Crag ruins?"

"Yes, Mr. Hacket," replied several voices.

"Well, raise your banners; it is high time! Here is gold! Here is your invincible chief! Courage! March to the rescue of the noble Schumacker, the unfortunate Count Griffenfeld!"

"Hurrah! hurrah for Schumacker!" repeated many voices; and the name of Schumacker echoed and re-echoed from the subterranean arches.

Ordener, more and more curious, more and more amazed, listened, hardly daring to breathe. He could neither believe nor understand what he heard. Schumacker connected with Kennybol and Hans of Iceland! What was this dark drama, one scene in which he, an unsuspected spectator, had witnessed? Whose life did they wish to shield? Whose head was at stake?

"In me," continued the same voice, "you see the friend and confidant of the noble Count Griffenfeld."

The voice was wholly unfamiliar to Ordener. It went on: "Put implicit trust in me, as he does. Friends, everything is in your favor; you will reach Throndhjem without meeting an enemy."

"Let us be off, Mr. Hacket," interrupted a voice. "Peters told me that he saw the whole regiment from Munkholm marching through the mountain-passes to attack us."

"He deceived you," replied the other, in authoritative tones. "The government as yet knows nothing of your revolt, and it is so wholly unsuspicious that the man who rejected your just complaints—your oppressor, the oppressor of the illustrious and unfortunate Schumacker, General Levin de Knud—has left Throndhjem for the capital, to join in the festivities on the occasion of the marriage of his ward, Ordener Guldenlew, and Ulrica d'Ahlefeld."

Ordener's feelings may be imagined. To hear all these names which interested him so deeply, and even his own, uttered by unknown voices in this wild, desolate region, in this mysterious tunnel! A frightful thought pierced his soul. Could it be true? Was it indeed an agent of Count Griffenfeld whose voice he heard? What! could Schumacker, that venerable old man, his noble Ethel's noble father, revolt against his royal master, hire brigands, and kindle a civil war? And it was for this hypocrite, this rebel, that he, the son of the Norwegian viceroy, the pupil of General Levin, had compromised his future and risked his life! It was for his sake that he had sought and fought with that Iceland bandit with whom Schumacker seemed to be in league, since he placed him at the head of these scoundrels! Who knows but that casket for which he, Ordener, was on the point of shedding his lifeblood, contained some of the base secrets of this vile plot? Or had the revengeful prisoner of Munkholm made a fool of him? Perhaps he had found out his name; perhaps—and this thought was painful indeed to the generous youth—he wished to ruin the son of an enemy by urging him to this fatal journey!

Alas! when we have long loved and revered the name of an unfortunate man, when in our secret soul we have vowed everlasting devotion to his misfortunes, it is bitter to be repaid with ingratitude, to feel that we are forever disenchanted with generosity, and that we must renounce the pure, sweet joys of loyal self-sacrifice. We grow old in an instant with the most melancholy form of old age; we grow old in experience, and we lose the most beautiful illusion of a life whose only beauty lies in its illusions.

Such were the dispiriting thoughts that crowded confusedly upon Ordener's mind. The noble youth longed to die at that instant; he felt that his happiness had vanished. True, there were many things in the assertions of the man who described himself as Griffenfeld's envoy which struck him as false or doubtful; but these statements, being only meant to deceive a set of poor rustics, Schumacker was but the more guilty in his eyes; and this same Schumacker was his Ethel's father!

These reflections agitated him the more violently because they all thronged upon him at once. He reeled against the rounds of the ladder on which he stood, and listened still; for we sometimes wait with inexplicable impatience and fearful eagerness for the misfortunes which we dread the most.

"Yes," added the voice of the envoy, "you are to be commanded by the much-dreaded Hans of Iceland. Who will dare resist you? You fight for your wives and your children, basely despoiled of their inheritance; for a noble and unfortunate man, who for twenty years has languished unjustly in an infamous prison. Come, for Schumacker and liberty await you. Death to tyrants!"

"Death!" repeated a thousand voices; and the clash of arms rang through the winding cave, mingled with the hoarse note of the mountaineer's horn.

"Stop!" cried Ordener.

He hurriedly descended the remainder of the ladder; for the idea that he might save Schumacker from committing a crime and spare his country untold misery had taken entire possession of him. But as he stood at the mouth of the cave, fear lest he might destroy his Ethel's father, and perhaps his Ethel herself, by rash invectives, took the place of every other consideration, and he remained rooted to the spot, pale, and casting an amazed glance at the singular scene before him.

It was like a vast square in some underground city, whose limits were lost amid endless columns supporting the vaulted roof. These pillars glittered like crystal in the rays of countless torches borne by a multitude of men, armed with strange weapons, and scattered in confusion about the cave. From all these points of light and all these fearful figures straying among the shadows, it might have passed for one of the legendary gatherings described by ancient chroniclers,—an assembly of wizards and demons, bearing stars for torches, and illuminating antique groves and ruined castles by night.

A prolonged shout arose.

"A stranger! Kill him! kill him!"

A hundred arms were raised to strike Ordener down. He put his hand to his side in search of his sword Noble youth! In his generous ardor he had forgotten that he was alone and unarmed.

"Stay! stay!" cried a voice,—the voice of one whom Ordener recognized as Schumacker's envoy.

He was a short, stout man, dressed in black, with a deceitful smile. He advanced toward Ordener, saying: "Who are you?"

Ordener made no answer; he was threatened on every side, and there was not an inch of his breast uncovered by a sword-point or the mouth of a pistol.

"Are you afraid?" asked the little man, with a sneer.

"If your hand were upon my heart, instead of these swords," coldly answered Ordener, "you would see that it beats no faster than your own, if indeed you have a heart."

"Ah, ha!" said the little man; "so you defy us! Well, then let him die!" And he turned his back.

"Give me death," returned Ordener; "it is the only thing that I would accept from you."

"One moment, Mr. Hacket," said an old man, with a thick beard, who stood leaning on a long musket. "You are my guests, and I alone have the right to send this fellow to tell the dead what he has seen."

Mr. Hacket laughed.

"Faith, my dear Jonas, let it be as you please! It matters little to me who judges this spy, so long as he is condemned."

The old man turned to Ordener.

"Come, tell us who you are, since you are so boldly curious to know who we are."

Ordener was silent. Surrounded by the strange allies of that Schumacker for whom he would so willingly have shed his blood, he felt only an infinite longing to die.

"His worship will not answer," said the old man. "When the fox is caught, he cries no more. Kill him!"

"My brave Jonas," rejoined Hacket, "let this man's death be Hans of Iceland's first exploit among you."

"Yes, yes!" cried many voices.

Ordener, astounded, but still undaunted, looked about him for Hans of Iceland, with whom he had so valiantly disputed his life that very morning, and saw with increased surprise a man of colossal size, dressed in the garb of the mountaineers. This giant stared at Ordener with brutal stupidity, and called for an axe.

"You are not Hans of Iceland!" emphatically exclaimed Ordener.

"Kill him! kill him!" cried Hacket, angrily.

Ordener saw that he must die. He put his hand in his bosom to draw out his Ethel's hair and give it one last kiss. As he did so, a paper fell from his belt.

"What is that paper?" asked Hacket. "Norbith, seize that paper."

Norbith was a young man, whose stern, dark features bore the stamp of true nobility. He picked up the paper and unfolded it. "Good God!" he exclaimed, "it is the passport of my poor friend, Christopher Nedlam, that unfortunate fellow who was beheaded not a week ago in Skongen market-place, for coining counterfeit money."

"Well," said Hacket, in a disappointed tone, "you may keep the bit of paper. I thought it was something more important. Come, my dear Hans, despatch your man."

Young Norbith threw himself before Ordener, crying: "This man is under my protection. My head shall fall before you touch a hair of his. I will not suffer the safe-conduct of my friend Christopher Nedlam to be violated."

Ordener, so miraculously preserved, hung his head and felt humiliated; for he remembered how contemptuously he had inwardly received Chaplain Athanasius Munder's touching prayer,—"May the gift of the dying benefit the traveller!"

"Pooh! pooh!" said Hacket, "you talk nonsense, good Norbith. The man is a spy; he must die."

"Give me my axe," repeated the giant.

"He shall not die!" cried Norbith. "What would the spirit of my poor Nedlam say, whom they hung in such cowardly fashion? I tell you he shall not die; for Nedlam will not let him die!"

"As far as that goes," said old Jonas, "Norbith is right. Why should we kill this stranger, Mr. Hacket? He has Christopher Nedlam's pass."

"But he is a spy, a spy!" repeated Hacket.

The old man took his stand with the young one at Ordener's side, and both said quietly: "He has the pass of Christopher Nedlam, who was hung at Skongen."

Hacket saw that he must needs submit; for all the others began to murmur, and to say that this stranger should not die, as he had the safe-conduct of Nedlam the counterfeiter.

"Very well," he hissed through his teeth with concentrated rage; "then let him live. After all, it is your business, and not mine."

"If he were the Devil himself I would not kill him," said the triumphant Norbith.

With these words he turned to Ordener.

"Look here," he added, "you must be a good fellow as you have my poor friend Nedlam's pass. We are the royal miners. We have rebelled to rid ourselves of the protectorate of the Crown. Mr. Hacket, here, says that we have taken up arms for a certain Count Schumacker; but I for one know nothing about him. Stranger, our cause is just. Hear me, and answer as if you were answering your patron saint. Will you join us?"

An idea flashed through Ordener's mind.

"Yes," replied he.

Norbith offered him a sword, which Ordener silently accepted.

"Brother," said the youthful leader; "if you mean to betray us, begin by killing me."

At this instant the sound of the horn rang through the arched galleries of the mine, and distant voices were heard exclaiming, "Here comes Kennybol!"

XXXII

There are thoughts as high as heaven. — *Old Spanish Romanes.*

THE soul sometimes has sudden inspirations, brilliant flashes whose extent can no more be expressed, whose depth can no more be sounded by an entire volume of thoughts and reflections, than the brightness of a thousand torches can reproduce the intense, swift radiance of a flash of lightning.

We will not, therefore, try to analyze the overwhelming and secret impulse which upon young Norbith's proposal led the noble son of the Norwegian viceroy to join a party of bandits who had risen in revolt to defend a proscribed man. It was doubtless a generous desire to fathom this dark scheme at any cost, mixed with a bitter loathing for life, a reckless indifference to the future; perhaps some vague doubt of Schumacker's guilt, inspired by all the various incidents which struck the young man as equivocal and false, by a strange instinct for the truth, and above all by his love for Ethel. In short, it was certainly a secret sense of the help which a clear-sighted friend, in the midst of his blind partisans, might render Schumacker.

XXXIII

Is that the chief? His look alarms me; I dare not speak to
him.—Maturin: *Bertram*.

ON hearing the shouts which announced the arrival of the famous
hunter Kennybol, Hacket sprang forward to meet him, leaving Ordener
with the two other leaders.

"Here you are at last, my dear Kennybol! Come, let me present you to
your much-dreaded commander, Hans of Iceland."

At this name, Kennybol, pale, breathless, his hair standing on end, his
face bathed in perspiration, and his hands stained with blood, started back.

"Hans of Iceland!"

"Come," said Hacket, "don't be alarmed! He is here to help you. You
must look upon him as a friend and comrade."

Kennybol did not heed him.

"Hans of Iceland here!" he repeated.

"To be sure," said Hacket, with ill-suppressed laughter; "are you afraid
of him?"

"What!" for the third time interrupted the hunter; "do you really mean
it,—is Hans of Iceland here, in this mine?"

Hacket turned to the bystanders: "Has our brave Kennybol lost his
wits?"

Then, addressing Kennybol: "I see that it was your dread of Hans of
Iceland which made you so late."

Kennybol raised his hands to heaven.

"By Ethelreda, the holy Norwegian saint and martyr, it was not fear of
Hans of Iceland, but Hans of Iceland himself, I swear, that delayed me so
long."

These words caused a murmur of surprise to run through the crowd
of miners and mountaineers surrounding the two speakers, and clouded

Hacket's face as the sight and the rescue of Ordener had but a moment before.

"What! What do you mean?" he asked, dropping his voice.

"I mean, Mr. Hacket, that but for your confounded Hans of Iceland I should have been here before the owl's first hoot."

"Indeed! and what did he do to you?"

"Oh, do not ask me. I only hope that my beard may turn as white as an ermine's skin in a single day if I am ever caught again hunting a white bear, since I escaped this time with my life."

"Did you come near being eaten by a bear?"

Kennybol shrugged his shoulders contemptuously.

"A bear! a terrible foe that would be! Kennybol eaten by a bear! For what do you take me, Mr. Hacket?"

"Oh, pardon me!" said Hacket, with a smile.

"If you knew what had happened to me, good sir," interrupted the old hunter, in a low voice, "you would not persist in telling me that Hans of Iceland is here."

Hacket again seemed embarrassed. He seized Kennybol abruptly by the arm, as if he feared lest he should approach the spot where the giant's huge head now loomed up above those of the miners.

"My dear Kennybol," said he, solemnly, "tell me, I entreat you, what caused your delay. You must understand that at this time anything may be of the utmost importance."

"That is true," said Kennybol, after a brief pause.

Then, yielding to Hacket's repeated requests, he told him how that very morning, aided by six comrades, he had pursued a white bear into the immediate vicinity of Walderhog cave, without noticing, in the excitement of the chase, that they were so near that dreadful place; how the growls of the bear at bay had attracted a little man, a monster, or demon, who, armed with a stone axe, had rushed upon them to defend the bear. The appearance of this devil, who could be no other than Hans, the demon of Iceland, had petrified all seven of them with terror. Finally, his six companions had fallen victims to the two monsters, and he, Kennybol, only owed his safety to speedy flight, assisted by his own nimbleness, Hans of Iceland's fatigue, and above all, by the protection of that blessed patron saint of hunters, Saint Sylvester.

"You see, Mr. Hacket," he concluded his tale, which was still somewhat incoherent from fright, and adorned with all the flowers of the mountain dialect, — "you see that if I am late you should not blame me, and that it is impossible for the demon of Iceland, whom I left this morning with his bear wreaking their fury upon the corpses of my six poor friends on Walderhog heath, to be here now in the guise of a friend. I protest that it cannot be. I know him now, that fiend incarnate; I have seen him!"

Hacket, who had listened attentively, said gravely: "My brave friend Kennybol, nothing is impossible to Hans or to the Devil; I knew all this before."

The savage features of the old hunter from the mountains of Kiölen assumed an expression of extreme amazement and childlike credulity. "What!" he exclaimed.

"Yes," added Hacket, in whose face a more skilful observer might have read grim triumph; "I knew it all, except that you were the hero of this unfortunate adventure. Hans of Iceland told me the whole story on our way here."

"Really!" said Kennybol; and he gazed at Hacket with respect and awe.

Hacket continued with the same perfect composure: "To be sure. But now calm yourself; I will present you to this dreadful Hans of Iceland."

Kennybol uttered an exclamation of fright.

"Be calm, I say," repeated Hacket. "Consider him as your friend and leader; but be careful not to remind him in any way of what occurred this morning. Do you understand?"

Resistance was useless; but it was not without a severe mental struggle that he agreed to be presented to the demon. They advanced to the group where Ordener stood with Jonas and Norbith.

"May God guard you, good Jonas, dear Norbith!" said Kennybol.

"We need his protection, Kennybol," said Jonas.

At this instant Kennybol's eye met that of Ordener, who was trying to attract his attention.

"Ah! there you are, young man," said he, going up to him eagerly and offering him his hard, wrinkled hand; "welcome! It seems that your courage met with its reward."

Ordener, who could not imagine how this mountaineer happened to understand him so well, was about to ask an explanation, when Norbith exclaimed: "Then you know this stranger, Kennybol?"

"By my patron saint, I do! I love and esteem him. He is devoted, like ourselves, to the good cause which we all serve."

And he cast another meaning look at Ordener, which the latter was on the point of answering, when Hacket, who had gone in search of his giant, whose company all the insurgents seemed to avoid, came up to our four friends, saying: "Kennybol, my valiant hunter, here is your leader, the famous Hans of Klipstadur!"

Kennybol glanced at the huge brigand with more surprise than terror, and whispered in Hacket's ear: "Mr. Hacket, the Hans of Iceland whom I met this morning was a short man."

Hacket answered in low tones: "You forget, Kennybol; he is a demon!"

"True," said the credulous hunter; "I suppose he has changed his shape."

And he turned aside with a shudder to cross himself secretly.

XXXIV

The mask approaches; it is Angelo himself. The rascal knows
his business well; he must be sure of his facts.—Lessing.

IN a dark grove of old oaks, whose dense leaves the pale light of dawn
can scarcely penetrate, a short man approaches another man who is alone,
and seems to waiting for him. The following conversation begins in low
tones:—

"Your worship must excuse me for keeping you waiting; several things
detained me."

"Such as what?"

"The leader of the mountain men, Kennybol, did not reach the appointed
place until midnight; and we were also disturbed by an unlooked-for
witness."

"Who?"

"A fellow who thrust himself like a fool into the mine in the midst of
our secret meeting. At first I took him for a spy, and would have put him
to death; but he turned out to be the bearer of a safe-conduct from some
gallows-bird held in great respect by our miners, and they instantly took
him under their protection. When I came to consider the matter, I made up
my mind that he was probably a curious traveller or a learned fool. At any
rate, I have taken all necessary precautions in regard to him."

"Is everything else going well?"

"Very well. The miners from Guldsbrandsdal and the Färöe Islands, led
by young Norbith and old Jonas, with the mountain men from Kiölen, under
Kennybol, are probably on the march at this moment. Four miles from Blue
Star, their comrades from Hubfallo and Sund-Moer will join them; those
from Kongsberg and the iron-workers from Lake Miösen, who have already
compelled the Wahlstrom garrison to retreat, as your lordship knows, will
await them a few miles farther on; and finally, my dear and honored master,
these combined forces will halt for the night some two miles away from
Skongen, in the gorges of Black Pillar."

"But how did they receive your Hans of Iceland?"

"With perfect confidence."

"Would that I could avenge my son's death on that monster! What a pity that he should escape us!"

"My noble lord, first use Hans of Iceland's name to wreak your revenge upon Schumacker; then it will be time enough to think of vengeance against Hans himself. The insurgents will march all day, and halt to-night in Black Pillar Pass, two miles from Skongen."

"What! can you venture to let so large a force advance so close to Skongen? Musdœmon, take care!"

"You are suspicious, noble Count. Your worship may send a messenger at once to Colonel Vœthaün, whose regiment is probably at Skongen now; inform him that the rebel forces will encamp to-night in Black Pillar Pass, and have no misgivings. The place seems made purposely for ambuscades."

"I understand you; but why, my dear fellow, did you muster the rebels in such numbers?"

"The greater the insurrection, sir, the greater will be Schumacker's crime and your merit. Besides, it is important that it should be crushed at a single blow."

"Very good; but why did you order them to halt so near Skongen?"

"Because it is the only spot in the mountains where all resistance is impossible. None will ever leave it alive but those whom we select to appear before the court."

"Capital! Something tells me, Musdœmon, to finish this business quickly. If all looks well in this quarter, it looks stormy in another. You know that we have been making secret search at Copenhagen for the papers which we feared had fallen into the possession of Dispolsen?"

"Well, sir?"

"Well, I have just discovered that the scheming fellow had mysterious relations with that accursed astrologer, Cumbysulsum."

"Who died recently?"

"Yes; and that the old sorcerer delivered certain papers to Schumacker's agent before he died."

"Damnation! He had letters of mine,—a statement of our plot!"

"*Your* plot, Musdœmon!"

"A thousand pardons, noble Count! But why did your worship put yourself in the power of such a humbug as Cumbysulsum?—the old traitor!"

"You see, Musdœmon, I am not a sceptic and unbeliever, like you. It is not without good reason, my dear fellow, that I have always put my trust in old Cumbysulsum's magic skill."

"I wish your worship had had as much doubt of his loyalty as you had trust in his skill. However, let us not take fright too soon, noble master. Dispolsen is dead, his papers are lost; in a few days we shall be safely rid of those whom they might benefit."

"In any event, what charge could be brought against me?"

"Or me, protected as I am by your Grace?"

"Oh, yes, my dear fellow, of course you can count upon me; but let us bring this business to a head. I will send the messenger to the colonel. Come, my people are waiting for me behind those bushes, and we must return to Throndhjem, which the Mecklenburger must have left ere now. Continue to serve me faithfully, and in spite of all the Cumbysulsums and Dispolsens upon earth, you can count on me in life and death!"

"I beg your Grace to believe—The Devil!"

Here they plunged into the thicket, among whose branches their voices gradually died away; and soon after, no sound was heard save the tread of their departing steeds.

XXXV

Beat the drums! They come, they come! They have all sworn, and all the same oath, never to return to Castile without the captive count, their lord.

They have his marble statue in a chariot, and are resolved never to turn back until they see the statue itself turn back.

And in token that the first man who retraces his steps will be regarded as a traitor, they have all raised their right hand and taken an oath.

And they marched toward Arlançon as swiftly as the oxen which drag the chariot could go; they tarry no more than does the sun.

Burgos is deserted; only the women and children remain behind; and so too in the suburbs. They talk, as they go, of horses and falcons, and question whether they should free Castile from the tribute she pays Leon.

And before they enter Navarre, they meet upon the frontier....

Old Spanish Romance.

WHILE the preceding conversation was going on in one of the forests on the outskirts of Lake Miösen, the rebels, divided into three columns, left Apsyl-Corh lead-mine by the chief entrance, which opens, on a level with the ground, in a deep ravine.

Ordener, who, in spite of his desire for a closer acquaintance with Kennybol, had been placed under Norbith's command, at first saw nothing but a long line of torches, whose beams, vying with the early light of dawn, were reflected back from hatchets, pitchforks, mattocks, clubs with iron heads, huge hammers, pickaxes, crowbars, and all the rude implements which could be borrowed from their daily toil, mingled with genuine weapons of warfare, such as muskets, pikes, swords, carbines, and guns, which showed that this revolt was a conspiracy. When the sun rose, and the glow of the torches was no more than smoke, he could better observe the aspect of this strange army, which advanced in disorder, with hoarse songs and fierce shouts, like a band of hungry wolves in pursuit of a dead body.

It was divided into three parts. First came the mountaineers from Kiölen, under command of Kennybol, whom they all resembled in their dress of wild beasts' skins, and in their bold, savage mien. Then followed the young miners led by Norbith, and the older ones under Jonas, with their broad-brimmed hats, loose trousers, bare arms, and blackened faces, gazing at the sun in mute surprise. Above this noisy band floated a confused sea of scarlet banners, bearing various mottoes, such as, "Long live Schumacker!" "Let us free our Deliverer!" "Freedom for Miners!" "Liberty for Count Griffenfeld!" "Death to Guldenlew!" "Death to all Oppressors!" "Death to d'Ahlefeld!" The rebels seemed to regard these standards rather in the light of a burden than an ornament, and they were passed frequently from hand to hand when the color-bearers were tired, or desired to mingle the discordant notes of their horns with the psalm-singing and shouts of their comrades.

The rear-guard of this strange army consisted of ten or a dozen carts drawn by reindeer and strong mules, doubtless meant to carry ammunition; and the vanguard, of the giant, escorted by Hacket, who marched alone, armed with a mace and an axe, followed at a considerable distance, with no small terror, by the men under command of Kennybol, who never took his eyes from him, as if anxious not to lose sight of his diabolical leader during the various transformations which he might be pleased to undergo.

This stream of insurgents poured down the mountainside with many confused noises, filling the pine woods with the sound of their horns. Their numbers were soon swelled by various reinforcements from Sund-Moer, Hubfallo, Kongsberg, and a troop of iron-workers from Lake Miösen, who presented a singular contrast to the rest of the rebels. They were tall, powerful men, armed with hammers and tongs, their broad leather aprons being their only shield, a huge wooden cross their only standard, as they marched soberly and rhythmically, with a regular tread more religious than military, their only war-song being Biblical psalms and canticles. They had no leader but their cross-bearer, who walked before them unarmed.

The rebel troop met not a single human being on their road. As they approached, the goat-herd drove his flocks into a cave, and the peasant forsook his village; for the inhabitant of the valley and plain is everywhere alike,—he fears the bandit's horn as much as the bowman's blast.

Thus they traversed hills and forests, with here and there a small settlement, followed winding roads where traces of wild beasts were more frequent than the footprint of man, skirted lakes, crossed torrents, ravines, and marshes. Ordener recognized none of these places. Once only his eye, as he looked up, caught upon the horizon the dim, blue outline of a great sloping rock. He turned to one of his rude companions, and asked, "My friend, what is that rock to the south, on our right?"

"That is the Vulture's Neck, Oëlmœ Cliff," was the reply.

Ordener sighed heavily.

XXXVI

God keep and bless you, my daughter.—Régnier.

MONKEY, paroquets, combs, and ribbons, all were ready to receive Lieutenant Frederic. His mother had sent, at great expense, for the famous Scudéry's latest novel. By her order it had been richly bound, with silvergilt clasps, and placed, with the bottles of perfume and boxes of patches, upon the elegant toilet-table, with gilded feet, and richly inlaid, with which she had furnished her dear son Frederic's future sitting-room. When she had thus fulfilled the careful round of petty maternal cares which had for a moment caused her to forget her hate, she remembered that she had now nothing else to do but to injure Schumacker and Ethel. General Levin's departure left them at her mercy.

So many things had happened recently at Munkholm of which she could learn but little! Who was the serf, vassal, or peasant, who, if she was to credit Frederic's very ambiguous and embarrassed phrases, had won the love of the ex-chancellor's daughter? What were Baron Ordener's relations with the prisoners of Munkholm? What were the incomprehensible motives for Ordener's most peculiar absence at a time when both kingdoms were given over to preparations for his marriage to that Ulrica d'Ahlefeld whom he seemed to disdain? And lastly, what had occurred between Levin de Knud and Schumacker? The countess was lost in conjectures. She finally resolved, in order to clear up all these mysteries, to risk a descent upon Munkholm,—a step to which she was counselled both by her curiosity as a woman and her interests as an enemy.

One evening, as Ethel, alone in the donjon garden, had just written, for the sixth time, with a diamond ring, some mysterious monogram upon the dusty window in the postern gate through which her Ordener had disappeared, it opened. The young girl started. It was the first time that this gate had been opened since it closed upon him.

A tall, pale woman, dressed in white, stood before her. She gave Ethel a smile as sweet as poisoned honey, and behind her mask of quiet friendliness there lurked an expression of hatred, spite, and involuntary admiration.

Ethel looked at her in astonishment, almost fear. Except her old nurse, who had died in her arms, this was the first woman she had seen within the gloomy walls of Munkholm.

"My child," gently asked the stranger, "are you the daughter of the prisoner of Munkholm?"

Ethel could not help turning away her head; she instinctively shrank from the stranger, and she felt as if there were venom in the breath which uttered such sweet tones. She answered: "I am Ethel Schumacker. My father tells me that in my cradle I was called Countess of Tönsberg and Princess of Wollin."

"Your father tells you so!" exclaimed the tall woman, with a sneer which she at once repressed. Then she added: "You have had many misfortunes!"

"Misfortune received me, at my birth, in its cruel arms," replied the youthful captive; "my noble father says that it will never leave me while I live."

A smile flitted across the lips of the stranger, as she rejoined in a pitying tone: "And do you never murmur against those who flung you into this cell? Do you not curse the authors of your misery?"

"No, for fear that our curse might draw down upon their heads evils like those which they make us endure."

"And," continued the pale woman, with unmoved face, "do you know the authors of these evils of which you complain?"

Ethel considered a moment, and said: "All that has happened to us is by the will of Heaven."

"Does your father never speak to you of the king?"

"The king? I pray for him every morning and evening, although I do not know him."

Ethel did not understand why the stranger bit her lip at this reply.

"Does your unhappy father never, in his anger, mention his relentless foes, General Arensdorf, Bishop Spolleyson, and Chancellor d'Ahlefeld?"

"I don't know whom you mean."

"And do you know the name of Levin de Knud?"

The recollection of the scene which had occurred but two days before, between Schumacker and the governor of Throndhjem, was so fresh in Ethel's mind that she could not but be struck by the name of Levin de Knud.

"Levin de Knud?" said she; "I think that he is the man for whom my father feels so much esteem, almost affection."

"What!" cried the tall woman.

"Yes," resumed the girl; "it was Levin de Knud whom my father defended so warmly, day before yesterday, against the governor of Throndhjem."

These words increased her hearer's surprise.

"Against the governor of Throndhjem! Do not trifle with me, girl. I am here in your interests. Your father took General Levin de Knud's part against the governor of Throndhjem, you say?"

"General! I thought he was a captain. But no; you are right. My father," added Ethel, "seemed to feel as much attachment for this General Levin de Knud as dislike for the governor of Throndhjem."

"Here is a strange mystery indeed!" thought the tall, pale woman, whose curiosity increased momentarily. "My dear child, what happened between your father and the governor?"

All these questions wearied poor Ethel, who looked fixedly at the tall woman, saying: "Am I a criminal, that you should cross-examine me thus?"

At these simple words the stranger seemed thunderstruck, as if she saw the reward of her skill slipping through her fingers. She replied, nevertheless, in a tremulous voice: "You would not speak to me so if you knew why and for whom I come."

"What!" said Ethel; "do you come from him? Do you bring me a message from him?" And all the blood in her body rushed to her fair face; her heart throbbed in her bosom with impatience and alarm.

"From whom?" asked the stranger.

The young girl hesitated as she was about to utter the adored name. She saw a flash of wicked joy gleam in the stranger's eye like a ray from hell. She said sadly:—

"You do not know the person whom I mean."

An expression of disappointment again appeared upon the stranger's apparently friendly face.

"Poor young girl!" she cried; "what can I do to help you?"

Ethel did not hear her. Her thoughts were beyond the mountains of the North, in quest of the daring traveller. Her head sank upon her breast, and her hands were unconsciously clasped.

"Does your father hope to escape from this prison?"

This question, twice repeated by the stranger, brought Ethel to herself.

"Yes," said she, and tears sparkled on her cheek.

The stranger's eyes flashed.

"He does! Tell me how; by what means; when!"

"He hopes to escape from this prison because he hopes ere long to die."

There is sometimes a power in the very simplicity of a gentle young spirit which outwits the artifices of a heart grown old in wickedness. This thought seemed to occur to the great lady, for her expression suddenly changed, and laying her cold hand on Ethel's arm, she said in a tone which was almost sincere: "Tell me, have you heard that your father's life is again threatened by a fresh judicial inquiry? That he is suspected of having stirred up a revolt among the miners of the North?"

The words "revolt" and "inquiry" conveyed no clear idea to Ethel's mind. She raised her great dark eyes to the stranger's face as she asked: "What do you mean?"

"That your father is conspiring against the State; that his crime is all but discovered; that this crime will be punished with death."

"Death! crime!" cried the poor girl.

"Crime and death," said the strange lady, seriously.

"My father! my noble father!" continued Ethel. "Alas! he spends his days in hearing me read the Edda and the Gospel! He conspire! What has he done to you?"

"Do not look at me so fiercely. I tell you again I am not your enemy. Your father is suspected of a grave crime; I am here to warn you of it. Perhaps, instead of such a show of dislike, I might lay claim to your gratitude."

This reproach touched Ethel.

"Oh, forgive me, noble lady, forgive me! What human being have I ever seen who was not an enemy? I have doubted you. You will forgive me, will you not?"

The stranger smiled.

"What, my girl! have you never met a friend until to-day?"

A hot blush mantled Ethel's brow. She hesitated an instant.

"Yes. God knows the truth, we have found a friend, noble lady,—one only!"

"One only!" said the great lady, hastily. "His name, I implore. You do not know how important it is; it is for your father's safety. Who is this friend?"

"I do not know," said Ethel.

The stranger turned pale.

"Is it because I wish to serve you that you trifle with me? Consider that your father's life is at stake. Tell me, who is this friend of whom you speak?"

"Heaven knows, noble lady, that I know nothing of him but his name, which is Ordener."

Ethel uttered these words with that difficulty which we all feel in pronouncing before an indifferent person the sacred name which wakes within us every emotion of love.

"Ordener! Ordener!" repeated the stranger, with singular agitation, while her hands crumpled the white embroideries of her veil. "And what is his father's name?" she asked in a troubled voice.

"I do not know," replied the girl. "What are his family and his father to me? This Ordener, noble lady, is the most generous of men."

Alas! the accent with which these words were spoken revealed Ethel's secret to the sharp-sighted stranger.

She assumed an air of calm composure, and asked, without taking her eyes from the girl's face: "Have you heard of the approaching marriage of the viceroy's son to the daughter of the present lord chancellor, d'Ahlefeld?"

She was obliged to repeat her question before Ethel's mind could grasp an idea which did not interest her.

"I believe I have," was her answer.

Her calmness, and her indifferent manner, seemed to surprise the stranger.

"Well, what do you think of this marriage?"

It was impossible to note the slightest change in Ethel's large eyes as she replied: "Nothing, truly. May their union be a happy one!"

"Counts Guldenlew and d'Ahlefeld, the fathers of the young couple, are both bitter enemies of your father."

"May their marriage be blessed!" gently repeated Ethel.

"I have an idea," continued the crafty stranger. "If your father's life be really threatened, you might obtain his pardon through the viceroy's son upon the occasion of this great marriage."

"May the saints reward you for your kind thought for us, noble lady; but how should my petition reach the viceroy's son?"

These words were spoken in such good faith that they drew a gesture of surprise from the stranger.

"What! do you not know him?"

"That powerful lord!" cried Ethel. "You forget that I have never been outside the walls of this fortress."

"Truly," muttered the tall woman between her teeth. "What did that old fool of a Levin tell me? She does not know him. Still, that is impossible," said she; then, raising her voice: "You must have seen the viceroy's son; he has been here."

"That may be, noble lady; of all the men who have been here, I have never seen but one,—my Ordener."

"Your Ordener!" interrupted the stranger. She added, without seeming to notice Ethel's blushes: "Do you know a young man with noble face, elegant figure, grave and dignified bearing? His expression is gentle, yet firm; his complexion fresh as that of a maiden; his hair chestnut."

"Oh!" cried poor Ethel, "that is he; it is my betrothed, my adored Ordener! Where did you meet him? He told you that he loved me, did he not? He told you that he has my whole heart. Alas! a poor prisoner has nothing but her love to give. My noble friend! It was but a week ago,—I can see him still on this very spot, with his green mantle, beneath which beats so generous a heart, and that black plume, which waved so gracefully above his broad brow."

She did not finish her sentence. The tall stranger tottered, turned pale, then red, and cried in her ears in tones of thunder: "Wretched girl, you love Ordener Guldenlew, the betrothed of Ulrica d'Ahlefeld, the son of your father's deadly foe, the viceroy of Norway!"

Ethel fell fainting on the ground.

XXXVII

Caupolican. Walk so cautiously that the earth itself may not catch your footfall. Redouble your precautions, friends. If we arrive unheard, I will answer for the victory.

Tucapel. Night veils all; fearful darkness covers the earth. We hear no sentinel; we have seen no spies.

Ringo. Let us advance!

Tucapel. What do I hear? Are we discovered?

Lope da Vega: The Conquest of Arauco.

"I SAY, Guldon Stayper, old fellow, the evening breeze is beginning to blow my hairy cap about my head rather vigorously."

These words were spoken by Kennybol, as his eyes wandered for a moment from the giant who marched at the head of the insurgents, and half turned toward a mountaineer whom the accident of a disorderly progress had placed beside him.

His friend shook his head and shifted his banner from one shoulder to the other, with a deep sigh of fatigue, as he answered:—

"Hum! I fancy, Captain, that in these confounded Black Pillar gorges, through which the wind rushes like a torrent let loose, we shall not be as warm to-night as if we were flames dancing on the hearth."

"We must make such rousing fires that the old owls will be scared from their nests among the rocks in their ruined palace. I can't endure owls. On that horrid night when I saw the fairy Ubfem she took the shape of an owl."

"By Saint Sylvester!" interrupted Guldon Stayper, turning his head, "the angel of the storm beats his wings most furiously! Take my advice, Captain Kennybol, and set fire to all the pine-trees on the mountain. It would be a fine sight to see an army warm itself with a whole forest."

"Heaven forbid, my dear Guldon! Think of the deer, and the gerfalcons, and the pheasants! Roast the game, if you will, but do not burn it alive."

Old Guidon laughed: "Oh, Captain, you are the same devil of a Kennybol,—the wolf of deer, the bear of wolves, and the buffalo of bears!"

"Are we far from Black Pillar?" asked a voice from the huntsmen.

"Comrade," replied Kennybol, "we shall enter the gorge at nightfall; we shall reach the Four Crosses directly."

There was a brief silence, during which nothing was heard but the tramp of many feet, the moaning of the wind, and the distant song of the regiment of iron-workers from Lake Miösen.

"Friend Guldon Stayper," resumed Kennybol, when he had whistled an old hunting-song, "you have just passed a few days at Throndhjem, have you not?"

"Yes, Captain; my brother George, the fisherman, was ill, and I took his place in the boat for a short time, so that his poor family might not starve while he was ill."

"Well, as you come from Throndhjem, did you happen to see this count, the prisoner—Schumacker—Gleffenhem—what is his name, now? I mean that man in whose behalf we have rebelled against the royal protectorate, and whose arms I suppose you have on that big red flag."

"It is heavy enough, I can tell you!" said Guldon. "Do you mean the prisoner in Munkholm fortress,—the count, if you choose to call him so; and how do you suppose, Captain, that I should see him? I should have needed," he added, lowering his voice, "the eyes of that demon marching in front of us, though he does not leave a smell of brimstone behind him; of that Hans of Iceland, who can see through stone walls; or the ring of Queen Mab, who passes through keyholes. There is but one man among us now, I am sure, who ever saw the count,—the prisoner to whom you refer."

"But one? Ah! Mr. Hacket? But this Hacket is no longer with us; he left us to-day to return to—"

"I do not mean Mr. Hacket, Captain."

"And who then?"

"That young man in the green mantle, with the black plume, who burst into our midst last night."

"Well?"

"Well!" said Guldon, drawing closer to Kennybol; "he knows the count,—this famous count, as well as I know you, Captain Kennybol."

Kennybol looked at Guldon, winked his left eye, smacked his lips, and clapped his friend on the shoulder with that triumphant exclamation which so often escapes us when we are satisfied with our own penetration,—"I thought as much!"

"Yes, Captain," continued Guldon Stayper, changing his flame-colored banner to the other shoulder; "I assure you that the young man in green has seen Count—I don't know what you call him, the one for whom we are fighting—in Munkholm keep; and he seemed to think no more of walking into that prison than you or I would of shooting in a royal park."

"And how happen you to know this, brother Guldon?"

The old mountaineer seized Kennybol by the arm, and half opening his otter-skin waistcoat with a caution which was almost suspicious, he said, "Look there!"

"By my most holy patron saint!" exclaimed Kennybol; "it glitters like diamonds!"

It was indeed a superb diamond buckle, which fastened Guldon Stayper's rough belt.

"And they are real diamonds," he replied, closing his waistcoat. "I am just as sure of it as I am that the moon is two days' journey from the earth, and that my belt is made of buffalo leather."

Kennybol's face clouded, and his expression changed from surprise to distress. He cast down his eyes, and said with savage sternness: "Guldon Stayper, of Chol-Sœ village, in the Kiölen mountains, your father, Medprath Stayper, died at the age of one hundred and two, without reproach; for it was no crime to kill one of the king's deer or elk by mistake. Guldon Stayper, fifty-seven good years have passed over your gray head, which cannot be called youth except for an owl. Guldon Stayper, old friend, I would rather for your sake that the diamonds in that buckle were grains of millet, if you did not come by them honestly,—as honestly as a royal pheasant comes by a leaden bullet."

As he pronounced this strange sermon, the mountaineer's tone was both impressive and menacing.

"As truly as Captain Kennybol is the boldest hunter in Kiölen," replied Guldon, unmoved, "and as truly as these diamonds are diamonds, they are my lawful property."

"Indeed!" said Kennybol, in accents which wavered between confidence and doubt.

"God and my patron saint know," replied Guldon, "that one evening, just as I was pointing out the Throndhjem Spladgest to some sons of our good mother Norway, who were carrying thither the body of an officer found dead on Urchtal Sands,—this was about a week ago,—a young man stepped up to my boat. 'To Munkholm!' says he to me. I was not at all anxious to obey, Captain; a free bird never likes to fly into the neighborhood of a cage. But the young gentleman had a haughty, lordly manner; he was followed by a servant leading two horses; he leaped into my boat with an air of authority; I took up my oars, that is to say, my brother's oars. It was my good angel that willed me to do so. When we reached the fortress, my young passenger, after exchanging a few words with the officer on guard, flung me in payment—as God hears me, he did, Captain—this diamond buckle which I showed you, and which would have belonged to my brother George, and not to me, if at the time that the traveller—Heaven help him!— engaged me, the day's work which I was doing for George had not been done. This is the truth, Captain Kennybol."

"Very good."

Little by little the captain's features had cleared as much as their naturally hard and gloomy expression would permit, and he asked Guidon in a softened voice: "And are you sure, old fellow, that this young man is the same who is now behind us with Norbith's followers?"

"Sure! I could not mistake among a thousand faces the face of him who made my fortune; besides, it is the same cloak, the same black plume."

"I believe you, Guldon!"

"And it is clear that he went there to see the famous prisoner; for if he were not bound on some very mysterious errand, he would never have rewarded so handsomely the boatman who rowed him over and besides, now that he has joined us—"

"You are right."

"And I imagine, Captain, that this young stranger may have far greater influence with the count whom we are about to set free than Mr. Hacket, who strikes me, by my soul! as only fit to mew like a wildcat."

Kennybol nodded his head expressively.

"Comrade, you have said just what I meant to say. I should be much more inclined in this whole matter to obey that young gentleman than the envoy Hacket. Saint Sylvester and Saint Olaf help me! but if the Iceland demon be our commander, I believe, friend Guldon, that we owe it far less to that magpie Hacket than to this stranger."

"Really, Captain?" inquired Guldon.

Kennybol opened his mouth to answer, when he felt a hand on his shoulder; it was Norbith.

"Kennybol, we are betrayed! Gormon Woëstrœm has just come from the South. The entire regiment of musketeers is marching against us. The Schleswig lancers are at Sparbo; three companies of Danish dragoons await the cavalry at Loevig. All along the road he saw as many green jackets as there were bushes. Let us hasten toward Skongen; let us not pause until we reach that point. There, at least, we can defend ourselves. One thing more; Gormon thinks that he saw the gleam of muskets among the briers as he came through the defiles of Black Pillar."

The young leader was pale and agitated; but his face and voice still showed courage and resolution.

"Impossible!" cried Kennybol.

"It is certain! certain!" said Norbith.

"But Mr. Hacket—"

"Is a traitor or a coward. Depend on what I say, friend Kennybol. Where is this Hacket?"

At this moment old Jonas approached the two chiefs. By the deep discouragement stamped upon his features it was easily seen that he had learned the fatal news.

The eyes of the two elder men, Jonas and Kennybol, met, and they shook their heads with one accord.

"Well, Jonas! Well, Kennybol!" said Norbith.

But the aged leader of the Färöe miners slowly passed his hand across his wrinkled brow, and in a low voice answered the appealing look of the aged leader of the Kiölen mountaineers: "Yes, it is but too true; it is but too certain. Gormon Woëstrœm saw them."

"If it be so," said Kennybol, "what is to be done?"

"What is to be done?" answered Jonas.

"I consider, friend Jonas, that we should do well to halt."

"And better still, brother Kennybol, to retreat."

"Halt! retreat!" exclaimed Norbith; "we must push forward."

The two elders looked at the young man in cold surprise.

"Push forward!" said Kennybol; "and how about the Munkholm musketeers?"

"And the Schleswig lancers?" added Jonas.

"And the Danish dragoons?" continued Kennybol.

Norbith stamped his foot.

"And the royal protectorate; and my mother dying of cold and hunger?"

"The devil, the royal protectorate!" said the miner Jonas, with a shudder.

"Never mind!" said Kennybol.

Jonas took Kennybol by the hand, saying: "Old fellow, you have not the honor to be a ward of our glorious sovereign, Christian IV. May the blessed king Olaf, in heaven, deliver us from the protectorate!"

"You had better trust to your sword for that benefit!" said Norbith, in a fierce tone.

"Bold words are easy to a young man, friend Norbith," answered Kennybol; "but consider that if we advance, all these green jackets—"

"I think that it would be useless for us to return to our mountains, like foxes running from wolves, for our names and our revolt are known; and if we needs must die, I prefer a musket-ball to the hangman's rope."

Jonas nodded assent.

"The devil! the protectorate for our brothers, the gallows for us! Norbith may be right, after all."

"Give me your hand, good Norbith," said Kennybol; "there is danger in either course. We may as well march straight to the edge of the precipice as fall over it backwards."

"Come on! come on!" cried old Jonas, striking his sword-hilt.

Norbith grasped them by the hand.

"Listen, brothers! Be bold, like me; I will be prudent, like you. Let us not pause until we reach Skongen; the garrison is weak, and we will overwhelm it. Let us pass, since we must, through the defiles of Black Pillar, but in utter silence. We must traverse them, even if they be guarded by the enemy."

"I do not think that the musketeers have come so far as Ordals bridge, beyond Skongen; but it matters not. Silence!"

"Silence! so be it!" repeated Kennybol.

"Now, Jonas," said Norbith, "let us return to our posts. To-morrow we may be at Throndhjem in spite of musketeers, lancers, dragoons, and all the green jerkins of the South."

The three chiefs parted. Soon the watchword, "Silence!" passed from rank to rank, and the insurgents, a moment before so tumultuous, looked, in those waste places darkened by approaching night, like a band of mute ghosts roaming noiselessly through the winding paths of a cemetery.

But their road became narrower every moment, and seemed by degrees to dive between two walls of rock which grew steeper and steeper. As the red moon rose among a mass of cold clouds hovering about her with weird inconstancy, Kennybol turned to Guldon Stayper, saying, "We are about to enter Black Pillar Pass. Silence!"

In fact, they already heard the roar of the torrent which follows every turn of the road between the two mountains, and they saw, to the south, the huge granite pyramid known as the Black Pillar, outlined against the gray sky and the surrounding snow-capped mountains; while the western horizon, veiled in mists, was bounded by the extreme verge of Sparbo forest, and by huge piles of rocks, terraced as if a stairway for giants.

The rebels, forced to stretch their columns over this crooked road compressed between two mountains, continued their march. They penetrated those dark valleys without lighting a torch, without uttering a sound. The very sound of their footsteps was unheard amid the deafening crash of waterfalls and the roar of a furious blast which bowed the Druidical woods, and drove the clouds in eddying whirls about tall peaks clad in snow and ice. Lost in the dark depths of the gorge, the light of the moon, which was veiled now and again, did not reach the heads of their pikes, and the white eagles flying overhead did not guess that so vast a multitude of men was troubling their solitude.

Once old Guldon Stayper touched Kennybol's shoulder with the butt-end of his carbine, saying, "Captain, Captain, something glimmers behind that tuft of holly and broom."

"So it does," replied the mountain chief; "it is the water of the stream reflecting the clouds." And they passed on.

Again Guldon grasped his leader quickly by the arm.

"Look!" he said; "are not those muskets, shining yonder in the shadow of that rock?"

Kennybol shook his head; then, after looking attentively, he said, "Never fear, brother Guldon; it is a moonbeam falling on an icy peak."

No further cause for alarm appeared, and the various bands, as they marched quietly through the winding gorge, insensibly forgot all the danger of their position.

After two hours of often painful progress, over the treetrunks and granite bowlders which blocked the road, the vanguard entered the mountainous group of pine-trees at the end of Black Pillar Pass, overhung by high, black, moss-grown cliffs.

Guldon Stayper approached Kennybol, declaring that he was delighted that they were at last almost out of this cursed cut-throat place, and that they must render thanks to Saint Sylvester that the Black Pillar had not been fatal to them.

Kennybol laughed, swearing that he had never shared such old-womanish fears; for with most men, when danger is over it ceases to exist, and they try to prove by their incredulity the courage which they perhaps failed to display before.

At this moment two small round lights, like two live coals, moving in the thick underwood, attracted his attention.

"By my soul's salvation!" he whispered, pulling Guldon's arm, "see; those two blazing eyes must surely belong to the fiercest wildcat that ever mewed in a thicket."

"You are right," replied old Stayper; "and if he were not marching in front of us, I should rather think that they were the wicked eyes of the demon of Ice—"

"Hush!" cried Kennybol. Then, seizing his carbine, he added, "Truly, it shall not be said that such fine game passed before Kennybol in vain."

The shot was fired before Guldon Stayper, who threw himself upon the rash hunter, could prevent it. It was not the shrill cry of a wildcat that answered the discharge of the gun; it was the fearful howl of a tiger, followed by a burst of human laughter more frightful still.

No one heard the report as its dying echoes were prolonged from rock to rock; for the flash of the powder had no sooner lighted up the darkness, the fatal crack of the gun had no sooner burst upon the silence, than a thousand terrible voices rang out unexpectedly from mountain, valley, and forest; a shout of "Long live the king!" loud as the rolling thunder, swept over the heads of the rebels, close beside them, behind and before them, and the murderous light of a dreadful volley of musketry, bursting from every hand, and striking them down, at the same time disclosed, amid red clouds of smoke, a battalion behind every rock, and a soldier behind every tree.

XXXVIII

To arms! to arms! ye captains!
The Prisoner of Ochali.

WE must now ask the reader to retrace with us the day which has just passed, and to return to Skongen, where, while the insurgents were leaving Apsyl-Corh lead-mine, the regiment of musketeers, which we saw on the march in an earlier chapter of this very truthful tale, had just arrived.

After giving a few orders in regard to billeting the soldiers under his command, Baron Vœthaün, colonel of the musketeers, was about to enter the house assigned to him, near the city gate, when a heavy hand was placed familiarly upon his shoulder. He turned and saw a short man, whose face was almost wholly hidden by a broad-brimmed straw hat. He had a bushy red beard, and was closely wrapped in the folds of a gray serge cloak, which, by the tattered cowl still hanging from it, seemed once to have been a hermit's gown. His hands were covered with thick gloves.

"Well, my good man," asked the colonel, sharply, "what the deuce do you want?"

"Colonel of the Munkholm musketeers," replied the fellow, with an odd look, "follow me for a moment; I have news for you."

At this singular request, the baron paused for a moment in silent surprise.

"Important news, Colonel!" repeated the man with the thick gloves.

This persistence decided Baron Vœthaün. At such a crisis, and with such a mission as his, no information was to be despised. "So be it," said he.

The little man preceded him, and as soon as they were outside the town, he stopped. "Colonel, would you really like to destroy all the insurgents at a single blow?"

The colonel laughed, saying, "Why, that would not be a bad way to open the campaign."

"Very well! Then station your men in ambush this very day, in Black Pillar Pass, two miles distant from the town; the rebels are to encamp there to-night. When you see their first fire blaze, fall upon them with your troops. Victory will be easy."

"Excellent advice, my good man, and I thank you for it; but how did you learn all this?"

"If you knew me, Colonel, you would rather ask me how I could fail to know it."

"Who are you, then?"

The man stamped his foot. "I did not come here to answer such questions."

"Fear nothing. Whoever you may be, the service which you have done us must be your safeguard. Perhaps you were one of the rebels?"

"I refused to join them."

"Then why conceal your name, if you are a loyal subject of the king?"

"What is that to you?"

The colonel made another attempt to gain a little information as to this singular giver of advice. "Tell me, is it true that the insurgents are under command of the famous Hans of Iceland?"

"Hans of Iceland!" repeated the little man, with peculiar emphasis.

The baron repeated his question. A burst of laughter, which might have passed for the roar of a wild beast, was the only answer which he could obtain. He ventured a few more questions as to the number and the leaders of the miners; the little man silenced him.

"Colonel of the Munkholm musketeers, I have told you all that I have to tell. Lie in wait to-day in Black Pillar Pass with your entire regiment, and you may destroy the whole rebel force."

"You will not tell me who you are; you thus prevent the king from proving his gratitude; but it is only right that I should reward you for the service which you have done me."

The colonel threw his purse at the small man's feet.

"Keep your gold, Colonel," said he; "I do not need it. And," he added, pointing to a large bag which hung from his rope girdle, "if you wish pay for killing these men, I have money enough, Colonel, to give you for their blood."

Before the colonel could recover from the surprise caused by this mysterious being's inexplicable words, he had vanished.

Baron Vœthaün slowly retraced his steps, wondering whether he should place any faith in the fellow's news. As he entered his quarters, he was handed a letter, sealed with the lord chancellor's arms. It contained a message from Count d'Ahlefeld, which the colonel found, with amazement that may be readily imagined, consisted of the same piece of news and the same advice just given him outside the city gate by the incomprehensible character with the straw hat and the thick gloves.

XXXIX

All must perish!
The sword cleaveth the helmet;
The strong armor is pierced by the lance;
Fire devoureth the dwelling of princes;
Engines break down the fences of the battle.
All must perish!
The race of Hengist is gone—
The name of Horsa is no more!
Shrink not then from your doom, sons of the sword!
Let your blades drink blood like wine;
Feast ye in the banquet of slaughter,
By the light of the blazing halls!
Strong be your swords while your blood is warm,
And spare neither for pity nor fear,
For vengeance hath but an hour;
Strong hate itself shall expire!
I also must perish!
     Walter Scott: *Ivanhoe.*

WE will not try to describe the fearful confusion which broke the already straggling ranks of the rebels, when the fatal defile suddenly revealed to them all its steep and bristling peaks, all its caverns peopled with unlooked-for foes. It would be hard to say whether the prolonged shout, made up of a thousand shrieks, which rose from the columns of men thus unexpectedly mowed down, was a yell of despair, of terror, or of rage. The dreadful fire vomited against them from every side by the now unmasked platoons of the royal troops, grew hotter every moment; and before another shot from their lines followed Kennybol's unfortunate volley, they were wrapped in a stifling cloud of burning smoke, through which death flew blindly, where each man, shut off from his friends, could but dimly distinguish the musketeers, lancers, and dragoons, moving vaguely among the cliffs and upon the edge of the thickets, like demons in a red-hot furnace.

The insurgents, thus scattered over a distance of a mile, upon a narrow, winding road, bordered on one side by a deep torrent, on the other by a rocky wall, which made it impossible for them to turn and fall back, were like a serpent destroyed by a blow on the back, when he has unwound all his spirals, and, though cut to pieces, still tries to turn and coil, striving to unite his separate fragments.

When their first surprise was past, a common despair seemed to animate all these men, naturally fierce and intrepid. Frantic with rage to be thus overwhelmed without the possibility of defence, the rebels uttered a simultaneous shout,—a shout which in an instant drowned the clamor of their triumphant foes; and when the latter saw these men, without leaders, in dire disorder, almost destitute of weapons, climbing perpendicular cliffs, under a terrible fire, clinging with tooth and nail to the bushes growing on the verge of the precipice, brandishing hammers and pitchforks, the well-armed troops, well-drilled, securely posted as they were, although they had not yet lost a single man, could not resist a moment of involuntary panic.

Several times these barbarians clambered over a bridge of dead bodies, or upon the shoulders of their comrades planted against the rock like a living ladder, to the heights held by their assailants; but they had scarcely cried, "Liberty!" had scarcely lifted their hatchets or their knotted clubs,— they had scarcely showed their blackened faces, foaming with convulsive rage, ere they were hurled into the abyss, dragging with them such of their rash companions as they encountered in their fall, hanging to some bush or hugging some cliff.

The efforts of these unfortunates to fly and to defend themselves were fruitless. Every outlet was guarded; every accessible point swarmed with soldiers. The greater part of the luckless rebels bit the dust, perishing when they had shattered scythe or cutlass upon some granite fragment; some, folding their arms, their eyes fixed upon the ground, sat by the roadside, silently waiting for a ball to hurl them into the torrent below; those whom Hacket's forethought had provided with wretched muskets, fired a few chance shots at the summit of the cliffs and the mouth of the caves, from which a ceaseless rain of shot fell upon their heads. A tremendous uproar, in which the furious shouts of the rebel leaders and the quiet commands of the king's officers were plainly distinguishable, was mingled with the intermittent and frequent din of musketry, while a bloody vapor rose and floated above the scene of carnage, veiling the face of the mountains in tremulous mists; and the stream, white with foam, flowed like an enemy between the two bodies of hostile men, bearing away upon its bosom its prey of corpses.

In the earlier stage of the action, or rather of the slaughter, the Kiölen mountaineers, under the brave and reckless Kennybol, were the greatest sufferers. It will be remembered that they formed the advance-guard of the rebel army, and that they had entered the pine wood at the head of the pass. The ill-fated Kennybol had no sooner fired his gun, than the forest, peopled as by magic with hostile sharpshooters, surrounded them with a ring of fire; while from a level height, commanded by a number of huge bowlders, an entire battalion of the Munkholm regiment, formed in a hollow square, battered them unceasingly with a fearful musketry. In this horrible emergency, Kennybol, distracted and aghast, gazed at the mysterious giant, his only hope of safety lying in some superhuman power such as that of Hans of Iceland; but, alas! the awful demon did not suddenly unfold broad wings and soar above the combatants, spitting forth fire and brimstone upon the musketeers; he did not grow and grow until he reached the clouds, and overthrow a mountain upon the foe, or stamp upon the earth and open a yawning gulf to swallow up the ambushed army. The dreadful Hans of Iceland shrank like Kennybol from the first volley of shot, and approaching him, with troubled countenance asked for a carbine, because, he said, in a very commonplace tone, at such a time his axe was quite as useless as any old woman's spindle.

Kennybol, amazed, but still credulous, offered his own musket to the giant with a terror which almost made him forget his fear of the balls showering about him. Still expecting a miracle, he looked to see his fatal weapon become as big as a cannon in the hands of Hans of Iceland, or to see it change into a winged dragon darting fire from eyes, mouth, and nostrils. Nothing of the sort occurred, and the poor hunter's astonishment reached its climax when he saw the demon load the gun with ordinary powder and shot, just as he himself might have done, take aim like himself, and fire, though with far less skill than he would have shown. He stared at him in stupid surprise, as this purely mechanical act was repeated again and again; and convinced at last that all hope of a miracle must be abandoned, he turned his thoughts to rescuing his companions and himself from their evil predicament by some human means. Already his poor old friend Guldon Stayper lay beside him, riddled with bullets; already his followers, terrified and unable to escape, surrounded on every hand, huddled together without a thought of defence, uttering distressing cries. Kennybol saw what an easy target this mass of men afforded the enemy's guns, each discharge destroying a score of the insurgents. He ordered his unfortunate companions to scatter, to take refuge in the bushes along the road, —much thicker and larger at this point than anywhere else in Black Pillar Pass, —to hide in the underbrush, and to reply as best they could to the more and more murderous fire from the sharpshooters and the Munkholm battalion. The mountaineers, for the most part well armed, being all hunters, carried out their leader's order with a readiness which they might not have displayed at a less critical moment; for in the face of danger men usually lose their head, and obey willingly any one who has presence of mind and self-possession to act for all.

Still, this wise measure was far from insuring victory, or even safety. More mountaineers lay stretched upon the ground than still lived, and in spite of the example and encouragement offered them by their leader and the giant, several of them, leaning on their useless guns or prostrate with the wounded, obstinately persisted in waiting to be killed without taking the trouble to kill others in return. It may seem amazing that these men, in the habit of exposing their life every day in their expeditions over the glaciers in pursuit of wild beasts, should lose heart so soon; but let no one forget that in vulgar hearts courage is purely local. A man may laugh at shot and shell, and shiver in the dark or on the edge of a precipice; a man may face fierce animals daily, leap across fearful abysses, and yet run from a volley of artillery. Fearlessness is often only a habit; and one who has ceased to fear death under certain forms, dreads it none the less.

Kennybol, surrounded by heaps of dying friends, began himself to despair, although as yet he had received only a slight scratch on his left arm, and the diabolical giant still kept up his fire with the most comforting composure. All at once he saw an extraordinary confusion in the fatal battalion posted on the heights, which could not be caused by the slight damage inflicted by the very feeble resistance of his followers. He heard fearful shrieks of agony, the curses of the dying, exclamations of terror, rise from the victors.

Soon their fire slackened, the smoke cleared away, and he distinctly saw huge masses of granite falling upon the Munkholm musketeers from the top of the high cliff overlooking the level height upon which they were stationed. These bowlders succeeded one another with awful rapidity; they crashed one upon the other, and rebounded among the soldiers, who breaking their lines rushed in dire disorder down the hill, and fled in every direction.

At this unexpected aid, Kennybol turned; but the giant was still there! The mountaineer was dumfounded; for he supposed that Hans of Iceland had at last found his wings and taken his place upon the cliff, from which he overwhelmed the enemy. He looked up to the spot whence those fearful masses fell, and saw nothing. He could therefore only suppose that a party of rebels had succeeded in reaching this dangerous position, although he saw no glitter of weapons, and heard no shouts of triumph.

However, the fire from the plateau had wholly ceased; the trees hid the remnant of the royal troops, who were probably rallying their forces at the foot of the hill. The musketry from the sharpshooters also became less frequent. Kennybol, like a skilful leader, took advantage of this unexpected interval; he encouraged his men, and showed them, by the sombre light which reddened the scene of slaughter, the pile of corpses heaped upon the height, and the bowlders which still fell at intervals.

Then the mountaineers in their turn answered the enemy's groans with shouts of victory. They formed in line, and although still harassed by sharpshooters scattered among the bushes, they resolved, filled with fresh courage, to force their way out of this ill-omened defile.

The column thus formed was about to move; Kennybol had already given the signal with his horn, amid loud cries of "Liberty! liberty! No more protectorate!" when the notes of trumpet and drum sounding a charge were heard directly in front of them. Then the rest of the battalion from the height, strengthened by reinforcements of fresh troops, appeared within gunshot at a turn in the road, displaying a bristling line of pikes and bayonets upheld by rank upon rank as far as the eye could reach. Arriving thus unexpectedly in sight of Kennybol's division, the troops halted, and a man, who seemed to be the commanding officer, stepped forward, waving a white flag and escorted by a trumpeter.

The unforeseen appearance of this troop did not dismay Kennybol. In time of danger there is a point where surprise and fear become impossible.

At the first sound of trumpet and drum the old fox of Kiölen halted his men. As the royal troops drew up before him in line of battle, he ordered every gun to be loaded, and formed his mountaineers in double ranks, so that they might not offer so broad a mark for the enemy's fire. He placed himself at the head, the giant at his side, as in the heat of action, for he began to feel quite familiar with him, and observed that his eyes did not flame quite so brightly as a smithy's forge, and that his pretended claws were by no means as unlike ordinary human fingernails as was claimed for them.

When the officer in command of the musketeers stepped forward as if to surrender, and the sharpshooters ceased firing, although their loud shouts, ringing out on every hand, declared them still ambushed in the forests, he suspended his preparations for defence.

Meantime, the officer with the white flag had reached the centre of the space between the two hostile columns; here he paused, and the trumpeter accompanying him blew three loud blasts. The officer then cried in a loud voice, distinctly heard by the mountaineers, in spite of the ever increasing tumult of the battle raging behind them in the mountain gorges: "In the king's name! The king graciously pardons all those rebels who throw down their arms and surrender their leaders to his Majesty's supreme justice!"

The bearer of the flag of truce had scarcely pronounced those words, when a shot was fired from a neighboring thicket. The officer staggered, took a few steps forward, raising his flag above his head, and fell, exclaiming: "Treason!"

No one knew whose hand had fired the fatal shot.

"Treason! Cowardly treason!" repeated the royal troops, with a thrill of indignation.

And a fearful volley of musketry overwhelmed the mountaineers.

"Treason!" replied the mountaineers in their turn, made furious as they saw their brothers fall.

And a general discharge answered the unexpected attack from the royal troops.

"At them, comrades! Death to those vile cowards! Death!" cried the officers of the musketeers.

And both parties rushed forward with drawn swords, the two contending columns meeting directly over the body of the unfortunate officer, with a fearful din of arms.

The broken ranks were soon inextricably confounded. Rebel chiefs, king's officers, soldiers, mountaineers, all pell-mell ran their heads together, seized one another, grappled like two bands of famished tigers meeting in the desert. Their long pikes, bayonets, and partisans were now useless; swords and hatchets alone gleamed above their heads, and many of the combatants, in their hand-to-hand struggle, could use no other weapon than their dagger or their teeth.

The same rage and fury inspired both mountaineers and musketeers; the common cry of "Treason! Vengeance!" sprang from every mouth. The fray had reached a point when every heart was full of brutal ferocity, when men walked with utter indifference over heaps of wounded and dead, amid which the dying revive only to make one last attack on him who tramples them under foot.

At this moment a short man, whom several combatants, amid the smoke and streaming blood, took for a wild beast, in his dress of skins, flung himself into the thick of the carnage, with awful laughter and yells of joy. None knew whence he came, nor upon which side he fought; for his stone axe did not choose its victims, but smote alike the skull of a rebel and the head of a musketeer. He seemed, however, to prefer slaying the Munkholm troops. All gave way before him; he rushed through the fray like a disembodied spirit; and his bloody axe whirled about him without a pause, scattering fragments of flesh, lacerated limbs, and shattered bones on every side.

He shrieked "Vengeance!" as did all the rest, and uttered strange words, the name of "Gill" recurring frequently. This fearful stranger seemed to regard the slaughter as a feast.

A mountaineer upon whom his murderous glance fell threw himself at the feet of the giant in whom Kennybol had placed such vain trust, crying: "Hans of Iceland, save me!"

"Hans of Iceland!" repeated the little man.

He approached the giant.

"Are you Hans of Iceland?" he asked.

The giant, by way of answer, raised his axe. The small man sprang back, and the blade, as it fell, was buried in the skull of the wretch who had implored his aid.

The unknown laughed aloud.

"Ho! ho! by Ingulf! I thought Hans of Iceland was more skilful."

"It is thus that Hans of Iceland saves those who pray to him for help!" said the giant.

"You are right."

The two dreadful champions attacked each other madly. Stone axe and steel axe met; they clashed so fiercely that both blades flew in fragments, with a myriad sparks.

Quicker than thought, the little man, finding himself disarmed, seized a heavy wooden club, dropped by some dying man, and evading the giant, who stooped to grasp him in his arms, dealt a furious blow with both hands on the broad brow of his colossal antagonist.

The giant uttered a stifled shriek, and fell. The little man trampled him under foot in triumph, foaming with joy, and exclaiming, "You bore a name too heavy for you!" and brandishing his victorious mace, he rushed in search of fresh victims.

The giant was not dead. The force of the blow had stunned him, and he dropped senseless, but soon opened his eyes, and gave faint signs of returning life. A musketeer, seeing him through the uproar, threw himself upon him, shouting, "Hans of Iceland is taken! Victory!"

"Hans of Iceland is taken!" repeated every voice, whether in tones of triumph or distress.

The little man had vanished.

For some time the mountaineers had realized that they must perforce submit to superior numbers; for the Munkholm musketeers had been joined by the sharpshooters from the forest, and by detachments of lancers and foot dragoons, who poured in from deep gorges, where the surrender of many of the rebel leaders had put a stop to slaughter. Brave Kennybol, wounded early in the fight, was made a prisoner. Hans of Iceland's capture deprived the mountaineers of such courage as they still possessed, and they threw down their arms.

When the first beams of the rising sun gilded the sharp peaks of lofty glaciers still half submerged in darkness, mournful peace and fearful silence reigned in Black Pillar Pass, broken only by feeble moans borne away by the chill breeze.

Black clouds of crows flocked to those fatal gorges from every quarter of the horizon; and a few poor goat-herds, who passed the cliffs at twilight, hastened home in terror, declaring that they had seen an animal with the face of a man in Black Pillar Pass, seated on a heap of slain, drinking their blood.

XL

Let him who will, burn beneath these smouldering fires.—
Brantome.

"OPEN the window, daughter; those panes are very dirty, and I would fain see the day."

"See the day, father! It will soon be night."

"The sun still lies on the hills along the fjord. I long to breathe the free air through my prison bars. The sky is so clear!"

"Father, a storm is at hand."

"A storm, Ethel! Where do you see it?"

"It is because the sky is clear, father, that I foresee a storm."

The old man looked at his daughter in surprise.

"Had I reasoned thus in my youth, I should not be here." Then he added in a firmer tone: "What you say is correct, but it is not a common inference for one of your age. I do not understand why your youthful reasoning should be so like my aged experience."

Ethel's eyes fell, as if she were troubled by this serious and simple remark. She clasped her hands sadly, and a deep sigh heaved her breast.

"Daughter," said the aged prisoner, "for some days you have looked pale, as if life had never warmed the blood in your veins. For several mornings you have approached me with red and swollen lids, with eyes that have wept and watched. I have passed several days in silence, Ethel, with no effort on your part to rouse me from my gloomy meditations on the past. You sit beside me more melancholy even than myself; and yet you are not, like your father, weighed down by the burden of a whole lifetime of empty inaction. Morning clouds vanish quickly. You are at that period of existence when you can choose in dreams a future independent of the present, be it what it may. What troubles you, my daughter? Thanks to your constant captivity, you are sheltered from all sudden calamity. What error have you committed? I cannot think that you are grieving for me; you must by this time be accustomed to my incurable misfortunes. Hope, to be sure, can no longer be the subject of my discourse; but that is no reason why I should read despair in your eyes."

As he spoke these words, the prisoner's stern voice melted with paternal love. Ethel stood silently before him. All at once she turned away with an almost convulsive motion, fell upon her knees on the stone floor, and hid her face in her hands, as if to stifle the tears and sobs which burst from her.

Too much woe filled full the wretched girl's heart. What had she done to that fatal stranger, that she should reveal to her the secret that was eating away her very life? Alas! since she had known her Ordener's true name, the poor child had not closed her eyes, nor had her soul known rest. Night brought her no alleviation, save that then she could weep freely and unseen. All was over! He was not hers, he who was hers by all her memories, by all her pangs, by all her prayers, he whose wife she had held herself to be upon the faith of her dreams. For the evening when Ordener had clasped her so tenderly in his arms was no more than a dream to her now. And in truth that sweet dream had been repeated nightly in her sleep. Was it a guilty love which she still cherished for that absent friend, struggle against it as she might? Her Ordener was betrothed to another! And who can tell what that virginal heart endured when the strange and unknown sentiment of jealousy found entrance there like a poisonous viper? When she tossed for long sleepless hours upon her fevered bed, picturing her Ordener, perhaps even then, in the arms of another, fairer, richer, nobler than herself? For, thought she, I was mad indeed to suppose that he would brave death for me. Ordener is the son of a viceroy, of a great lord, and I am nothing but a poor prisoner, nothing but the daughter of a proscribed and exiled man. He has left me, for he is free; and left me, no doubt, to wed his lovely betrothed, — the daughter of a chancellor, a minister, a haughty count! Has my Ordener deceived me, then? Oh, God! who would have thought that such a voice was capable of deceit?

And the wretched Ethel wept and wept again, and saw her Ordener before her, the man whom she had made the unwitting divinity of her whole being, that Ordener adorned with all the splendor of his rank, advancing to the altar amid festal preparations, and gazing upon her rival with the smile that had once been her delight.

However, in spite of her unspeakable agony, she never for an instant forgot her filial affection. The weak girl made the most heroic efforts to conceal her distress from her unfortunate father; for there is nothing more painful than to repress all outward signs of grief, and tears unshed are far more bitter than those that flow. Several days had passed before the silent old man observed the change in his Ethel, and at his affectionate questions her long-repressed grief had at last burst forth.

For some time he watched her emotion with a bitter smile and a shake of the head; but at last he said: "Ethel, you do not live among men; why do you weep?"

He had scarcely finished these words, when the sweet and noble girl rose. By a great effort she checked her tears, and dried her eyes with her scarf, saying: "Father, forgive me; it was a momentary weakness." And she looked at him with an attempt to smile.

She went to the back of the room, found the Edda, seated herself by her taciturn father, and opened the book at random; then, mastering her voice, she began to read. But her useless task was unheeded by her and by the old man, who waved his hand.

"Enough, enough, my daughter!"

She closed her book.

"Ethel," added Schumacker, "do you ever think of Ordener?"

The young girl started in confusion.

"Yes," he continued, "of that Ordener who went—"

"Father," interrupted Ethel, "why should we trouble ourselves about him? I think as you do,—that he left us, never to return."

"Never to return, my daughter! I cannot have said such a thing. On the contrary, I have a strange presentiment that he will come back."

"That was not your opinion, father, when you spoke so distrustingly of the young man."

"Did I speak distrustfully of him?"

"Yes, father, and I agree with you; I think that he deceived us."

"That he deceived us, daughter! If I judged him thus, I acted like most men who condemn without proof. I have received nothing but professions of devotion from this Ordener."

"And how do you know, father, that those cordial words did not hide treacherous thoughts?"

"Usually men disregard misfortune and disgrace. If this Ordener were not attached to me, he would not have visited my prison without a purpose."

"Are you sure," replied Ethel, feebly, "that he had no purpose in coming here?"

"What could it be?" eagerly asked the old man.

Ethel was silent.

It was too great an effort for her to continue to accuse her beloved Ordener, whom she had formerly defended against her father.

"I am no longer Count Griffenfeld," he resumed. "I am no longer lord chancellor of Denmark and Norway, the favored dispenser of royal bounty, the all-powerful minister. I am a miserable prisoner of State, a proscribed man, to be shunned like one stricken with the plague. It shows courage even to mention my name without execration to the men whom I overwhelmed with honors and wealth; it shows devotion for a man to cross the threshold of this dungeon unless he be a jailer or an executioner; it shows heroism, my girl, for a man to cross it and call himself my friend. No; I will not be ungrateful, like the rest of humanity. That young man merits my gratitude, were it only for letting me see a kindly face and hear a consoling voice."

Ethel listened in agony to these words, which would have charmed her a few days earlier, when this Ordener was still cherished as her Ordener. The old man, after a brief pause, resumed in a solemn tone: "Listen to me, my daughter; for what I have to say to you is serious. I feel that I am fading slowly; my life is ebbing. Yes, daughter, my end is at hand."

Ethel interrupted him with a stifled groan.

"Oh God, father, say not so! For mercy's sake, spare your poor daughter! Alas! would you forsake me? What would become of me, alone in the world, if I were deprived of your protection?"

"The protection of a proscribed man!" said her father, shaking his head. "However, that is the very thing of which I have been thinking. Yes, your future happiness occupies me even more than my past misfortunes; hear me, therefore, and do not interrupt me again. This Ordener does not deserve that you should judge him so severely, my daughter, and I had not hitherto thought that you felt such dislike to him. His appearance is frank and noble, which proves nothing, truly; but I must say that he does not strike me as without merit, although it is enough that he has a human soul, for it to contain the seeds of every vice and every crime. There is no flame without smoke."

The old man again paused, and fixing his eyes upon his daughter, added: "Warned from within of approaching death, I have pondered much, Ethel; and if he return, as I hope he may, I shall make him your protector and husband."

Ethel trembled and turned pale; at the very moment when her dream of happiness had fled forever, her father strove to realize it. The bitter reflection, "I might have been happy!" revived all the violence of her despair. For some moments she was unable to speak, lest the burning tears which filled her eyes should flow afresh.

Her father waited for her answer.

"What!" she said at last in a faint voice, "would you have chosen him for my husband, father, without knowing his birth, his family, his name?"

"I not only chose him, my daughter, I choose him still."

The old man's tone was almost imperious. Ethel sighed.

"I choose him for you, I say; and what is his birth to me? I do not care to know his family, since I know him. Think of it; he is the only anchor of salvation left to you. Fortunately, I believe that he does not feel the same aversion for you which you show for him."

The poor girl raised her eyes to heaven.

"You hear me, Ethel! I repeat, what is his birth to me? He is doubtless of obscure rank, for those born in palaces are not taught to frequent prisons. Do not show such proud regret, my daughter; do not forget that Ethel Schumacker is no longer Princess of Wollin and Countess of Tönsberg. You have fallen lower than the point from which your father rose by his own efforts. Consider yourself happy if this man accept your hand, be his family what it may. If he be of humble birth, so much the better, my daughter; at least your days will be sheltered from the storms which have tormented your father. Far from the envy and hatred of men, under some unknown name, you will lead a modest existence, very different from mine, for its end will be better than its beginning."

Ethel fell on her knees.

"Oh, father, have mercy!"

He opened his arms to her in amazement.

"What do you mean, my daughter?"

"In Heaven's name, do not describe a happiness which is not for me!"

"Ethel," sternly answered the old man, "do not risk your whole life. I refused the hand of a princess of the blood royal, a princess of Holstein Augustenburg,—do you hear that?—and my pride was cruelly punished. You despise an obscure but loyal man; tremble lest yours be as sadly chastised."

"Would to Heaven," sighed Ethel, "that he were an obscure and loyal man!"

The old man rose, and paced the room in agitation. "My daughter," said he, "your poor father implores and commands you. Do not let me die uncertain as to your future; promise me that you will accept this stranger as your husband."

"I will obey you always, father; but do not hope that he will return."

"I have weighed the probabilities, and I think from the tone in which Ordener uttered your name—"

"That he loves me!" bitterly interrupted Ethel. "Oh, no; do not believe it."

The father answered coldly: "I do not know whether, to use your girlish expression, he loves you; but I know that he will return."

"Give up that idea, father; besides, you would not wish him for your son-in-law if you knew who he is."

"Ethel, he shall be my son-in-law, be his name and rank what they may."

"Well!" she replied, "how if this young man, whom you regard as your solace, whom you consider as your daughter's support, be the son of one of your mortal foes,—of the viceroy of Norway, Count Guldenlew?"

Schumacker started back.

"Heavens! what do you say? Ordener! that Ordener! It is impossible!"

The look of unutterable hatred which flashed from the old man's faded eyes froze Ethel's trembling heart, and she vainly repented the rash words which she had uttered.

The blow was struck. For a few moments Schumacker stood motionless, with folded arms; his whole body quivered as if laid upon live coals; his flaming eyes started from their sockets; and his gaze, riveted to the pavement, seemed as if it would pierce the stones. At last these words issued from his livid lips in a voice as faint as that of a man who dreams. "Ordener! Yes, it must be so; Ordener Guldenlew! It is well. Come, Schumacker, old fool, open your arms to him; the loyal youth has come to stab you to the heart."

Suddenly he stamped upon the ground, and went on in tones of thunder: "So they send their whole infamous race to insult me in my disgrace and captivity! I have already seen a d'Ahlefeld; I almost smiled upon a Guldenlew! Monsters! Who would ever have thought that this Ordener possessed such a soul and bore such a name? Wretched me! Wretched he!"

Then he fell exhausted into his chair, and while his breast heaved with sighs, poor Ethel, trembling with fright, wept at his feet.

"Do not weep, my daughter," said he, in gloomy tones "come, oh, come to my heart!"

And he clasped her in his arms.

Ethel knew not how to explain this caress at a moment of rage, but he resumed: "At least, girl, you were more clear-sighted than your old father. You were not deceived by that serpent with gentle but venomous eyes. Come! let me thank you for the hatred which you have shown me that you feel for that contemptible Ordener."

She shuddered at these praises, alas! so ill-deserved.

"Father," said she, "be calm!"

"Promise me," added Schumacker, "that you will always retain the same feeling for the son of Guldenlew. Swear it!"

"God forbids us to swear, father."

"Swear, swear, girl!" vehemently repeated Schumacker. "Will you always retain the same feeling for Ordener Guldenlew?"

Ethel had scarcely strength to falter, "Always."

The old man drew her to his heart.

"It is well, my daughter! Let me at least bequeath to you my hate, if I cannot leave you the wealth and honors of which I was robbed. Listen! they deprived your old father of rank and glory; they dragged him in irons to the gallows, as if to stain him with every infamy and make him endure every torment. Wretches! Oh, may heaven and hell hear me, and may they be cursed in this life and cursed in their posterity!"

He was silent for a moment; then, embracing his poor daughter, terrified by his curses: "But Ethel, my only glory and my only treasure, tell me, how was your instinct so much more skilful than mine? How did you discover that this traitor bears one of the abhorred names inscribed upon my heart in gall? How did you penetrate his secret?"

She was summoning all her strength to answer, when the door opened.

A man dressed in black, carrying in his hand an ebony wand, and wearing about his neck a chain of unpolished steel, appeared upon the threshold, escorted by halberdiers also dressed in black.

"What do you want?" asked the captive, sharply, and in astonishment.

The man, without replying or looking at him, unrolled a long parchment, to which was fastened by silken threads a seal of green wax, and read aloud: "In the name of his Majesty, our most gracious sovereign and lord, Christian the king. Schumacker, prisoner of State in the royal fortress of Munkholm, and his daughter, are commanded to follow the bearer of the said command."

Schumacker repeated his question: "What do you want?"

The man in black, still immovable, prepared to re-read the document.

"That will do," said the old man.

Then, rising, he signed to the surprised and startled Ethel to follow with him this dismal escort.

Schumacker and his Daughter made Prisoners.
Photo-Etching.—From drawing by Démarest.

XLI

A doleful signal was given, an abject minister of justice knocked at his door and informed him that he was wanted. — Joseph de Maistre.

NIGHT had fallen; a cold wind whistled around the Cursed Tower, and the doors of Vygla ruin rattled on their hinges, as if the same hand had shaken all of them at once.

The wild inhabitants of the tower, the hangman and his family, had gathered about the fire lighted in the middle of the room on the first floor, which cast a fitful glow upon their dark faces and scarlet garments. The children's features were fierce as their father's laughter and haggard as their mother's gaze. Their eyes, as well as those of Becky were fixed on Orugix, who, seated on a wooden stool, seemed to be recovering his breath, his feet covered with dust, showing that he had but just returned from some distant trip.

"Wife, listen; listen, children. I've not been gone two whole days merely to bring back bad news. If I am not made executioner to the king before another month is out, I wish I may never tie another slip-noose or handle an axe again. Rejoice, my little wolf-cubs; your father may leave you the Copenhagen scaffold by way of an inheritance, after all."

"Nychol," asked Becky, "what has happened?"

"And you, my old gypsy," rejoined Nychol, with his boisterous laugh, "rejoice too! You can buy any number of blue glass necklaces to adorn your long, skinny neck. Our agreement will soon be up; but never fear, in a month, when you see me chief hangman of both kingdoms, you will not refuse to break another jug with me."[1]

"What is it, what is it, father?" asked the children, the older of whom was playing with a bloody rack, while the little one amused himself by plucking alive a young bird which he had stolen from the nest.

"What is it, children?—Kill that bird, Haspar; it makes as much noise as a rusty saw; and besides, you should never be cruel. Kill it.—What is it, you say? Nothing,—a trifle, truly; nothing, dame Becky, save that within a week from this time ex-chancellor Schumacker, who is a prisoner at Munkholm, after looking me so closely in the face at Copenhagen, and the famous brigand of Iceland, Hans of Klipstadur, may perhaps both pass through my hands at once."

The red woman's wandering eye assumed an expression of surprised curiosity.

"Schumacker! Hans of Iceland! How is that, Nychol?"

"I'll tell you all about it. Yesterday morning, on the road to Skongen, at Ordals bridge, I met the whole regiment of musketeers from Munkholm marching back to Throndhjem with a very victorious air. I questioned one of the soldiers, who condescended to answer, probably because he did not know why my jerkin and my cart were red. I learned that the musketeers were returning from Black Pillar Pass, where they had cut to pieces various bands of brigands,—that is to say, insurgent miners. Now, you must know, gypsy Becky, that these rebels revolted in Schumacker's name, and were commanded by Hans of Iceland. You must know that his uprising renders Hans of Iceland guilty of the crime of insurrection against royal authority, and Schumacker guilty of high treason, which will naturally lead those two honorable gentlemen to the scaffold or the block. Add to these two superb executions, which cannot fail to bring me in at least fifteen gold ducats each, and to entitle me to the greatest honor in both kingdoms, several other though less important ones—"

"But do tell me," interrupted Becky, "has Hans of Iceland been captured?"

"Why do you interrupt your lord and master, miserable woman?" said the hangman. "Yes, to be sure, the famous, the impregnable Hans of Iceland is a prisoner, together with several other leaders of the brigands, his lieutenants, who will also bring me in twelve crowns apiece, to say nothing of the sale of their bodies. He was captured, I tell you; and I saw him, if you must know all the particulars, march by between a double file of soldiers."

The woman and children crowded eagerly about Orugix.

"What! did you really see him, father?" asked the children.

"Be quiet, boys. You shriek like a rogue protesting his innocence. I saw him; he is a giant. His hands were tied behind his back, and his forehead was bandaged. I suppose he was wounded in the head. But never fear, I will soon heal his hurt for him." Accompanying these brutal words with a brutal gesture, the hangman added: "There were four of his comrades behind him, prisoners too and wounded, like him, who were being taken, like him, to

Throndhjem, where they are to be tried with ex-chancellor Schumacker by a court of justice presided over by the lord mayor and the present chancellor."

"Father, what did the other prisoners look like?"

"The first two were a couple of old men, one of whom wore a miner's broad felt hat, and the other a mountaineer's cap; both seemed utterly disheartened. Of the other two, one was a young miner, who marched along with head up, whistling; the other,—do you remember, Becky, those travellers who came to this tower some ten days ago, on the night of that terrible storm?"

"As Satan remembers the day of his fall," replied the woman.

"Did you notice a young man in company with that crazy old doctor with the big periwig,—a young fellow, I say, who wore a great green cloak, and a cap with a black feather?"

"Yes, indeed; I can see him now, saying: 'Woman, we have plenty of gold!'"

"Well, old woman, I hope I may never wring the neck of anything worse than a grouse, if the fourth prisoner was not that young man. His face, to be sure, was entirely hidden by his feather, his cap, his hair, and his cloak; besides, he hung his head. But it was the very same dress, the same boots, the same manner. I'll swallow the stone gallows at Skongen at a single mouthful if it be not the same man! What do you say to that, Becky? Wouldn't it be a joke if after I had given him something to sustain life he should also receive from me something to cut it short, and should exercise my skill after having tasted my hospitality?"

The hangman's coarse laughter was loud and long; then he resumed: "Come, make merry, all of you, and let us drink. Yes, Becky, give me a glass of that beer which scrapes a man's throat as if he were drinking files, and let me drain it to my future advancement. Come, here's to the health and prosperity of Nychol Orugix, executioner royal that is to be! I will confess, you old sinner, that I found it hard work to go to Nœs village to hang a contemptible clown for stealing cabbage and chicory. Still, when I thought it over, I felt that thirty-two escalins were not to be sneezed at, and that my hands would not be degraded by turning off mere thieves and riff-raff of that kind until after they had actually beheaded the noble count and ex-chancellor, and the famous demon of Iceland. I therefore resigned myself, while waiting for my certificate as hangman to the king, to despatch the poor wretch at Nœs village. And here," he added, drawing a leather purse from his wallet, "are the thirty-two escalins for you, old girl."

At this moment three blasts from a horn were heard outside.

"Woman," cried Orugix, "those are the bowmen of the lord mayor."

With these words he hurried downstairs.

An instant later he reappeared, carrying a large parchment, of which he had broken the seal.

"There," said he to his wife, "there's what the lord mayor has sent me. Do you decipher it; for you can read Satan's scrawl. Perhaps it is my promotion already; for since the court is to have a chancellor to preside over it and a chancellor as prisoner at the bar, it is only proper that the man who carries out the sentence should be an executioner royal."

The woman took the parchment, and after studying it for some time, read aloud, while the children stared at her in stupid wonder: "In the name of the Council of the province of Throndhjem, Nychol Orugix, hangman for the province, is hereby ordered to repair at once to Throndhjem, and to carry with him his best axe, block, and black hangings."

"Is that all?" asked the hangman, in a dissatisfied tone.

"That is all," replied Becky.

"Hangman for the province!" muttered Orugix.

He cast an angry glance at the official document, but at last exclaimed: "Well, I must obey and be off. After all, they tell me to bring my best axe and the black hangings. Take care, Becky, that you rub off the spots of rust which have dimmed my axe, and see that the hangings are not stained with blood. We must not be discouraged; perhaps they mean to promote me in payment for this fine execution. So much the worse for the prisoners; they will not have the satisfaction of dying by the hand of an executioner royal."

XLII

Elvira. What has become of poor Sancho? He has not appeared in town?

Nuno. Sancho has doubtless contrived to find shelter.

Lope de Vega: *The Best Alcalde is the King.*

COUNT d'Ahlefeld, dragging behind him an ample robe of black satin lined with ermine, his head and shoulders concealed by a large judicial wig, his breast covered with stars and decorations, among which were the collars of the Royal Orders of the Elephant and the Dannebrog, clad, in a word, in the complete costume of the lord chancellor of Denmark and Norway, paced with an anxious air up and down the apartment of Countess d'Ahlefeld, who was alone with him at the moment.

"Come, it is nine o'clock; the court is about to open; it must not be kept waiting, for sentence must be pronounced to-night, so that it may be carried out by to-morrow morning at latest. The mayor assures me that the hangman will be here before dawn. Elphega, did you order the boat to take me to Munkholm?"

"My lord, it has been waiting for you at least half an hour," replied the countess, rising from her seat.

"And is my litter at the door?"

"Yes, my lord."

"Good! So you say, Elphega," added the count, clapping his hand to his head, "that there is a love-affair between Ordener Guldenlew and Schumacker's daughter?"

"A very serious one, I assure you," replied the countess, with a smile of anger and contempt.

"Who would ever have imagined it? And yet I tell you that I suspected it."

"And so did I," said the countess. "This is a trick played upon us by that confounded Levin."

"Old scamp of a Mecklenburger!" muttered the chancellor; "never fear, I'll recommend you to Arensdorf. If I could only succeed in disgracing him! Ah! see here, Elphega, I have an inspiration."

"What is it?"

"You know that the persons whom we are to try at Munkholm Castle are six in number,—Schumacker, whom I hope I shall have no further cause to fear, to-morrow, at this hour; the colossal mountaineer, our false Hans of Iceland, who has sworn to sustain his character to the end, in the hope that Musdœmon, from whom he has already received large sums of money, will help him to escape,—that Musdœmon really has the most devilish ideas! The other four prisoners are the three rebel chiefs, and a certain unknown character, who stumbled, no one knows how, into the midst of the assembly at Apsyl-Corh, and whom Musdœmon's precautions have thrown into our hands. Musdœmon thinks that the fellow is a spy of Levin de Knud. And indeed, when brought here a prisoner, his first words were to ask for the general; and when he learned of the Mecklenburger's absence, he seemed dumfounded. Moreover, he has refused to answer any of Musdœmon's questions."

"My dear lord," interrupted the countess, "why have you not questioned him yourself?"

"Really, Elphega, how could I, in the midst of all the business which has overwhelmed me since my arrival? I trusted the affair to Musdœmon, whom it interests as much as it does me. Besides, my dear, the fellow is not of the slightest consequence in himself; he is merely some poor vagabond. We can only turn him to account by representing him to be an agent of Levin de Knud, and as he was captured in the rebel ranks, it would go to prove a guilty connivance between Schumacker and the Mecklenburger, which will suffice to bring about, if not the arraignment, at least the disgrace, of that confounded Levin."

The countess meditated for a moment. "You are right; my lord. But how about this fatal passion of Baron Thorwick for Ethel Schumacker?"

The chancellor again rubbed his head. Then, shrugging his shoulders, he said: "See here, Elphega; neither you nor I are young novices, and we ought to understand men. When Schumacker has been condemned for high treason for the second time; when he has undergone an infamous death on the gallows; when his daughter, reduced to the lowest ranks of society, is forever publicly disgraced by her father's shame,—do you suppose,

Elphega, that Ordener Guldenlew will then recall for a single instant this childish flirtation which you call passion, judging it by the extravagant talk of a crazy girl, or that he will hesitate a single day between the dishonored daughter of a wretched criminal and the illustrious daughter of a great chancellor? We must judge others by ourselves; where do you find that the human heart is so constituted?"

"I trust that you may be right. But I think you will not disapprove of my request to the mayor that Schumacker's daughter might be present at her father's trial, and might be placed in the same gallery with me. I am curious to study the creature."

"All that can throw light upon the affair is valuable," said the chancellor, calmly. "But tell me, does anybody know where Ordener is at present?"

"No one knows; he is the worthy pupil of that old Levin, a knight-errant like him. I believe that he is visiting Wardhus just now."

"Well, well, our Ulrica will settle him. But come, I forget that the court is waiting for me."

The countess detained the chancellor. "One word more, my lord. I asked you yesterday, but your mind was full of other things, and I could not get an answer,—where is my Frederic?"

"Frederic!" said the count, with a melancholy expression, and hiding his face with his hand.

"Yes, answer me; my Frederic? His regiment has returned to Throndhjem without him. Swear to me that Frederic was not in that horrible affair at Black Pillar Pass. Why do you change color at his name? I am in mortal terror."

The chancellor's features resumed their wonted composure. "Make yourself easy, Elphega. I swear that he was not at Black Pillar Pass. Besides, the list of officers killed or wounded in that skirmish has been published."

"Yes," said the countess, growing calmer, "you reassure me. Only two officers were killed,—Captain Lory and that young Baron Randmer, who played so many mad pranks with my poor Frederic at the Copenhagen balls. Oh, I have read and re-read the list, I assure you. But tell me, my lord, did my boy remain at Wahlstrom?"

"He did," replied the count.

"Well, my friend," said the mother, with a smile which she tried to render affectionate, "I have but one favor to ask of you,—that is, to recall Frederic as soon as may be from that frightful region."

The chancellor broke from her suppliant arms, saying, "Madam, the court waits. Farewell. What you ask does not depend on my will." And he quitted the room abruptly.

The countess was left in a sad and pensive mood. "It does not depend upon his will!" said she; "and he has but to utter a word to restore my son to my arms! I always thought that man was genuinely bad."

XLIII

Is it thus you treat a man in my position? Is it thus you forget
the respect due to justice?—Calderon: *Louis Perez of Galicia.*

THE trembling Ethel, separated from her father by the guards upon
leaving the Lion of Schleswig tower, was conducted through dim passages,
hitherto unknown to her, to a small, dark cell, which was closed as soon as
she had entered it. In the wall opposite the door was a large grated opening,
through which came the light of links and torches. Before this opening was
a bench, upon which sat a woman, veiled and dressed in black, who signed
to her to be seated beside her. Ethel obeyed in silent dismay. She looked
through the grated window and saw a solemn and imposing scene.

At the farther end of a room hung with black and dimly lighted by
copper lamps suspended from the vaulted roof, was a black platform in
the shape of a horseshoe, occupied by seven judges in black gowns, one of
whom, placed in the centre upon a higher seat, wore on his breast glittering
diamond chains and gold medals. The judge on his right differed from the
others in the wearing of a white girdle and an ermine mantle, showing
him to be the lord mayor of the province. To the right of the bench was a
platform covered with a daïs, upon which sat an old man, in bishop's dress;
to the left, a table covered with papers, behind which stood a short man
with a huge wig, and enveloped in a long black gown.

Opposite the judges was a wooden bench, surrounded by halberdiers
holding torches, whose light, reflected back from a forest of pikes, muskets,
and partisans, shed a faint glimmer upon the tumultuous heads of a mob of
spectators, crowded against the iron railing dividing them from the court-
room.

Ethel looked at this spectacle as she might have beheld some waking
dream; yet she was far from feeling indifferent to what was about to happen.
A secret voice warned her to listen well, because a crisis in her life was at
hand. Her heart was a prey to contending emotions; she longed to know
instantly what interest she had in the scene before her, or never to know it
at all. For some days, the idea that her Ordener was forever lost to her had
inspired her with a desperate desire to be done with existence once for all,
and to read the book of her fate at a single glance. Therefore, realizing that

this was a decisive hour, she watched the sombre picture before her, not so much with aversion as with a sort of impatient, melancholy joy.

She saw the president rise and proclaim in the king's name that the court was opened.

She heard the short, dark man to the left of the bench read, in a low, rapid voice, a long discourse in which her father's name, mixed with the words "conspiracy," "revolt in the mines," and "high treason," frequently recurred. Then she remembered what the dread stranger had told her, in the donjon garden, of the charges against her father; and she shuddered as she heard the man in the black robe conclude his speech with the word "death," pronounced with great emphasis.

She turned in terror to the veiled lady, from whom she shrank with unaccountable fear. "Where are we? What does all this mean?" she timidly asked.

A gesture from her mysterious companion commanded her to be silent and attentive. She again turned her eyes to the court-room. The venerable bishop rose, and Ethel caught these words: "In the name of omnipotent and most merciful God, I, Pamphilus-Luther, bishop of the royal province and town of Throndhjem, do greet the worthy court assembled here in the name of the king, our lord, under God.

"And I say, that having observed that the prisoners brought to this bar are men and Christians, and that they have no counsel, I declare to the worthy judges that it is my purpose to aid them with my poor strength in the cruel position in which it has pleased Heaven to place them.

"Praying that God will deign to strengthen my great weakness, and enlighten my great blindness, I, bishop of this royal diocese, greet this wise and worthy court."

So saying, the bishop stepped from his episcopal throne, and took his seat upon the prisoners' bench, amid a murmur of applause from the people.

The president then rose, and said in dry tones, "Halberdiers, command silence! My lord bishop, the court thanks your reverence, in the name of the prisoners. Inhabitants of the province of Throndhjem, pay good heed to the king's justice; there can be no appeal from the sentence of the court. Bowmen, bring in the prisoners."

There was an expectant and terrified hush; the heads of the crowd swayed to and fro in the darkness like the waves of a stormy sea, upon which the thunder is about to burst.

Soon Ethel heard a dull sound and a strange stir below her, in the gloomy aisles of the court; the audience moved aside with a thrill of impatient curiosity; there was a noise of many feet; halberds and muskets gleamed, and six men, chained and surrounded by guards, entered the room bareheaded. Ethel had eyes for the first of the six alone, a white-headed old man in a black gown. It was her father.

She leaned, almost fainting, against the stone balustrade in front of her; everything swam before her in a confused cloud, and it seemed as if her heart were in her throat. She said in a feeble voice, "O God! help me!"

The veiled woman bent over her and gave her salts to smell, which roused her from her lethargy.

"Noble lady," said she, reviving, "for mercy's sake, speak but one word to convince me that I am not the sport of spirits from hell."

The stranger, deaf to her entreaty, again turned her head toward the court; and poor Ethel, who had somewhat recovered her strength, resigned herself to do the same in silence.

The president rose, and said in slow, solemn tones, "Prisoners, you are brought before us that we may decide whether or not you are guilty of high treason, conspiracy, and armed rebellion against the authority of the king, our sovereign lord. Examine your consciences well, for the charge of leze-majesty rests upon your heads."

At this moment a gleam of light fell upon the face of one of the six prisoners, a young man who held his head down, as if to veil his features with his long hair. Ethel started, and a cold sweat oozed from every pore. She thought she recognized—But no; it was a cruel illusion. The room was but dimly lighted, and men moved about it like shadows; the great polished ebony Christ hanging over the president's chair was scarcely visible.

And yet that young man was wrapped in a mantle which at this distance seemed to be green; his disordered hair was chestnut, and the unexpected gleam which revealed his features—But no; it was not true. It could not be! It was some horrid delusion!

The prisoners were seated on the bench beside the bishop. Schumacker took his place at one end; he was separated from the chestnut-haired young man by his four companions in misfortune, who wore coarse clothes, and among whom was one of gigantic stature. The bishop sat at the other end of the bench.

Ethel saw the president turn to her father, saying in a stern voice: "Old man, tell us your name, and who you are."

The old man raised his venerable head.

"Once," he replied, looking steadily at the president, "I was Count Griffenfeld and Tönsberg, Prince of Wollin, Prince of the Holy German Empire, Knight of the Royal Orders of the Elephant and the Dannebrog, Knight of the Golden Fleece in Germany and of the Garter in England, Prime Minister, Lord Rector of all our Universities, Lord High Chancellor of Denmark, and—"

The president interrupted him: "Prisoner, the court does not ask who you were, nor what your name once was, but who you are and what it now is."

"Well," answered the old man, quickly, "my name is John Schumacker now; I am sixty-nine years old, and I am nothing but your former benefactor, Chancellor d'Ahlefeld."

The president seemed confused.

"I recognized you, Count," added the ex-chancellor, "and as I thought you did not know me, I took the liberty to remind your Grace that we are old acquaintances."

"Schumacker," said the president, in a voice trembling with concentrated fury, "do not trifle with the court."

The aged prisoner again interrupted him: "We have changed places, noble Chancellor; I used to call you 'd'Ahlefeld,' and you addressed me as 'Count.'"

"Prisoner," replied the president, "you only injure your cause by recalling the infamous decree which already brands your name."

"If that sentence entailed infamy on any one, Count d'Ahlefeld, it was not on me."

The old man half rose as he spoke these words with great emphasis.

The president waved his hand.

"Sit down. Do not insult, in the presence of the court, the judges who condemned you, and the king who surrendered you to those judges. Recollect that his Majesty deigned to grant you your life, and confine yourself to defending it."

Schumacker's only answer was a shrug of the shoulders.

"Have you," asked the president, "anything to say in regard to the charges preferred against you?"

Seeing that Schumacker was silent, the president repeated his question.

"Are you speaking to me?" said the ex-chancellor. "I supposed, noble Count d'Ahlefeld, that you were speaking to yourself. Of what crime do you accuse me? Did I ever give a Judas kiss to a friend? Have I imprisoned, condemned, and dishonored a benefactor,—robbed him to whom I owed everything? In truth, my lord chancellor, I know not why I am brought here. Doubtless it is to judge of your skill in lopping off innocent heads. Indeed, I shall not be sorry to see whether you find it as easy to ruin me as to ruin the kingdom, and whether a single comma will be a sufficient pretext for my death, as one letter of the alphabet was enough for you to bring on a war with Sweden."[2]

He had scarcely uttered this bitter jest, when the man seated at the table to the left of the bench arose.

"My lord president," said he, bowing low, "my lord judges, I move that John Schumacker be forbidden to speak, if he continue to insult his Grace, the president of this worshipful court."

The calm voice of the bishop answered: "Mr. Private Secretary, no prisoner can be deprived of the right to speak."

"True, Reverend Bishop," hastily exclaimed the president. "We propose to allow the defence the utmost liberty. I would merely advise the prisoner to moderate his expressions if he understands his own interest."

Schumacker shook his head, and said coldly: "It seems that Count d'Ahlefeld is more sure of his game than he was in 1677."

"Silence!" said the president; and instantly addressing the prisoner next to the old man, he asked his name.

A mountaineer of colossal stature, whose forehead was swathed in bandages, rose, saying, "I am Hans, from Klipstadur, in Iceland."

A shudder of horror ran through the crowd, and Schumacher, lifting his head, which had sunk upon his breast, cast a sudden glance at his dreadful neighbor, from whom all his other fellow-prisoners shrank.

"Hans of Iceland," asked the president, when the confusion ceased, "what have you to say for yourself?"

Ethel was as much startled as any of the spectators by the appearance of the famous brigand, who had so long played a prominent part in all her visions of alarm. She fixed her eyes with timid dread upon the monstrous giant, with whom her Ordener had possibly fought, whose victim he perhaps was. This idea again took possession of her soul in all its painful shapes. Thus, wholly absorbed by countless heart-rending emotions, she hardly heeded the coarse, blundering answer of this Hans of Iceland, whom she regarded almost as her Ordener's murderer. She only understood that the brigand declared himself to be the leader of the rebel forces.

"Was it of your own free will," asked the president, "or by the suggestion of others, that you took command of the insurgents?"

The brigand answered: "It was not of my own free will."

"Who persuaded you to commit such a crime?"

"A man named Hacket."

"Who was this Hacket?"

"An agent of Schumacker, whom he also called Count Griffenfeld."

The president turned to Schumacker: "Schumacker, do you know this Hacket?"

"You have forestalled me, Count d'Ahlefeld," rejoined the old man; "I was about to ask you the same question."

"John Schumacker," said the president, "your hatred is ill advised. The court will put the proper value upon your system of defence."

The bishop then said, turning to the short man, who seemed to fill the office of recorder and prosecutor: "Mr. Private Secretary, is this Hacket one of your clients?"

"No, your reverence," replied the secretary.

"Does any one know what has become of him?"

"He was not captured; he has disappeared."

It seemed as if the private secretary tried to steady his voice as he said this.

"I rather think that he has vanished altogether," said Schumacker.

The bishop continued: "Mr. Secretary, is any one in pursuit of this Hacket? Has any one a description of him?"

Before the private secretary could answer, one of the prisoners rose. He was a young miner, with a stern, proud face.

"He is easily described," said he, in a firm voice. "This contemptible Hacket, Schumacker's agent, is a man of low stature, with an open countenance, like the mouth of hell. Stay, Mr. Bishop; his voice is very like that of the gentleman writing at the table over there, whom your reverence calls, I believe, 'private secretary.' And truly, if the room were not so dark, and the private secretary had less hair to hide his face, I could almost swear that he looked very much like the traitor Hacket."

"Our brother speaks truly," cried the prisoners on either side of the young miner.

"Indeed!" muttered Schumacker, with a look of triumph.

The secretary involuntarily started, whether from fear, or from the indignation which he felt at being compared to Hacket. The president, who himself seemed disturbed, hurriedly exclaimed: "Prisoners, remember that you are only to speak in answer to a question from the court; and do not insult the officers of the law by unworthy comparisons."

"But, Mr. President," said the bishop, "this is a mere matter of description. If the guilty Hacket has points of resemblance to your secretary, it may be useful to—"

The president cut him short.

"Hans of Iceland, you, who have had such frequent intercourse with Hacket, tell us, to satisfy the worthy bishop, whether the fellow really resembles our honorable private secretary."

"Not at all, sir," unhesitatingly answered the giant.

"You see, my lord bishop," added the president.

The bishop acknowledged his satisfaction by a bow, and the president, addressing another prisoner, pronounced the usual formula: "What is your name?"

"Wilfred Kennybol, from the Kiölen Mountains."

"Were you among the insurgents?"

"Yes, sir; the truth at all costs. I was captured in the cursed defile of Black Pillar. I was the chief of the mountaineers."

"Who urged you to the crime of rebellion?"

"Our brothers the miners complained of the royal protectorate; and that was very natural, was it not, your worship? If you had nothing but a mud hut and a couple of paltry fox-skins, you would not like to have them taken from you. The government would not listen to their petitions. Then, sir, they made up their minds to rebel, and begged us to help them. Such a slight favor could not be refused by brothers who say the same prayers and worship the same saints. That's the whole story."

"Did nobody," said the president, "excite, encourage, and direct your insurrection?"

"There was a Mr. Hacket, who was forever talking to us about rescuing a count who was imprisoned at Munkholm, whose messenger he said he was. We promised to do as he asked, because it was nothing to us to set one more captive free."

"Was not this count's name Schumacker or Griffenfeld, fellow?"

"Exactly so, your worship."

"Did you never see him?"

"No, sir; but if he be that old man who told you that he had so many names just now, I must confess—"

"What?" interrupted the president.

"That he has a very beautiful white beard, sir; almost as handsome a one as my sister Maase's husband's father, of the village of Surb; and he lived to be one hundred and twenty years old."

The darkness of the room prevented any one from seeing whether the president looked disappointed at the mountaineer's simple answer. He ordered the archers to produce certain scarlet flags.

"Wilfred Kennybol," he asked, "do you recognize these flags?"

"Yes, your Grace; they were given to us by Hacket in Count Schumacker's name. The count also distributed arms to the miners; for we did not need them, we mountaineers, who live by our gun and game-bag. And I myself, sir, such as you see me, trussed as I am like a miserable fowl to be roasted, have more than once, in one of our deep valleys, brought down an old eagle flying so high that it looked like a lark or a thrush."

"You hear, judges," remarked the private secretary; "the prisoner Schumacker distributed arms and banners to the rebels, through Hacket."

"Kennybol," asked the president, "have you anything more to say?"

"Nothing, your Grace, except that I do not deserve death. I only lent a hand in brotherly love to the miners, and I'll venture to say before all your worships that my bullet, old hunter as I am, never touched one of the king's deer."

The president, without answering this plea, cross-examined Kennybol's two companions; they were the leaders of the miners. The older of the two, who stated that his name was Jonas, repeated Kennybol's testimony in slightly different words. The other,—the same young man who had noticed such a strong resemblance between the private secretary and the treacherous Hacket,—called himself Norbith, and proudly avowed his share in the rebellion, but refused to reveal anything regarding Hacket and Schumacker, saying that he had sworn secrecy, and had forgotten everything but that oath. In vain the president tried threats and entreaties; the obstinate youth was not to be moved. Moreover, he insisted that he had not rebelled on Schumacker's account, but simply because his old mother was cold and hungry. He did not deny that he might deserve to die; but he declared that it would be unjust to kill him, because in killing him they would also kill his poor mother, who had done nothing to merit punishment.

When Norbith ceased speaking, the private secretary briefly summed up the heavy charges against the prisoners, and more especially against Schumacker. He read some of the seditious mottoes on the flags, and showed how the general agreement of the answers of the ex-chancellor's accomplices, and even the silence of Norbith bound by a fanatical oath, tended to inculpate him. "There now remains," he said in close, "but a single prisoner to be examined, and we have strong reasons for thinking him the secret agent of the authority who has ill protected the peace of the province of Throndhjem. This authority has favored, if not by his guilty connivance, at least by his fatal negligence, the outbreak of the revolt which must destroy all these unhappy men, and restore Schumacker to the scaffold from which the king's clemency so generously preserved him."

Ethel, whose fears for Ordener were now converted into cruel apprehensions for her father, shuddered at these ominous words, and wept floods of tears when her father rose and said quietly: "Chancellor d'Ahlefeld, I admire your skill. Have you summoned the hangman?"

The unfortunate girl thought her cup of bitterness was full: she was mistaken.

The sixth prisoner now stood up. With a superb gesture he swept back the hair which covered his face, and replied to the president's questions in a clear, firm voice: "My name is Ordener Guldenlew, Baron Thorwick, Knight of the Dannebrog."

An exclamation of surprise escaped the secretary: "The viceroy's son!"

"The viceroy's son!" repeated every voice, as if the words were taken up by countless echoes.

The president shrank back in his seat; the judges, hitherto motionless upon the bench, bent toward one another in confusion, like trees beaten by opposing winds. The commotion was even greater in the audience. The spectators climbed upon stone cornices and iron rails; the entire assembly spoke through a single mouth; and the guards, forgetting to insist upon silence, added their ejaculations to the general uproar.

Only those accustomed to sudden emotions can imagine Ethel's feelings. Who could describe that unwonted mixture of agonizing joy and delicious grief; that anxious expectation, which was alike fear and hope, and yet not quite either? He stood before her, but he could not see her. There was her beloved Ordener,—her Ordener,—whom she had believed dead, whom she knew was lost to her; her friend who had deceived her, and whom she adored with renewed adoration. He was there; yes, he was there. She was not the victim of a vain dream. Oh, it was really he,—that Ordener, alas! whom she had seen in dreams more often than in reality. But did he appear within these gloomy precincts as an angel of deliverance, or a spirit of evil? Was she to hope in him, or to tremble for him? A thousand conjectures crowded upon her at once, and oppressed her mind like a flame choked by too much fuel; all the ideas and sensations which we have suggested flashed through her brain as the son of the Norwegian viceroy pronounced his name. She was the first to recognize him, and before any one else had recognized him, she had fainted.

She soon recovered her senses for the second time, thanks to the attentions of her mysterious neighbor. With pale cheeks, she again opened her eyes, in which the tears had been suddenly dried. She cast an eager glance at the young man still standing unmoved amid the general confusion; and after all agitation had ceased in the court and among the people, Ordener Guldenlew's name still rang in her ears. With painful alarm she observed that he wore his arm in a sling, and that his wrists were chained; she noticed that his mantle was torn in several places, and that his faithful sword no longer hung at his side. Nothing escaped her solicitude, for the eye of a lover is like that of a mother. Her whole soul flew to the rescue of him whom she could not shield with her body; and, be it said to the glory and the shame of love, in that room, which contained her father and her father's persecutors, Ethel saw but one man.

Silence was gradually restored. The president resumed his examination of the viceroy's son. "My lord Baron," said he, in a tremulous voice.

"I am not 'my lord Baron' here," firmly answered Ordener. "I am Ordener Guldenlew, just as he who was once Count Griffenfeld is John Schumacker here."

The president hesitated for a moment, then went on: "Well, Ordener Guldenlew, it is doubtless by some unlucky accident that you are brought before us. The rebels must have captured you while you were travelling, and forced you to join them, and it is probably in this way that you were found in their ranks."

The secretary rose: "Noble judges, the mere name of the viceroy's son is a sufficient plea for him. Baron Ordener Guldenlew cannot by any possibility be a rebel. Our illustrious president has given a clear explanation of his unfortunate arrest among the rebels. The noble prisoner's only error is in not sooner revealing his name. We request that he may be set free at once, abandoning all charges against him, and only regretting that he should have been seated upon a bench degraded by the criminal Schumacker and his accomplices."

"What would you do?" cried Ordener.

"The private secretary," said the president, "withdraws the charges against you."

"He is wrong," replied Ordener, in a loud, clear voice; "I alone of all here should be accused, judged, and condemned." He paused a moment, and added in a less resolute tone, "For I alone am guilty."

"You alone guilty!" exclaimed the president.

"You alone guilty!" repeated the secretary.

A fresh burst of astonishment was heard in the audience. The wretched Ethel shuddered; she did not reflect that this declaration from her lover would save her father. She thought only of her Ordener's death.

"Silence in the court!" said the president, possibly taking advantage of this brief tumult to collect his thoughts and recover his self-possession. "Ordener Guldenlew," he resumed, "explain yourself."

The young man mused an instant, then sighed heavily, and uttered these words in a tone of calm submission: "Yes, I know that an infamous death awaits me; I know that my life might have been bright and fair. But God reads my heart; God alone! I am about to accomplish the most urgent duty of my life. I am about to sacrifice to it my blood, perhaps my honor; but I feel that I shall die without regret or remorse. Do not be surprised at my words, judges; there are mysteries in the soul and in the destiny of man which men cannot penetrate, and which are judged in heaven alone. Hear me, therefore, and act toward me as your conscience may dictate when you have pardoned these unfortunate men, and more especially the much injured Schumacker, who has already, in his long captivity, expiated many more crimes than any one man could ever commit. Yes, I am guilty, noble judges, and I alone. Schumacker is innocent; these other unhappy men were merely led astray. I am the author of the insurrection among the miners."

"You!" exclaimed the president and his private secretary, with a singular look upon their faces.

"I! and do not interrupt me again, gentlemen. I am in haste to finish; for by accusing myself I exonerate these poor prisoners. I excited the miners in Schumacker's name; I distributed those banners to the rebels; I sent them money and arms in the name of the prisoner of Munkholm. Hacket was my agent."

At the name of Hacket, the private secretary made a gesture of stupefied amazement.

Ordener continued: "I will not trespass on your time, gentlemen. I was captured among the miners, whom I persuaded to revolt. I alone did everything. Now judge me. If I have proved my guilt, I have also proved the innocence of Schumacker and the poor wretches whom you deem his accomplices."

The young man spoke these words, his eyes raised to heaven. Ethel, almost lifeless, scarcely breathed; but it seemed to her that Ordener, although he exculpated her father, pronounced his name most bitterly. The young man's language terrified and amazed her, although she could not comprehend it. Of all she heard, she grasped nothing but misery.

A sentiment of similar nature seemed to engross the president. He was scarcely able to believe his ears. Nevertheless, he asked the viceroy's son: "If you are indeed the sole author of this revolt, what was your object in instigating it?"

"I cannot tell you."

Ethel shivered when she heard the president reply in a somewhat angry tone: "Had you not an intrigue with Schumacker's daughter?"

But Ordener, though in chains, advanced toward the bench, and exclaimed, in accents of indignation: "Chancellor d'Ahlefeld, content yourself with my life, which I place in your hands; respect a noble and innocent girl. Do not a second time attempt to dishonor her."

Ethel, who felt the blood rise to her face, did not comprehend the meaning of the words, "a second time," upon which her defender laid such emphasis; but by the rage expressed in the president's features, it seemed that he understood them.

"Ordener Guldenlew, do not forget the respect due to the king's justice and the officers of the law. I reprimand you in the name of the court. I now summon you anew to declare your purpose in committing the crime of which you accuse yourself."

"I repeat that I cannot tell you."

"Was it not to deliver Schumacker?" inquired the secretary.

Ordener was silent.

"Do not persist in silence, prisoner," said the president; "it is proved that you have been in communication with Schumacker, and your confession of guilt rather implicates than exonerates the prisoner of Munkholm. You have paid frequent visits to Munkholm, and your motive was surely more than mere curiosity. Let this diamond buckle bear witness."

The president took from the table a diamond buckle.

"Do you recognize it as your property?"

"Yes. By what chance?"

"Well! One of the rebels gave it, before he died, to our private secretary, averring that he received it from you in payment for rowing you across from Throndhjem to Munkholm fortress. Now I ask you, judges, if such a price paid to a common sailor does not prove the importance laid by the prisoner, Ordener Guldenlew, upon his reaching that prison, which is the one where Schumacker was confined?"

"Ah!" exclaimed the prisoner Kennybol, "what your grace says is true; I recognize the buckle. It is the same story which our poor brother Guidon Stayper told me."

"Silence," said the president; "let Ordener Guldenlew answer."

"I will not deny," replied Ordener, "that I desired to see Schumacker. But this buckle has no significance. It is forbidden to enter the fort wearing diamonds. The sailor who rowed me across complained of his poverty during our passage. I flung him this buckle, which I was not allowed to wear."

"Pardon me, your Grace," interrupted the private secretary, "the rule does not include the viceroy's son. You could therefore—"

"I did not wish to give my name."

"Why not?" asked the president.

"I cannot tell you."

"Your relations with Schumacker and his daughter prove that the object of your conspiracy was to set them free."

Schumacker, who had hitherto shown no sign of attention save an occasional scornful shrug of the shoulders, rose: "To set me free! The object of this infernal plot was to compromise and ruin me, as it still is. Do you think that Ordener Guldenlew would confess his share in this crime unless he had been captured among the rebels? Oh, I see that he inherits his father's hatred of me! And as for the relations which you suppose exist between him and myself and my daughter, let him know, that accursed Guldenlew, that my daughter also inherits my loathing for him,—for the whole race of Guldenlews and d'Ahlefelds!"

Ordener sighed deeply, while Ethel in her heart disclaimed her father's assertion; and he fell back upon his bench, quivering with wrath.

"The court will decide for itself," said the president.

Ordener, who, at Schumacker's words, had silently cast down his eyes, seemed to awake: "Oh, hear me, noble judges! You are about to examine your consciences; do not forget that Ordener Guldenlew is alone guilty; Schumacker is innocent. These other unfortunate men were deceived by my agent, Hacket. I did everything else."

Kennybol interrupted him: "His worship says truly, judges, for it was he who undertook to bring Hans of Iceland to us; I only hope that name may not bring me ill luck. I know that it was this young man who ventured to seek him out in Walderhog cave, to persuade him to be our leader. He confided the secret of his undertaking to me in Surb village, at the house of my brother Braal. And for the rest, too, the young gentleman says truly; we were deceived by that confounded Hacket, whence it follows that we do not deserve death."

"Mr. Secretary," said the president, "the hearing is ended. What are your conclusions?"

The secretary rose, bowed several times to the court, passed his finger under the folds of his lace band, without taking his eyes from the president's face. At last he pronounced the following words in a dull, measured voice: "Mr. President, most worthy judges! It is a true bill. Ordener Guldenlew, who has forever tarnished the glory of an illustrious name, has only succeeded in establishing his own guilt without proving the innocence of ex-chancellor Schumacker and his accomplices, Hans of Iceland, Wilfred Kennybol, Jonas, and Norbith. I require the court to declare the six prisoners guilty of the crime of high treason in the first degree."

A vague murmur rose from the crowd. The president was about to dismiss the court, when the bishop asked for a brief hearing.

"Learned judges, it is proper that the prisoners' defence should be heard last. I could wish that they had a better advocate, for I am old and feeble, and have no other strength than that which proceeds from God. I am confounded at the secretary's severe sentence. There is no proof of my client Schumacker's crime. There is no evidence that he has had any direct share in the insurrection; and since my other client, Ordener Guldenlew, confesses that he made unlawful use of Schumacker's name, and moreover that he is the sole author of this damnable sedition, all evidence against Schumacker disappears; you should therefore acquit him. I recommend to your Christian indulgence the other prisoners, who were only led astray like the Good Shepherd's sheep; and even young Ordener Guldenlew, who has at least the merit, very great in the sight of God, of confessing his crime. Reflect, judges, that he is still at the age when a man may err, and even fall; but God does not refuse to support or to raise him up. Ordener Guldenlew bears scarce a fourth the burden of years which weigh down my head. Place in the balance of your judgment his youth and inexperience, and do not so soon deprive him of the life which the Lord has but lately given him."

The old man ceased, and took his place beside Ordener, who smiled; while at the invitation of the president, the judges rose from the bench, and silently crossed the threshold of the dread scene of their deliberations.

While a handful of men were deciding the fate of six fellow-beings within that terrible sanctuary, the prisoners remained motionless upon their seat between two files of halberdiers. Schumacker, his head on his breast, seemed absorbed in meditation. The giant stared to the right and left with stupid assurance; Jonas and Kennybol, with clasped hands, prayed in low tones, while their comrade, Norbith, stamped his foot or shook his chains with a convulsive start. Between him and the venerable bishop, who was reading the penitential psalms, sat Ordener, with folded arms and eyes lifted to heaven.

Behind them was the noise of the crowd, which swelled high when the judges left the room. The famous prisoner of Munkholm, the much-dreaded demon of Iceland, and above all the viceroy's son, were the objects of every thought, every speech, and every glance. The uproar, mingled with groans, laughter, and confused cries, rose and fell like a flame flickering in the wind.

Thus passed several hours of anxious expectation, so long that every one was astonished that they could be contained in a single night. From time to time a glance was cast toward the door of the anteroom; but there was nothing to be seen, save the two soldiers pacing to and fro with their glittering partisans before the fatal entrance, like two silent ghosts.

At last the lamps and torches began to burn dim, and the first pale rays of dawn were piercing the narrow windows of the room when the awful door opened. Profound silence instantly, and as if by magic, took the place of all the confusion; and the only sounds heard were the hurried breathing and the vague slight stir of the multitude in suspense.

The judges, proceeding slowly from the anteroom, resumed their places on the bench, the president at their head.

The private secretary, who had seemed absorbed in thought during their absence, bowed and said: "Mr. President, what sentence does the court, from whose decision there is no appeal, pronounce in the king's name? We are ready to hear it with religious respect."

The judge, seated at the president's right hand, rose, holding a roll of parchment: "His Grace, our illustrious president, exhausted by the length of this session, has deigned to commission me, lord mayor of the province of Throndhjem, and the natural president of this worshipful court, to read in his stead the sentence pronounced in the name of the king. I am about to fulfil this honorable but painful duty, requesting the audience to hear the king's impeccable justice in silence."

The lord mayor's voice then assumed a grave and solemn intonation, and every heart beat faster.

"In the name of our revered master and lawful sovereign, King Christian, we, the judges of the Supreme Court of the province of Throndhjem, summoned to decide in the cases of John Schumacker, prisoner of the State; Wilfred Kennybol, native of the Kiölen Mountains; Jonas, royal miner; Norbith, royal miner; Hans of Klipstadur, in Iceland; and Ordener Guldenlew, Baron Thorwick, Knight of the Dannebrog, all accused of high treason and leze-majesty in the first degree (Hans of Iceland being moreover charged with the crimes of murder, arson, and robbery), do find:—

"I. That John Schumacker is not guilty;

"II. That Wilfred Kennybol, Jonas, and Norbith are guilty, but are recommended to mercy, because they were led astray;

"III. That Hans of Iceland is guilty of all the crimes laid to his charge;

"IV. That Ordener Guldenlew is guilty of high treason and leze-majesty in the first degree."

The judge paused an instant as if to take breath. Ordener fixed upon him a look of celestial joy.

"John Schumacker," resumed the judge, "the court acquits you and remands you to prison;

"Kennybol, Jonas, and Norbith, the court commutes the penalty which you have incurred, to imprisonment for life, and a fine of one thousand crowns each;

"Hans of Klipstadur, murderer and incendiary, you will be taken this night to Munkholm parade-ground, and hanged by the neck until you are dead, dead, dead!

"Ordener Guldenlew, traitor, after having been stripped of your titles in presence of this court, you will be conducted this very night to the same place, with a lighted torch in your hand, and there your head shall be hewn off, your body burned, your ashes strewn to the winds, and your head exposed upon a stake. Let all withdraw. Such is the sentence rendered by the king's justice."

The lord mayor had scarcely ended these fatal words, when a shriek rang through the room. This shriek horrified the spectators even more than did the fearful terms of the death sentence; this shriek for a brief moment turned the calm and radiant face of the condemned Ordener pale.

XLIV

Misfortune made them equals.—Charles Nodier.

ALL was over now; Ordener's work was done. He had saved the father of the woman he loved; he had saved her too by preserving her father to protect her. The young man's noble plot to save Schumacker's life had succeeded; nothing else mattered now; it only remained for him to die.

Let those who deem him guilty or foolish judge the generous Ordener now, as he judges himself in his own soul with holy rapture. For it had been his one thought, when he entered the rebel ranks, that if he could not prevent Schumacker from carrying out his guilty purpose, he might at least help him to escape punishment by drawing it upon his own head.

"Alas!" he thought, "Schumacker is undoubtedly guilty; but embittered as he is by misfortune and imprisonment, his crime is excusable. He sighs to be set free; he struggles to acquire his liberty, even by rebellion. Besides, what would become of my Ethel if her father were taken from her; if she should lose him by the gallows, if fresh disgrace should blast his name, what would become of her, helpless and unprotected, alone in her cell or roaming through a world of foes?" This thought determined him to make the sacrifice, and he joyfully prepared for it. It is a lover's greatest happiness to lay down his life, I do not say for the life, but for a smile or a tear, of the loved object.

He was accordingly captured with the rebels, was dragged before the judges assembled to condemn Schumacker, his generous falsehood was uttered, he was sentenced, he must die a cruel death, suffer shameful torments, leave behind him a stained name; but what cared the noble youth? He had saved his Ethel's father.

He sat chained in a damp dungeon, where light and air never entered save through dark holes; beside him was a supply of food for the remnant of his existence,—a loaf of black bread and a jug of water; an iron collar weighed down his neck; iron fetters were about his hands and feet. Every hour that passed robbed him of a greater portion of his life than a year would bear away from other mortals. He was lost in a delicious dream.

"Perhaps my memory will not die with me, at least in one human heart. Perhaps she will deign to shed a tear in return for the blood I so freely shed for her; perhaps she will sometimes heave a sigh for him who sacrificed his life for her; perhaps in her virgin thoughts the dim image of her friend may sometimes appear. And who knows what lies behind the veil of death? Who knows if our souls, freed from their material prison, may not sometimes return to watch over the souls of those they love, and hold mysterious communion with those sweet companions still prisoned in the flesh, and in secret bring them angelic comfort and heavenly bliss?"

And yet bitter reflections would sometimes mingle with these consoling meditations. The hatred which Schumacker had expressed for him at the very moment of his self-sacrifice oppressed him. The agonized shriek which he had heard at the same instant with his death sentence had moved him deeply; for he alone, of all the assembly, recognized that voice and understood that misery. And should he never again see his Ethel? Must his last moments be passed within the self-same walls that contained her, and he be still unable to touch her soft hand once more, once more to hear the gentle voice of her for whom he was about to die?

He had yielded thus to those vague, sad musings which are to the mind what sleep is to the body, when the hoarse creak of rusty bolts struck harshly on his ear, already attuned to the music of the sphere to which he was so soon to take his flight. The heavy iron door grated upon its hinges. The young prisoner rose calmly, almost gladly, for he thought that the executioner had come for him, and he had already cast aside his life like the cloak beneath his feet.

He was mistaken. A slender white figure stood upon the threshold, like a radiant vision. Ordener doubted his own eyes, and wondered if he were not already in heaven. It was she; it was his Ethel!

The girl fell into his fettered embrace; she covered his hands with tears, and dried them with her long black hair. Kissing his chains, she bruised her pure lips upon those infamous irons; she did not speak, but her whole heart seemed ready to burst forth in the first word which might break through her sobs.

He felt the most celestial joy which he had known since his birth. He gently pressed his Ethel to his breast, and the combined powers of earth and hell could not at that moment have loosed the arms which encircled her. The knowledge of his approaching death lent a certain solemnity to his rapture; and he held his Ethel as close as if he had already taken possession of her for all eternity.

He did not ask this angel how she had gained access to him. She was there: could he waste a thought on anything else? Nor was he surprised. He never asked how this proscribed, feeble, lonely girl, in spite of triple doors of iron and triple ranks of soldiers, had contrived to open her own prison and that of her lover; it seemed to him quite simple; he had a perfect appreciation of the power of love.

Why speak with the voice when the soul can speak as readily? Why not allow the body to listen silently to the mysterious language of the spirit? Both were silent, because there are certain emotions which can find expression in silence only.

At last the young girl lifted her head from her lover's throbbing heart. "Ordener," said she, "I am here to save you;" and she uttered these words of hope with a pang.

Ordener smiled, and shook his head.

"To save me, Ethel! You deceive yourself; escape is impossible."

"Alas! I am but too well aware of that. This castle is crowded with soldiers, and every door is guarded by archers and jailers who never sleep." She added with an effort: "But I bring you another means of safety."

"No, no; your hope is vain. Do not delude yourself with idle fancies, Ethel; a few hours hence the axe will cruelly dispel them."

"Oh, do not say so, Ordener! You shall not die. Oh, spare me that dreadful thought! Or rather, no; let me behold it in all its horror, to give me strength to save you and sacrifice myself."

There was a strange expression in the young girl's voice.

Ordener gazed at her tenderly. "Sacrifice yourself! What do you mean?"

She hid her face in her hands, and sobbed almost inarticulately, "Oh, God!"

The struggle was brief; she overcame her emotion; her eyes sparkled, her lips wore a smile. She was as beautiful as an angel ascending from hell to heaven.

"Listen, my own Ordener: your scaffold shall never be reared. If you will but promise to marry Ulrica d'Ahlefeld, you may live."

"Ulrica d'Ahlefeld! That name from your lips, my Ethel!"

"Do not interrupt me," she continued, with the calm of a martyr undergoing the last pang; "I am sent here by Countess d'Ahlefeld. She promises to gain your pardon from the king, if in return you will agree to bestow your hand upon her daughter. I am here to obtain your oath to marry Ulrica and live for her. She chose me as her messenger because she thought that my voice might have some influence over you."

"Ethel," said the condemned man, in icy tones, "farewell! When you leave this cell, bid the hangman hasten his coming."

She rose, stood before him one moment, pale and trembling, then her knees gave way beneath her, and she sank to the stone floor with clasped hands.

"What have I done to him?" she muttered faintly.

Ordener silently fixed his eyes upon the flags.

"My lord," she said, dragging herself to him on her knees, "you do not answer me. Will you not speak to me once more? Then there is nothing left for me but to die."

A tear stood in the young man's eye.

"Ethel, you no longer love me."

"Oh, God!" cried the poor girl, clasping his knees. "No longer love you! You say that I no longer love you, Ordener! Did you really say those words?"

"You no longer love me, for you despise me."

He repented these cruel words as soon as he had uttered them; for Ethel's tone was heart-rending, as she threw her adored arms around his neck, and exclaimed in a voice broken by tears: "Forgive me, my beloved Ordener; forgive me as I forgive you. I despise you! Great heavens! Are you not my pride, my idol, my all? Tell me, was there aught in my words but deep love and ardent adoration? Alas! your stern language wounds me sorely, when I came here to save you, my idolized Ordener, by sacrificing my whole life for yours."

"Well," replied the young man, softened by her tears, and kissing them away, "was it not a want of esteem to suppose that I would buy my life by forsaking you, by basely renouncing my oaths, by sacrificing my love?" He added, fixing his eye on Ethel: "My love, for which I am about to shed my blood!"

Ethel uttered a deep groan as she answered: "Hear me, Ordener, before you judge me so rashly. Perhaps I have more strength than usually falls to the lot of a weak woman. From our lofty prison window I saw them build your scaffold on the parade. Ordener, you do not know what fearful agony it is to see the slow preparations for the death of one whose life is an indissoluble part of your own! Countess d'Ahlefeld, at whose side I sat when I heard the judge pronounce your death sentence, came to the cell to which I had returned with my father. She asked me if I would save you; she proposed this hateful means. Ordener, my poor happiness must perish; I must give you up, renounce you forever; yield to another my Ordener, poor lonely Ethel's only joy, or deliver you to the executioner. They bid me choose between my own misery and your death. I cannot hesitate."

He kissed this angel's hand with respectful worship.

"Neither do I hesitate, Ethel. You would not offer me life with Ulrica d'Ahlefeld's hand if you knew why I die."

"What? What secret mystery—"

"Let me keep this one secret from you, my beloved Ethel. I must die without letting you know whether you owe me gratitude or hatred for my death."

"You must die! Must you then die? Oh, God! it is but too true, and the scaffold stands ready even now; and no human power can save my Ordener, whom they will slay! Tell me,—cast one look upon your slave, your wife, and tell me, promise me, beloved Ordener, that you will listen to me without anger. Are you very sure—answer me as you would answer to God—that you could not be happy with that woman, that Ulrica d'Ahlefeld? Are you very sure, Ordener? Perhaps she is, she surely is, handsome, amiable, virtuous. She is far superior to her for whom you perish. Do not turn away your head, dear friend, dear Ordener. You are so noble and so young to mount the scaffold. Think! you might live with her in some gay city where you would lose all memory of this fatal dungeon; your days would flow by peacefully, without a thought of me. I consent,—you may drive me from your heart, erase my image from your thoughts, Ordener. Only live! Leave me here alone; let me be the one to die. And believe me, when I know that you are in the arms of another, you need not fear for me; I shall not suffer long."

She paused; her voice was drowned in tears. Still her grief-stricken countenance was radiant with her longing to win the ill-omened victory which must be her death.

Ordener said: "No more of this, Ethel. Let no name but yours and mine pass our lips at such a moment."

"Alas! alas!" she replied, "then you persist in dying?"

"I must; I shall go to the scaffold gladly for your sake; I should go to the altar with any other woman with horror and aversion. Say no more; you wound and distress me."

She wept, and murmured: "He will die, oh, God, a death of infamy!"

The condemned man answered with a smile: "Believe me, Ethel, there is less dishonor in my death than in such a life as you propose."

At this instant his eye, glancing away from his weeping Ethel, observed an old man in clerical dress standing in the shadow under the low, arched door. "What do you want?" said he, hastily.

"My lord, I came with the Countess d'Ahlefeld's messenger. You did not see me, and I waited silently until you should notice me."

In fact, Ordener had eyes for Ethel only; and she, at the sight of Ordener, had forgotten her companion.

"I am," continued the old man, "the minister whose duty it is—"

"I understand," said the young man; "I am ready."

The minister advanced toward him.

"God is also ready to receive you, my son."

"Sir," said Ordener, "your face is not unknown to me; I must have seen you elsewhere."

The minister bowed. "I too recognize you, my son; we met in Vygla tower. We both proved upon that occasion the fallibility of human words. You promised me the pardon of twelve unhappy prisoners, and I put no faith in your promise, being unable to guess that you were the viceroy's son; and you, my lord, who reckoned upon your power and your rank when you made me that promise—"

Ordener finished the thought which Athanasius Munder dared not put into words.

"Cannot now obtain pardon even for myself. You are right, sir. I had too little reverence for the future, it has punished me by showing me that its power is greater than mine."

The minister bent his head. "God is great!" said he.

Then he raised his kind eyes to Ordener, adding, "God is good!"

Ordener, who seemed preoccupied, exclaimed, after a brief pause: "Listen, sir; I will keep the promise which I made you in Vygla tower. When I am dead, go to Bergen, seek out my father, the viceroy of Norway, and tell him that the last favor which his son asks of him is to pardon your twelve protégés. He will grant it, I am sure."

A tear of emotion moistened the wrinkled cheek of Athanasius.

"My son, your soul must be filled with noble thoughts, if in the self-same hour you can reject your own pardon and generously implore that of others. For I heard your refusal; and although I blame such dangerous and inordinate affection, I was deeply touched by it. Now I ask myself,—*unde scelus?*—how could a man who approaches so near to the model of true justice soil his conscience with the crime for which you are condemned?"

"Father, I did not tell my secret to this angel; I cannot reveal it to you. But believe that I am not condemned for any crime of mine."

"What? Explain yourself, my son!"

"Do not urge me," firmly answered the young man. "Let me take my secret with me to the grave."

"This man cannot be guilty," muttered the minister.

Then drawing from his breast a black crucifix, he placed it on a sort of altar rudely shaped from a granite slab resting against the damp prison wall. Beside the crucifix he laid a small lighted lamp which he had brought with him, and an open Bible. "My son, meditate and pray; I will return a few hours hence. Come," he added, turning to Ethel, who during this conversation had preserved a solemn silence, "we must leave the prisoner. Our time has passed."

She rose, calm and radiant; a divine spark flashed from her eyes as she said: "Sir, I cannot go yet; you must first unite Ethel Schumacker to her husband, Ordener Guldenlew."

She looked at Ordener.

"If you were still free, happy, and powerful, my Ordener, I should weep, and I should shrink from linking

The Marriage of Ethel and Ordener.

Photo-Etching.—From drawing by Démarest.

my fatal destiny with yours. But now that you need no longer dread the contagion of my misfortune; that you, like me, are a captive, disgraced and oppressed; now that you are about to die, I come to you, hoping that you will at least deign, Ordener, my lord and husband, to allow her who could never have shared your life, to be your companion in death; for you love me too much, do you not, to doubt for an instant that I shall die with you?"

The prisoner fell at her feet, and kissed the hem of her gown.

"You, old man," she resumed, "must take the place of family and parents. This cell shall be our temple, this stone our altar. Here is my ring;

we kneel before God and before you. Bless us, and pronounce the sacred words which shall unite Ethel Schumacker and Ordener Guldenlew, her lord."

And they knelt together before the priest, who regarded them with mingled astonishment and pity.

"How, my children! What would you do?"

"Father," said the girl, "time presses. God and death wait for us."

In this life we sometimes meet with irresistible powers, supreme wills to which we yield instantly as if they were more than human. The priest raised his eyes, sighing: "May the Lord forgive me if I do wrong! You love each other; you have but little time to love on earth. I do not think I shall fail in my allegiance to God if I legalize your love."

The sweet and solemn ceremony was performed. With the final blessing of the priest, they rose a wedded pair.

The prisoner's face beamed with painful joy; he seemed for the first time conscious of the bitterness of death, now that he realized the sweetness of life. The features of his companion were sublime in their expression of grandeur and simplicity; she still felt the modesty of a maiden, and already exulted as a young wife.

"Hear me, Ordener," said she; "is it not fortunate that we must die, since we could never have been united in life? Do you know, love, what I will do? I will stand at the window of my cell, where I can see you mount the scaffold, so that our spirits may wing their flight to heaven together. If I should die before the axe falls, I will wait for you; for we are husband and wife, my adored Ordener, and this night our coffin shall be our bridal bed."

He pressed her to his throbbing heart, and could only utter these words, which for him summed up all human happiness: "Ethel, you are mine!"

"My children," said the chaplain, in a broken voice, "say farewell; it is time."

"Alas!" cried Ethel.

All her angelic strength returned, and she knelt before the prisoner: "Farewell, my beloved Ordener! My lord, give me your blessing."

The prisoner yielded to this touching request, then turned to take leave of the venerable Athanasius Munder. The old man was kneeling at his feet.

"What do you wish, father?" he asked in surprise.

The old man gazed at him with sweet humility: "Your blessing, my son."

"May Heaven bless you, and grant you all the happiness which your prayers call down upon your brother men!" replied Ordener, in touched and solemn tones.

Soon the sepulchral arches heard their last kisses and their last farewells; soon the rude bolts creaked noisily into place, and the iron door separated the youthful pair who were to die, only to meet again in eternity.

XLV

I will give two thousand crowns to any man who shall deliver over to me Louis Perez, dead or alive.—Calderon: *Louis Perez of Galicia.*

"BARON VŒTHAÜN, colonel of the Munkholm musketeers, which of the men who fought under your command at Black Pillar Pass took Hans of Iceland prisoner? Name him to the court, that he may receive the thousand crowns reward offered for the capture."

The president of the court thus addressed the colonel of musketeers. The court was in session; for according to old Norwegian custom, a court from whose sentence there is no appeal cannot adjourn until the sentence has been carried out. Before the judges stood the giant, who had just been led in again, with the rope round his neck from which he was soon to hang.

The colonel, seated at the table with the private secretary, rose and bowed to the court and to the bishop, who had reascended his throne.

"My lord judges, the soldier who captured Hans of Iceland is present. His name is Toric-Belfast, second musketeer of my regiment."

"Let him stand forth," replied the president, "and receive the promised reward."

A young soldier in the Munkholm uniform stepped forward.

"You are Toric-Belfast?" asked the president.

"Yes, your worship."

"It was you who took Hans of Iceland prisoner?"

"Yes, by the aid of Saint Beelzebub, I did, please your worship."

A heavy bag of money was placed before the bench.

"Do you recognize this man as the famous Hans of Iceland?" added the president, pointing to the fettered giant.

"I am better acquainted with my Kitty's pretty face than with that of Hans of Iceland; but I declare, by the halo of Saint Belphegor, that if Hans of Iceland be anywhere, it is in the shape of that big devil."

"Advance, Toric-Belfast," said the president. "Here are the thousand crowns offered by the lord mayor."

The soldier hurried toward the bench, when a voice rose from the crowd: "Munkholm musketeer, you never captured Hans of Iceland."

"By all the blessed devils!" cried the soldier, turning around, "I own nothing but my pipe and the moment of time in which I speak; but still I promise to give ten thousand gold crowns to the man who says that, if he can prove his words."

And folding his arms, he cast an assured glance over the audience: "Well! let the man who spoke, show himself."

"It is I!" said a small man, elbowing his way through the crowd.

The new-comer was wrapped in sealskin, like a Greenlander, his outlandish garb hanging stiffly about him. His beard was black; and thick hair of the same color, falling over his red eyebrows, concealed a hideous face. Neither his hands nor his arms were visible.

"Oh, it is you, is it?" said the soldier, with a loud laugh. "And who, then, do you say it was, my fine gentleman, that had the honor of capturing that infernal giant?"

The little man shook his head, and said with a malicious smile: "It was I."

At this instant Baron Vœthaün fancied that he recognized the mysterious being who had warned him at Skongen of the arrival of the rebels; Chancellor d'Ahlefeld thought he recognized his host at Arbar ruin; and the private secretary, a certain peasant from Oëlmœ, who wore a similar dress, and who had pointed out the lair of Hans of Iceland. But the three being separated, they could not impart to one another this fleeting impression, which the differences of feature and costume, afterward observed, must have soon dissipated.

"Indeed! it was you, was it?" ironically observed the soldier. "If it were not for your Greenland seal's costume, by the look which you cast at me, I should be tempted to take you for another ridiculous dwarf, who tried to pick a quarrel with me at the Spladgest, a fortnight or so ago. It was the very day that they brought in the body of Gill Stadt, the miner."

"Gill Stadt!" broke in the little man, with a shudder.

"Yes, Gill Stadt!" repeated the soldier, with an air of indifference, — "the rejected lover of a girl who was sweetheart to a comrade of mine, and for whose sake he died, like the fool that he was."

The little man said in hollow tones: "Was there not also the body of an officer of your regiment at the Spladgest?"

"Exactly; I shall remember that day as long as I live. I forgot that it was the hour for the tattoo, and I was arrested when I got back to the fort. That officer was Captain Dispolsen."

At this name the private secretary rose.

"These two fellows abuse the patience of the court. We beg the president to cut short this idle chatter."

"By my Kitty's good name! I ask nothing better," said Toric-Belfast, "provided your worships will give me the thousand crowns offered for the head of Hans, for it was I who took him prisoner."

"You lie!" cried the little man.

The soldier clapped his hand to his sword: "It is very lucky for you, you rascal, that we are in the presence of the court, where a soldier, even a Munkholm musketeer, must never resort to force."

"The reward," coldly observed the little man, "belongs to me; for if it were not for me, you would never have won Hans of Iceland's head."

The indignant soldier swore that it was he who captured Hans of Iceland, when, wounded on the field of battle, he was just beginning to revive.

"Well," said his opponent, "you may have captured him, but it was I who struck him down. If it had not been for me, you could never have taken him prisoner; therefore the thousand crowns are mine."

"It is false," replied the soldier. "It was not you who struck him down; it was an evil spirit, clad in the skins of wild beasts."

"It was I!"

"No, no!"

The president ordered both parties to be silent; then, again asking Colonel Vœthaün whether it was really Toric-Belfast who brought Hans of Iceland into camp a prisoner, at his assent he declared that the prize belonged to the soldier.

The small man gnashed his teeth, and the musketeer greedily stretched out his hands for the sack.

"One moment!" cried the little man. "Mr. President, that money according to the lord mayor's proclamation, was to be given to him who took Hans of Iceland."

"Well?" said the judge.

The little man turned to the giant: "That man is not Hans of Iceland."

A murmur of surprise ran through the room. The president and private secretary moved uneasily in their chairs.

"No!" emphatically reiterated the small man, "the money does not belong to the cursed musketeer of Munkholm, for that man is not Hans of Iceland."

"Halberdiers," said the president, "remove this madman, he has lost his senses."

The bishop interposed: "Will you allow me, most worthy President, to remark that you may, by refusing to hear this man, destroy the prisoner's last chance? I demand that he be confronted with the stranger."

"Reverend Bishop, the court will grant your request," replied the president; and addressing the giant: "You have declared yourself to be Hans of Iceland; do you persist in that statement?"

The prisoner answered: "I do; I am Hans of Iceland."

"You hear, Bishop?"

The little man shouted in the same breath with the president: "You lie, mountaineer of Kiölen! you lie! Do not persist in bearing a name which must crush you; remember that it has been fatal to you already."

"I am Hans from Klipstadur, in Iceland," repeated the giant, his eye riveted on the private secretary.

The small man approached the Munkholm soldier, who, like the rest of the audience, had watched this scene with eager curiosity.

"Mountaineer of Kiölen," he cried, "they say that Hans of Iceland drinks human blood. If you be he, drink. Here it is."

And scarcely were the words out of his mouth, when, tossing his sealskin mantle over his shoulder, he plunged a dagger into the soldier's heart, and flung his dead body at the giant's feet.

A cry of fright and horror followed; the soldiers guarding the giant started back. The small man, swift as lightning, rushed upon the defenceless mountaineer, and with another blow of his dagger, laid him upon the first corpse. Then flinging off his cloak, his false hair, and black beard, he revealed his wiry limbs, hideously attired in the skins of wild beasts, and a face which inspired the beholders with even greater horror than did the bloody dagger which he brandished aloft, reeking with a double murder.

"Ha! judges, where is Hans of Iceland now?"

"Guards, seize that monster!" cried the startled judge.

Hans hurled his dagger into the centre of the room.

"It is useless to me if there are no more Munkholm soldiers here."

With these words, he yielded unresistingly to the halberdiers and bowmen who surrounded him, prepared to lay siege to him, as to a city. They chained the monster to the prisoner's bench; and a litter bore away his victims, one of whom, the mountaineer, still breathed.

It is impossible to describe the various emotions of terror, astonishment, and indignation which, during this fearful scene, agitated the people, the guards, and the judges. When the brigand had taken his place, calm and unmoved, upon the fatal bench, a feeling of curiosity overcame every other impression, and breathless attention restored quiet.

The venerable bishop rose: "My lord judges—"

The bandit interrupted him: "Bishop of Throndhjem, I am Hans of Iceland; do not take the trouble to plead for me."

The private secretary rose: "Noble President—"

The monster cut him short: "Private Secretary, I am Hans of Iceland; do not take the pains to accuse me."

Then, his feet in a pool of blood, he ran his bold, fierce eye over the court, the bowmen, and the crowd; and it seemed as if each of them trembled with fear at the glance of that one man, unarmed, chained, and alone.

"Listen, judges; expect no long speeches from me. I am the demon of Klipstadur. My mother was old Iceland, the land of volcanoes. Once that land was but one huge mountain; it was crushed by the hand of a giant, who fell from heaven, and rested on its highest peak. I need not speak of myself. I am a descendant of Ingulf the Destroyer, and I bear his spirit within me. I have committed more murders and kindled more fires than all of you put together ever uttered unjust sentences in your lives. I have secrets in common with Chancellor d'Ahlefeld. I could drink every drop of blood that flows in your veins with delight. It is my nature to hate mankind, my mission to harm them. Colonel of the Munkholm musketeers, it was I who warned you of the march of the miners through Black Pillar Pass, sure that you would kill numbers of men in those gorges; it was I who destroyed a whole battalion of your regiment by hurling granite bowlders upon their heads. I did it to avenge my son. Now, judges, my son is dead; I came here in search of death. The soul of Ingulf oppresses me, because I must bear it alone, and can never transmit it to an heir. I am tired of life, since it can no longer be an example and a lesson to a successor. I have drunk enough blood; my thirst is quenched. Now, here I am; you may drink mine."

He was silent, and every voice repeated his awful words.

The bishop said: "My son, what was your object in committing so many crimes?"

The brigand laughed: "I' faith, I swear, reverend Bishop, it was not like your brother, the bishop of Borglum, with a view to enrich myself.[3] There was something in me which drove me to it."

"God does not always dwell in his ministers," meekly replied the saintly old man. "You would insult me, but I only wish I could defend you."

"Your reverence wastes his breath. Go ask your other brother, the bishop of Scalholt, in Iceland, to defend me. By Ingulf! it is a strange thing that two bishops should protect me,—one in my cradle, the other at my tomb. Bishop, you are an old fool."

"My son, do you believe in God?"

"Why not? There must be a God for us to blaspheme."

"Cease, unhappy man! You are about to die, and you will not kiss the feet of Christ—"

Hans of Iceland shrugged his shoulders.

"If I did so, it would be after the fashion of the constable of Roll, who pulled the king over as he kissed his foot."

The bishop seated himself, deeply moved.

"Come, judges," continued Hans of Iceland, "why this delay? If I were in your place and you in mine, I would not keep you waiting so long for your death sentence."

The court withdrew. After a brief deliberation they returned, and the president read aloud the sentence, which declared that Hans of Iceland was to be "hung by the neck until he was dead, dead, dead."

"That's good," said the brigand. "Chancellor d'Ahlefeld, I know enough about you to obtain a like sentence for you. But live, since you do naught but injure men. Oh, I am sure now that I shall not go to Nistheim!"[4]

The private secretary ordered the guards who led him away to place him in the Lion of Schleswig tower, until a dungeon could be prepared for him in the quarters of the Munkholm regiment, where he might await his execution.

"In the quarters of the Munkholm musketeers!" repeated the monster, with a growl of pleasure.

XLVI

However, the corpse of Ponce de Leon, which had remained beside the fountain, having been disfigured by the sun, the Moors of Alpuxares took possession of it and bore it to Grenada.—É. H.: *The Captive of Ochali.*

BEFORE dawn of the day so many of whose events we have already traced, at the very hour when Ordener's sentence was pronounced at Munkholm, the new keeper of the Throndhjem Spladgest, Benignus Spiagudry's former assistant and present successor, Oglypiglap, was abruptly aroused from his mattress by a violent series of raps, which fairly shook the building. He rose reluctantly, took his copper lamp, whose dim light dazzled his drowsy eyes, and went, swearing at the dampness of the dead-house, to open to those who waked him so early from his sleep.

They were fishers from Sparbo, who carried upon a litter, strewed with reeds, rushes, and seaweed, a corpse which they had found in the waters of the lake.

They laid down their burden within the gloomy walls, and Oglypiglap gave them a receipt for it, so that they might claim their fee.

Left alone in the Spladgest, he began to undress the corpse, which was remarkable for its length and leanness. The first thing which caught his eye as he raised the cloth which covered it was a vast periwig.

"Why, really," said he, "this outlandish wig has passed through my hands before; it belonged to that young French dandy.... And," he added, continuing his investigations, "here are the high boots of poor postilion Cramner, who was killed by his horses, and—What the devil does this mean?—the full black suit of Professor Syngramtax, that learned old fogy, who drowned himself not long ago! Who can this new-comer be that comes here clad in the cast-off apparel of all my ancient acquaintance?"

He examined the face of the dead by the light of his lamp, but in vain; the features, already decomposed, had lost their original shape and color. He felt in the pockets, and drew out some scraps of parchment soaked with water and stained with mud; he wiped them carefully on his leather apron, and succeeded in deciphering on one of them these disconnected and half-effaced phrases: "Rudbeck, Saxon the grammarian. Arngrimmsson, bishop of Holum.—There are but two counties in Norway, Larvig and Jarlsberg, and but one barony.—Silver mines exist only at Kongsberg; loadstone and asbestos, at Sund-Moer; amethyst, at Guldbrandsdal; chalcedony, agate, and jasper, at the Färöe Islands.—At Noukahiva, in time of famine, men eat their wives and children.—Thormodr Torfusson; Isleif, bishop of Scalholt, first historian of Iceland.—Mercury played at chess with the Moon, and won the seventy-second part of a day.—Maëlstrom, whirlpool.—*Hirundo, hirudo.*—Cicero, chick pea; glory.—The learned Frode.—Odin consulted the head of Mimer, the wise.—(Mahomet and his dove, Sertorius and his hind.)—The more the soil—the less gypsum it contains—"

"I can scarcely believe my eyes!" he cried, dropping the parchment; "it is the writing of my old master, Benignus Spiagudry!"

Then, examining the corpse afresh, he recognized the long lean hands, the scanty hair, and the whole build of the unfortunate man.

"They were not so much out of the way, after all," thought he, shaking his head, "who charged him with sacrilege and necromancy. The Devil carried him off to drown him in Lake Sparbo. What poor fools we mortals be! Who would ever have thought that Dr. Spiagudry, after taking so many people to board in his hostelry of the dead, would come here at last from afar to be cared for himself!"

The little Lapp philosopher lifted the body, to remove it to one of his six granite beds, when he found that something heavy was fastened about the unhappy Spiagudry's neck by a leather cord.

"Probably the stone with which the Devil pitched him into the lake," he muttered.

He was mistaken; it was a small iron box, upon which, on examining it closely, after wiping it carefully, he discovered a large shield-shaped padlock.

"Of course there is some deviltry in this box," said he; "the man was a sacrilegious sorcerer. I will hand it over to the bishop; it may contain an evil spirit."

Then, taking it from the corpse, which he placed in the inner room, he hurried away to the bishop's palace, muttering a prayer as he went, as a charm against the dreadful box under his arm.

XLVII

Is it a man or an infernal spirit that speaks thus? What mischievous spirit torments thee thus? Show me the relentless foe who inhabits thy heart.—Maturin.

HANS of Iceland and Schumacker were in the same cell in the Schleswig tower. The acquitted ex-chancellor paced slowly to and fro, his eyes heavy with bitter tears; the condemned brigand laughed at his chains, though surrounded by guards.

The two prisoners studied each other long and silently; it seemed as if both felt themselves and mutually recognized each other as enemies of mankind.

"Who are you?" at length asked the ex-chancellor.

"I will tell you my name," replied the bandit, "to make you shun me. I am Hans of Iceland."

Schumacker advanced toward him.

"Take my hand," said he.

"Do you wish me to devour it?"

"Hans of Iceland," rejoined Schumacker, "I like you because you hate mankind."

"And for that reason I hate you."

"Hark ye, I hate men, as you do, because they have returned me evil for good."

"You do not hate them as I do; I hate them because they have returned me good for evil."

Schumacker shuddered at the monster's expression. In vain he conquered his natural disposition; he could not sympathize with this fiend.

"Yes," he exclaimed, "I abhor men because they are false, ungrateful, cruel. I owe to them all the misery of my life."

"So much the better! I owe them all the pleasure of mine."

"What pleasure?"

"The pleasure of feeling their quivering flesh throb beneath my teeth, their hot blood moisten my parched throat; the rapture of crushing living beings against sharp rocks, and hearing the shriek of my victims mingle with the sound of their breaking limbs. These are the pleasures which I owe to men."

Schumacker shrank in horror from the monster whom he had approached with something like pride in his resemblance to him. Pierced with shame, he hid his wrinkled face in his hands; for his eyes were full of tears of anger, not against mankind, but against himself. His great and noble heart began to revolt at the hatred he had so long cherished, when he saw it reflected in Hans of Iceland's heart as in a fearful mirror.

"Well," said the monster, with a sneer, — "well, enemy of man, dare you boast your likeness to me?"

The old man shuddered. "Oh, God! Rather than hate mankind as you do, let me love them."

Guards came to remove the monster to a more secure cell. Schumacker was left alone in his dungeon to dream; but he was no longer the enemy of mankind.

XLVIII

Keep me, O Lord, from the hands of the wicked,
Preserve me from the violent man;
Who have purposed to thrust aside my step.
The proud have hid a snare for me, and cords;
They have spread a net by the wayside;
They have set gins for me.
Psalms cxl. 4.

THE fatal hour had come; the sun showed but half his disk above the horizon. The guards were doubled throughout Munkholm castle; before each door paced fierce, silent sentinels. The noises of the town seemed louder and more confused than usual as they ascended to the dark towers of the fortress, itself a prey to strange excitement. The mournful sound of muffled drums was heard in every courtyard; now and again cannon growled; the heavy bell in the donjon tolled slowly, with sullen, measured strokes; and from every direction boats loaded with people hastened toward the fearful rock.

A scaffold hung with black, around which an impatient mob swarmed in ever-increasing numbers, rose from the castle parade-ground in the centre of a hollow square of troops. Upon the scaffold a man clad in red serge walked up and down, now leaning upon the axe in his hand, and now fingering a billet and block upon the funeral platform. Close at hand a stake was prepared, before which several pitch torches burned. Between the scaffold and the stake was planted a post, from which hung the inscription: "ORDENER GULDENLEW, TRAITOR." A black flag floated from the top of the Schleswig tower.

At this moment Ordener appeared before the judges, still assembled in the court-room. The bishop alone was absent; his office as counsel for the defence had ended.

The son of the viceroy was dressed in black, and wore upon his neck the collar of the Dannebrog. His face was pale but proud. He was alone; for he had been led forth to torture before Chaplain Athanasius Munder returned to his cell.

Ordener's sacrifice was already inwardly accomplished. And yet Ethel's husband still clung to life, and might perhaps have chosen another night than that of the tomb for his wedding night. He had prayed and dreamed many dreams in his dreary cell. Now he was beyond all prayers and all dreams. He was strong in the strength imparted by religion and by love.

The crowd, more deeply moved than the prisoner, eagerly gazed at him. His illustrious rank, his horrible fate, awakened universal envy and pity. Every spectator watched his punishment, without comprehending his crime. In every human heart lurks a strange feeling which urges its owner to behold the tortures of others as well as their pleasures. Men seek with awful avidity to read destruction upon the distorted features of one who is about to die, as if some revelation from heaven or from hell must appear at that awful moment in the poor wretch's eyes; as if they would learn what sort of shadow is cast by the death angel's wing as he hovers over a human head; as if they would search and know what is left to a man when hope is gone. That being, full of health and strength, moving, breathing, living, and which in another instant must cease to move, breathe, and live, surrounded by beings like himself, whom he never harmed, all of whom pity him, and none of whom can help him; that wretched being, dying, though not dead, bending alike beneath an earthly power and an invisible might; this life, which society could not give, but which it takes with all the pomp and ceremony of legal murder,—profoundly stir the popular imagination. Condemned, as all of us are, to death, with an indefinite reprieve, the unfortunate man who knows the exact hour when his reprieve expires is an object of strange and painful curiosity.

The reader may remember that before he mounted the scaffold, Ordener was to be taken before the court, there to be stripped of his titles and honors. Hardly had the stir excited in the assembly by his arrival given place to quiet, when the president ordered the book of heraldry of both kingdoms, and the statutes of the order of the Dannebrog, to be brought.

Then directing the prisoner to kneel upon one knee, he commanded the spectators to pay respectful heed, opened the book of the knights of the Dannebrog, and began to read in a loud, stern voice: "We, Christian, by the grace and mercy of Almighty God, king of Denmark and Norway, of Goths and Vandals, Duke of Schleswig, Holstein, Stormaria, and Dytmarsen, Count of Oldenburg and Delmenhurst, do declare:—

"That having re-established, at the suggestion of the lord chancellor, Count Griffenfeld [the president passed over this name so rapidly that it was scarcely audible], the royal order of the Dannebrog, founded by our illustrious ancestor, Saint Waldemar,

"Whereas we hold that inasmuch as the said venerable order was created in memory of the flag Dannebrog sent down from heaven to our blessed kingdom,

"It would belie the divine origin of the order should any knight forfeit his honor, or break the holy laws of Church and State with impunity,

"We therefore decree, kneeling before God, that whosoever of the knights of the order shall deliver his soul to the demon by any felony or treason, after a public reprimand from the court, shall be forever degraded from his rank as a knight of this our royal order of the Dannebrog."

The president closed the book. "Ordener Guldenlew, Baron Thorwick, Knight of the Dannebrog, you have been found guilty of high treason, for which crime your head shall be cut off, your body burned, and your ashes flung to the winds. Ordener Guldenlew, traitor, you have shown yourself unworthy to hold rank with the knights of the Dannebrog. I request you to humble yourself, for I am about to degrade you publicly in the name of the king."

The president stretched his hand over the book of the

order and prepared to pronounce the fatal formula against Ordener, who remained calm and motionless, when a side door opened to the right of the bench.

An officer of the Church entered and announced his reverence, the bishop of Throndhjem. He entered hurriedly, accompanied by another ecclesiastic, on whose arm he leaned.

"Stop, Mr. President!" he exclaimed with a strength of which a man of his age seemed hardly capable. "Stop! Heaven be praised! I am in time."

The audience listened with renewed interest, foreseeing some fresh development. The president turned angrily to the bishop: "Allow me to inform your reverence that your presence here is wholly unnecessary. The court is about to degrade from his rank the prisoner, who will suffer the penalty of his crime directly."

"Forbear," said the bishop, "to lay hands on one who is pure in the sight of God. The prisoner is innocent."

The cry of astonishment which burst from the spectators was only matched by the cry of terror uttered by the president and private secretary.

"Yes, tremble, judges!" resumed the bishop, before the president could recover his usual presence of mind; "tremble! for you are about to shed innocent blood."

As the president's agitation died away, Ordener arose in consternation. The noble youth feared lest his generous ruse had been discovered, and proofs of Schumacker's guilt had been found.

"Bishop," said the president, "in this affair crime seems to evade us, being transferred from one to another. Do not trust to any mere appearance. If Ordener Guldenlew be innocent, who, then, is guilty?"

"Your grace shall know," replied the bishop. Then showing the court an iron casket which a servant had brought in behind him: "Noble lords, you have judged in darkness; within this casket is the miraculous light which shall dissipate that darkness."

The president, private secretary, and Ordener, all seemed amazed at the sight of the mysterious casket.

The bishop added: "Noble judges, hear me. To-day, as I returned to my palace, to rest from the fatigues of the night and to pray for the prisoners, I received this sealed iron box. The keeper of the Spladgest, I was told, brought it to the palace this morning to be given to me, declaring that it undoubtedly contained some Satanic charm, as he had found it on the body of the sacrilegious Benignus Spiagudry, which had just been fished out of Lake Sparbo."

Ordener listened more eagerly than ever. All the spectators were as still as death. The president and private secretary hung their heads guiltily. They seemed to have lost all their cunning and audacity. There is a moment in the life of every sinner when his power vanishes.

"After blessing this casket," continued the bishop, "we broke the seal, which, as you can still see, bears the ancient and now extinct arms of Griffenfeld. We did indeed find a devilish secret within. You shall judge for yourselves, venerable sirs. Lend me your most earnest attention, for human blood is at stake, and the Lord will hold you accountable for every drop that you may shed."

Then opening the terrible casket, he drew forth a slip of parchment, upon which was written the following testimony:—

I, Blaxtham Cumbysulsum, doctor, being about to die, do declare that of my own free will and pleasure I have placed in the hands of Captain Dispolsen, the agent, at Copenhagen, of the former Count Griffenfeld, the enclosed document, drawn up wholly by the hand of Turiaf Musdœmon, servant of the chancellor, Count d'Ahlefeld, to the end that the said captain may make such use of it as shall seem to him best; and I pray God to pardon my crimes.

Given under my hand and seal at Copenhagen, this eleventh day of January, 1699.

Cumbysulsum.

The private secretary shook like a leaf. He tried to speak, but could not. The bishop handed the parchment to the pale and agitated president.

"What do I see?" exclaimed the latter, as he unfolded the parchment. "A note to the noble Count d'Ahlefeld, upon the means of legally ridding himself of Schumacker! I—I swear, reverend Bishop—"

The paper dropped from his trembling fingers.

"Read it, read it, sir," said the bishop. "I doubt not that your unworthy servant has abused your name as he has that of the unfortunate Schumacker. Only see the result of your uncharitable aversion to your fallen predecessor. One of your followers has plotted his ruin in your name, doubtless hoping to make a merit of it to your Grace."

These words revived the president, as showing him that the suspicions of the bishop, who was acquainted with the entire contents of the casket, had not fallen upon him. Ordener also breathed more freely. He began to see that the innocence of Ethel's father might be made manifest at the same time with his own. He felt a deep surprise at the singular fate which had led him to pursue a fearful brigand to recover this casket, which his old guide, Benignus Spiagudry, bore about him all the time; that it was actually following him while he was seeking for it. He also reflected on the solemn lesson of the events which, after ruining him by means of this same fatal casket, now proved the instrument of his salvation.

The president, recovering himself, read with much show of indignation, in which the entire audience shared, a lengthy memorandum, in which Musdœmon set forth all the details of the abominable scheme which we have seen him execute in the course of this story. Several times the private secretary attempted to rise and defend himself, but each time he was frowned down. At last the odious reading came to an end amid a murmur of universal horror.

"Halberdiers, seize that man!" said the president, pointing to the private secretary.

The wretch, speechless and almost lifeless, stepped from his place, and was cast into the criminal dock, followed by the hoots of the populace.

"Judges," said the bishop, "shudder and rejoice. The truth, which has just been brought home to your consciences, will now be even more strongly confirmed by the testimony of our honored brother, Athanasius Munder, chaplain to the prisons of this royal town."

It was indeed Athanasius Munder who accompanied the bishop. He bowed to his superior in the Church and to the court, then at a sign from the president, proceeded as follows: "What I am about to state is the truth. May Heaven punish me if I utter a word with any other object than to do my duty! From what I saw this morning in the cell of the viceroy's son, I was led to think that the young man was not guilty, although your lordships had condemned him upon his own confession. Now, I was called, a few hours since, to give the last spiritual consolations to the unfortunate mountaineer so cruelly murdered before your very eyes, and whom you condemned, worthy sirs, as being Hans of Iceland. The dying man said to me: 'I am not Hans of Iceland; I am justly punished for having assumed his name. I was paid to play the part by the chancellor's private secretary; he is called Musdœmon; and it was he who managed the whole revolt under the name of Hacket! I believe him to be the only guilty man in this whole matter.' Then he asked me to give him my blessing, and advised me to make haste and repeat his last words to the court. God is my witness. May I save the shedding of innocent blood, and not cause that of the guilty to flow!"

He ceased, again bowing to his bishop and the judges.

"Your Grace sees," said the bishop to the president, "that one of my clients was not mistaken when he found so much resemblance between Hacket and your private secretary."

"Turiaf Musdœmon," said the president to the prisoner, "what have you to say in your defence?"

Musdœmon looked at his master with an expression which alarmed him. He had recovered his usual impudence, and after a brief pause, answered: "Nothing, sir."

The president resumed in a weak and faltering voice: "Then you acknowledge yourself guilty of the crime with which you are charged? You confess yourself to be the author of a conspiracy alike against the State and against one John Schumacker?"

"I do, my lord," replied Musdœmon.

The bishop rose. "Mr. President, that there may be no shadow of doubt in this affair, will your grace ask the prisoner if he had any accomplices?"

"Accomplices?" repeated Musdœmon.

He hesitated a moment. The president wore a look of awful anxiety.

"No, my lord Bishop," he said at last.

The president's look of relief fell full upon him.

"No, I had no accomplices," repeated Musdœmon, still more emphatically. "I concocted this plot through affection for my master, who knew nothing of it, to destroy his enemy, Schumacker."

The eyes of prisoner and president met once more.

"Your Grace," said the bishop, "must see that as Musdœmon had no accomplices, Baron Ordener Guldenlew must be innocent."

"Then why, worthy Bishop, did he confess his guilt?"

"Mr. President, why did that mountaineer persist that he was Hans of Iceland at the risk of his life? God alone knows our secret motives."

Ordener took up the word: "Judges, I can tell you my motive, now that the real criminal has been discovered. I accused myself falsely to save the former chancellor, Schumacker, whose death would have left his daughter without a protector."

The president bit his lip.

"We request the court," said the bishop, "to proclaim the innocence of our client, Ordener Guldenlew."

The president responded with a nod; and at the request of the lord mayor, they finished their examination of the terrible casket, which contained nothing more except Schumacker's titles of nobility, and a few letters from the Munkholm prisoner to Captain Dispolsen, —bitter, but not criminal letters, which alarmed no one but Chancellor d'Ahlefeld.

The court then withdrew; and after a brief deliberation, while the curious crowd, gathered on the parade, waited with stubborn impatience to see the viceroy's son led forth to die, and the executioner nonchalantly paced the scaffold, the president pronounced in a scarcely audible voice the death sentence of Turiaf Musdœmon, the acquittal of Ordener Guldenlew, and the restoration of all his honors, titles, and privileges.

XLIX

What will you sell me your carcass for, my boy
I would not give you, in faith, a broken toy.
Saint Michael and Satan (Old Miracle Play).

THE remnant of the regiment of Munkholm musketeers had returned to their old quarters in the barracks, which stood in the centre of a vast, square courtyard within the fortress. At night-fall the doors of this building were barricaded, all the soldiers withdrawing into it, with the exception of the sentinels upon the various towers, and the handful of men on guard before the military prison adjoining the barracks. This, being the safest and best watched place of confinement in Munkholm, contained the two prisoners sentenced to be hanged on the following morning, Hans of Iceland and Musdœmon.

Hans of Iceland was alone in his cell. He was stretched upon the floor, chained, his head upon a stone; a feeble light filtered through a square grated opening, cut in the heavy oak door which divided his cell from the next room, where he heard his jailers laugh and swear, and heard the sound of the bottles which they drained, and the dice which they threw upon a drumhead. The monster silently writhed in the darkness, his limbs twitched convulsively, and he gnashed his teeth.

All at once he lifted his voice and called aloud. A turnkey appeared at the grating: "What do you want?" said he.

Hans of Iceland rose. "Mate, I am cold; my stone bed is hard and damp. Give me a bundle of straw to sleep on, and a little fire to warm myself."

"It is only fair," replied the turnkey, "to give a little comfort to a poor devil who is going to be hung, even if he be the Iceland Devil. I will bring you what you want. Have you any money?"

"No," replied the brigand.

"What! you, the most famous robber in Norway, and you have not a few scurvy gold ducats in your pouch?"

"No," repeated the brigand.

"A few little crowns?"

"I tell you, no!"

"Not even a few paltry escalins?"

"No, no, nothing; not enough to buy a rat's skin or a man's soul."

The turnkey shook his head: "That's a different matter; you have no right to complain. Your cell is not so cold as the one you will have to sleep in to-morrow, and yet I'll be bound you won't notice the hardness of that bed."

So saying, the jailer withdrew, followed by the curses of the monster, who continued to rattle his chains, which gave forth a hollow clang as if they were breaking slowly under repeated and violent jerks and pulls.

The door opened. A tall man, dressed in red serge, carrying a dark lantern, entered the cell, accompanied by the jailer who had refused the prisoner's request. The latter at once became perfectly quiet.

"Hans of Iceland," said the man in red, "I am Nychol Orugix, executioner of the province of Throndhjem; to-morrow, at sunrise, I am to have the honor of hanging your Excellency upon a fine new gallows in Throndhjem market-place."

"Are you very sure that you will hang me?" replied the brigand.

The executioner laughed. "I wish you were as sure to rise straight into heaven by Jacob's ladder as you are to mount the scaffold by Nychol Orugix's ladder."

"Indeed?" said the monster, with a malicious grin.

"I tell you again, Sir Brigand, that I am hangman for the province."

"If I were not myself I should like to be you," replied the brigand.

"I can't say the same for you," rejoined the hangman; then rubbing his hands with a conceited and complacent smirk, he added: "My friend, you are right; ours is a fine trade. Ah! my hand knows the weight of a man's head."

"Have you often tasted blood?" asked the brigand.

"No; but I have often used the rack."

"Have you ever devoured the entrails of a living child?"

"No; but I have crushed men's bones in a vise; I have broken their limbs upon the wheel; I have dulled steel saws upon their skulls; I have torn their quivering flesh with red-hot pincers; I have burned the blood in their open veins by pouring in a stream of molten lead and boiling oil."

"Yes," said the brigand, with a thoughtful look, "you have your pleasures too."

"In fact," added the hangman, "Hans of Iceland though you be, I imagine that my hands have released more human souls than yours, to say nothing of your own, which you must render up to-morrow."

"Always provided that I have one. Do you suppose, then, executioner of Throndhjem, that you can release the spirit of Ingulf from Hans of Iceland's mortal frame without its carrying off your own?"

The executioner laughed heartily. "Indeed, we shall see to-morrow."

"We shall see," said the brigand.

"Well," said the executioner, "I did not come here to talk of your spirit, but only of your body. Hearken! your body by law belongs to me after your death; but the law gives you the right to sell it to me. Tell me what you will take for it?"

"What I will take for my corpse?" said the brigand.

"Yes, and be reasonable."

Hans of Iceland turned to his jailer: "Tell me, mate, how much do you ask for a bundle of straw and a handful of fire?"

The jailer reflected. "Two gold ducats."

"Well," said the brigand to the hangman, "you must give me two gold ducats for my corpse."

"Two gold ducats!" cried the hangman. "It is horribly dear. Two gold ducats for a wretched corpse! No, indeed! I'll give no such price."

"Then," quietly responded the monster, "you shall not have it."

"Then you will be thrown into the common sewer, instead of adorning the Royal Museum at Copenhagen or the collection of curiosities at Bergen."

"What do I care?"

"Long after your death, people will flock to look at your skeleton, saying, 'Those are the remains of the famous Hans of Iceland!' Your bones will be nicely polished, and strung on copper wire; you will be placed in a big glass case, and dusted carefully every day. Instead of these honors, consider what awaits you if you refuse to sell me your body; you will be left to rot in some charnel-house, where you will be the prey of worms and other vermin."

"Well, I shall be like the living, who are perpetually preyed upon by their inferiors and devoured by their superiors."

"Two gold ducats!" muttered the hangman; "what an exorbitant price! If you will not come down in your terms, my dear fellow, we can never make a trade."

"It is my first and probably my last trade; I am bent on having it a good one."

"Consider that I may make you repent of your obstinacy. To-morrow you will be in my power."

"Do you think so?" These words were uttered with a look which escaped the hangman.

"Yes; and there is a certain way of tightening a slip-knot—but if you will only be reasonable, I will hang you in my best manner."

"Little do I care what you do to my neck to-morrow," replied the monster, with a mocking air.

"Come, won't you be satisfied with two crowns? What can you do with the money?"

"Ask your comrade there," said the brigand, pointing to the turnkey; "he charges me two gold ducats for a handful of straw and a fire."

"Now by Saint Joseph's saw," said the hangman, angrily addressing the turnkey, "it is shocking to make a man pay its weight in gold for a fire and a little worthless straw."

"Two ducats!" the turnkey replied sourly; "I've a good mind to make him pay four! It is you, Master Nychol, who act like a regular screw in refusing to give this poor prisoner two gold ducats for his corpse, when you can sell it for at least twenty to some learned old fogy or some doctor."

"I never paid more than twenty escalins for a corpse in my life," said the hangman.

"Yes," replied the jailer, "for the body of some paltry thief, or some miserable Jew, that may be; but everybody knows that you can get whatever you choose to ask for Hans of Iceland's body."

Hans of Iceland shook his head.

"What business is it of yours?" said Orugix, curtly; "do I interfere with your plunder,—with the clothes and jewels that you steal from the prisoners, and the dirty water which you pour into their thin soup, and the torture to which you put them, to extort money from them? No, I never will give two gold ducats."

"No straw and no fire for less than two gold ducats," replied the obstinate jailer.

"No corpse for less than two gold ducats," repeated the unmoved brigand.

The hangman, after a brief pause, stamped his foot angrily, saying: "Well, I've no time to waste with you. I am wanted elsewhere." He drew from his waistcoat a leather bag, which he opened slowly and reluctantly. "There, cursed demon of Iceland, there are your two ducats. Satan would never give you as much for your soul as I do for your body, I am sure."

The brigand accepted the gold. The turnkey instantly held out his hand to take it.

"One instant, mate; first give me what I asked for."

The jailer went out, and soon returned with a bundle of dry straw and a pan of live coals, which he placed beside the prisoner.

"That's it," said the brigand, giving him the two ducats; "I'll make a warm night of it. One word more," he added in an ominous tone. "Does not this prison adjoin the barracks of the Munkholm musketeers?"

"It does," said the jailer.

"And which way is the wind?"

"From the east, I think."

"Good," said the brigand.

"What are you aiming at, comrade?" asked the jailer.

"Oh, nothing," replied the brigand.

"Farewell, comrade, until to-morrow morning early."

"Yes, to-morrow," repeated the brigand.

And the noise of the heavy door, as it closed, prevented the jailer and his companion from hearing the fierce, jeering laughter which accompanied these words.

L

Do you hope to end with another crime? — Alex. Soumet.

LET us now take a look at the other cell in the military prison adjoining the barracks, which holds our old acquaintance, Turiaf Musdœmon.

It may seem surprising that Musdœmon, crafty and cowardly as he was, should so readily confess his crime to the court which condemned him, and so generously conceal the share of his ungrateful master, Chancellor d'Ahlefeld, in it.

However, Musdœmon had not experienced a change of heart. His noble frankness was perhaps the greatest proof of cunning which he could possibly have given. When he saw his infernal intrigue so unexpectedly exposed, beyond all hope of denial, he was for an instant stunned and terrified. Conquering his alarm, his extreme shrewdness soon showed him that as it was impossible to destroy his chosen victims, he must bend all his energies to saving himself. Two plans at once presented themselves: the first, to throw all the blame upon Count d'Ahlefeld, who had so basely deserted him; the second, to assume the whole burden of the crime himself. A vulgar mind would have grasped at the former; Musdœmon chose the latter. The chancellor was chancellor, after all; besides, there was nothing in the papers which directly implicated him, although they contained overwhelming evidence against his secretary. Then, his master had given him several meaning looks; this was enough to confirm him in his purpose to suffer himself to be condemned, confident that Count d'Ahlefeld would connive at his escape, though less from gratitude for past service than through his need for future aid.

He therefore paced his prison, which was dimly lighted by a wretched lamp, never doubting that the door would be thrown open during the night. He studied the architecture of the old stone cell, built by kings whose very names have almost vanished from the pages of history, and was much surprised to find a wooden plank, which echoed back his tread as if it covered some subterranean vault. He also observed a huge iron ring cemented into the arched roof, from which hung a fragment of rope. Time passed; and he listened impatiently to the clock on the tower as it slowly struck the hours, its mournful toll resounding through the silence of the night.

At last there was a footfall outside his cell; his heart beat high with hope. The massive bolt creaked; the padlock dropped; and as the door opened, his face beamed with delight. It was the same character in scarlet robes whom we have just encountered in Hans of Iceland's prison. He had a coil of hempen cord under his arm, and was accompanied by four halberdiers in black, armed with swords and partisans.

Musdœmon still wore the wig and gown of a magistrate. His dress seemed to impress the man in red, who bowed low as if accustomed to respect that garb, and said with some hesitation: "Sir, is our business with your worship?"

"Yes, yes," hastily replied Musdœmon, confirmed in his hope of escape by this polite address, and failing to observe the bloody hue of the speaker's garments.

"Your name," said the man, his eyes fixed on a parchment which he had just unrolled, "is Turiaf Musdœmon, I believe."

"Just so. Do you come from the chancellor, my friend?"

"Yes, your worship."

"Do not fail, when you have done your errand, to assure his Grace of my undying gratitude."

The man in red looked at him in amazement. "Your—gratitude!"

"Yes, to be sure, my friend; for it will probably be out of my power to thank him in person very soon."

"Probably," dryly replied the man.

"And you must feel," added Musdœmon, "that I owe him a deep debt of gratitude for such a service."

"By the cross of the repentant thief," cried the man, with a coarse laugh, "to hear you, one would think that the chancellor was doing something quite unusual for you!"

"Well, to be sure, it is no more than strict justice."

"Strict justice! that is the word; but you acknowledge that it is justice. It is the first admission of the kind that I ever heard in the six-and-twenty years that I have followed my profession. Come, sir, we waste our time in idle talk; are you ready?"

"I am," said the delighted Musdœmon, stepping to the door.

"Wait; wait a minute," exclaimed the man in red, stooping to lay his coil of rope on the floor.

Musdœmon paused.

"What are you going to do with all that rope?"

"Your worship may well ask. I know that there is much more than I shall need; but when I began on this affair I thought there would be a great many more prisoners."

"Come, make haste!" said Musdœmon.

"Your worship is in a wonderful hurry. Have you no last favor to ask?"

"None but the one I have already mentioned, that you will thank his Grace for me. For God's sake, make haste!" added Musdœmon; "I long to get away from here. Have we a long journey before us?"

"A long journey!" replied the man in red, straightening himself, and measuring off a few lengths of rope. "The journey will not tire your worship much; for we can make it without leaving this room."

Musdœmon shuddered.

"What do you mean?"

"What do you mean yourself?" asked the man.

"Oh, God!" said Musdœmon, turning pale, "who are you?"

"I am the hangman."

The poor wretch trembled like a dry leaf blown by the wind.

"Did you not come to help me to escape?" he feebly muttered.

The hangman laughed. "Yes, truly! to help you to escape into the spirit-land, whence I warrant you will not be brought back."

Musdœmon grovelled on the floor. "Mercy! Have pity on me! Mercy!"

"I' faith," coldly observed the hangman, "'tis the first time I was ever asked such a thing. Do you take me for the king?"

The unfortunate man dragged himself on his knees, trailing his gown in the dust, beating his head against the floor, and clasping the hangman's feet with muffled groans and broken sobs.

"Come, be quiet!" said the hangman. "I never before saw a black gown kneel to a red jerkin." He kicked the suppliant aside, adding: "Pray to God and the saints, fellow; they will be more apt to hear you than I."

Musdœmon still knelt, his face buried in his hands, weeping bitterly.

Meantime, the hangman, standing on tiptoe, passed his rope through the ring in the ceiling: he let it hang until it reached the floor, then secured it by a double turn, and made a slip-knot in the end.

"I am ready," said he, when these ominous preparations were over; "are you ready to lay down your life?"

"No!" said Musdœmon, springing up; "no; it cannot be! There is some horrible mistake. Chancellor d'Ahlefeld is not so base; I am too necessary to him. It is impossible that it was for me he sent you. Let me escape; do not fear that the chancellor will be angry."

"Did you not say," replied the executioner, "that you were Turiaf Musdœmon?"

The prisoner hesitated for an instant, then said suddenly: "No, no! my name is not Musdœmon; my name is Turiaf Orugix."

"Orugix!" cried the executioner, "Orugix!"

He snatched off the periwig which concealed the prisoner's face, and uttered an exclamation of surprise: "My brother!"

"Your brother!" replied the prisoner, with a mixture of shame and pleasure; "can you be—"

"Nychol Orugix, hangman for the province of Throndhjem, at your service, brother Turiaf."

The prisoner fell upon the executioner's neck, calling him his brother, his beloved brother. This fraternal recognition would not have gratified any one who witnessed it. Turiaf lavished countless caresses upon Nychol with a forced and timid smile, while Nychol responded with a gloomy and embarrassed look. It was like a tiger fondling an elephant, while the monster's ponderous foot is already planted upon its panting chest.

"What happiness, brother Nychol! I am glad indeed to see you."

"And I am sorry for you, brother Turiaf."

The prisoner pretended not to hear these words, and went on in trembling tones: "You have a wife and children, I suppose? You must take me to see my gentle sister, and let me kiss my dear nephews."

"The Devil fly away with you!" muttered the hangman.

"I will be a second father to them. Hark ye, brother, I am powerful; I have great influence—"

The brother replied with a sinister expression: "I know that you had! At present, you had better be thinking of that which you have doubtless contrived to curry with the saints."

All hope faded from the prisoner's face.

"Good God! what does this mean, dear Nychol? I am safe, since I have found you. Think that the same mother bore us; that we played together as children. Remember, Nychol, you are my brother!"

"You never remembered it until now," replied the brutal Nychol.

"No, I cannot die by my brother's hand!"

"It is your own fault, Turiaf. It was you who ruined my career; who prevented me from becoming royal executioner at Copenhagen; who caused me to be sent into this miserable region as a petty provincial hangman. If you had not been a bad brother, you would have no cause to complain of that which distresses you so much now. I should not be in Throndhjem, and some one else would have to finish your business. Now, enough, brother, you must die."

Death is hideous to the wicked for the same reason that it is beautiful to the good; both must put off their humanity, but the just man is delivered from his body as from a prison, while the wicked man is torn from it as from a jail. At the last moment hell yawns before the sinful soul which has dreamed of annihilation. It knocks anxiously at the dark portals of death; and it is not annihilation that answers.

The prisoner rolled upon the floor and wrung his hands, with moans more heart-rending than the everlasting wail of the damned.

"God have mercy! Holy angels in heaven, if you exist, have pity upon me! Nychol, brother Nychol, in our mother's name, oh, let me live!"

The hangman held out his warrant.

"I cannot; the order is peremptory."

"That warrant is not for me," stammered the despairing prisoner; "it is for one Musdœmon. That is not I; I am Turiaf Orugix."

"You jest," said Nychol, shrugging his shoulders. "I know perfectly well that it is meant for you. Besides," he added roughly, "yesterday you would not have been Turiaf Orugix to your brother; to-day he can only look upon you as Turiaf Musdœmon."

"Brother, brother!" groaned the wretch, "only wait until to-morrow! It is impossible that the chancellor could have given the order for my death; it is some frightful mistake. Count d'Ahlefeld loves me dearly. Dear Nychol, I implore you, spare my life! I shall soon be restored to favor, and I will do whatever you may ask—"

"You can do me but one service, Turiaf," broke in the hangman. "I have lost two executions already upon which I counted the most, those of ex-chancellor Schumacker and the viceroy's son. I am always unlucky. You and Hans of Iceland are all that are left. Your execution, being secret and by night, is worth at least twelve gold ducats to me. Let me hang you peaceably, that is the only favor I ask of you."

"Oh, God!" sighed the prisoner.

"It will be the first and last, in good sooth; but, in return, I promise that you shall not suffer. I will hang you like a brother; submit to your fate."

Musdœmon sprang to his feet; his nostrils were distended with rage; his livid lips quivered; his teeth chattered; his mouth foamed with despair.

"Satan! I saved that d'Ahlefeld; I have embraced my brother,—and they murder me! And I must die this very night in a dark dungeon, where none can hear my curses; where I may not cry out against them from one end of the kingdom to the other; where I may not tear asunder the veil that hides their crimes! Was it for such a death that I have stained my entire life? Wretch!" he added, turning to his brother, "would you become a fratricide?"

"I am the executioner," answered the phlegmatic Nychol.

"No!" exclaimed the prisoner; and he flung himself headlong upon the executioner, his eyes darting flame and streaming with tears, like those of a bull at bay,—"no, I will not die thus meekly; I have not lived like a poisonous serpent to die like a paltry worm trampled under foot! I will leave my life in my last sting; but it shall be mortal."

So saying, he grappled like a bitter foe with him whom he had just embraced as a brother; the fulsome, flattering Musdœmon now showed his true spirit. Despair stirred up the foul dregs of his soul; and after crawling prostrate like a tiger, like a tiger he sprang upon his enemy. It would have been hard to decide which of the two brothers was the most appalling, as they struggled, one with the brute ferocity of a wild beast, the other with the artful fury of a demon.

But the four halberdiers, hitherto passive spectators, did not remain motionless. They lent their aid to the executioner; and soon Musdœmon, whose rage was his only strength, was forced to quit his hold. He dashed himself against the wall, uttering inarticulate yells, and blunting his nails upon the stone.

"To die! Devils in hell, to die! My shrieks unheard outside this roof, my arms powerless to tear down these walls!"

He was seized, but offered no resistance; his useless efforts had exhausted him. He was stripped of his gown, and bound; at this moment a sealed packet fell from his bosom.

"What is that?" said the hangman.

An infernal light gleamed in the prisoner's haggard eyes. He muttered: "How could I forget that? Look here, brother Nychol," he added in an almost friendly tone; "these papers belong to the lord chancellor. Promise to give them to him, and you may do what you will with me."

"Since you are quiet now, I promise to grant your last wish, although you have been a bad brother to me. I will see that the chancellor has the papers, on the honor of an Orugix."

"Ask leave to hand them to him yourself," replied the prisoner, smiling at the executioner, who, from his nature, had little understanding of smiles. "The pleasure which they will afford his Grace may lead him to confer some favor on you."

"Really, brother?" said Orugix. "Thank you! Perhaps he will make me executioner royal after all, eh? Well, let us part good friends! I forgive you all the scratches which you gave me; forgive me for the hempen collar which I must give you."

"The chancellor promised me a very different sort of collar," said Musdœmon.

Then the halberdiers led him, bound, into the middle of the cell; the hangman placed the fatal noose round his neck.

"Are you ready, Turiaf?"

"One moment! one moment!" said the prisoner, whose tenor had revived; "for mercy's sake, brother, do not pull the rope until I tell you to do so!"

"I do not need to pull it," answered the hangman.

A moment later he repeated his question. "Are you ready?"

"One moment more! Alas! must I die?"

"Turiaf, I have no time to waste."

So saying, Orugix signed to the halberdiers to stand away from the prisoner.

"One word more, brother; do not forget to give the packet to Count d'Ahlefeld."

"Never fear," replied Nychol. He added for the third time: "Come, are you ready?"

The unfortunate man opened his lips, perhaps to plead for another brief delay, when the impatient hangman stooped and turned a brass button projecting from the floor.

The plank gave way beneath the victim; the poor wretch disappeared through a square trap-door with a dull twang from the rope, which was stretched suddenly and vibrated fearfully with the dying man's final convulsions.

Nothing was seen but the rope swinging to and fro in the dark opening, through which came a cool breeze and a sound as of running water.

The halberdiers themselves shrank back, horror-stricken. The hangman approached the abyss, seized the rope, which still vibrated, and swung himself into the hole, pressing both feet against his victim's shoulders; the fatal rope stretched to its utmost with a creak, and stood still. A stifled sob rose from the trap.

"All is over," said the hangman, climbing back into the cell. "Farewell, brother!"

He drew a cutlass from his belt. "Go feed the fishes in the fjord. Your body to the waves; your soul to the flames!"

With these words, he cut the taut rope. The fragment still fastened to the iron ring lashed the ceiling, while the deep, dark waters splashed high as the body fell, then swept on their underground course.

The hangman closed the trap as he had opened it; as he rose, he saw that the room was full of smoke.

"What is all this?" he asked the halberdiers. "Where does this smoke come from?"

They knew no better than he. In surprise, they opened the door; the corridors were also filled with thick and nauseating smoke. A secret outlet led them, greatly terrified, to the square courtyard, where a fearful sight met their gaze.

A vast conflagration, fanned by a violent east wind, was consuming the military prison and the barracks. The flames, driven in eddying whirls, climbed stone walls, crowned burning roofs, leaped from gaping window-frames; and the black towers of Munkholm now shone in a red and ominous light, now vanished in a dense cloud of smoke.

A turnkey, who was escaping by the courtyard, told them hastily that the fire had broken out in the monster's cell during the sleep of Hans of Iceland's keepers, he having been imprudently allowed to have a fire and straw.

"How unlucky I am!" cried Orugix, when he heard this story; "now I suppose Hans of Iceland has slipped through my hands too. The rascal must have been burned; and I sha'n't even get his body, for which I paid two ducats!"

Meantime, the unfortunate Munkholm musketeers, roused suddenly from their sleep by imminent death, crowded toward the door only to find it closely barred. Their shrieks of anguish and despair were heard outside; they stood at the blazing windows, wringing their hands, or dashed themselves madly upon the flagging of the court, escaping one death to meet another. The victorious flames devoured the entire structure before the rest of the garrison could come to the rescue.

All help was vain. Luckily, the building stood by itself. The door was broken in with hatchets, but it was too late; for as it opened, the burning roof and floors gave way, and fell upon the unfortunate men with a loud crash.

The entire building disappeared in a whirlwind of fiery dust and burning smoke, which stifled the faint moans of the expiring men.

Next morning nothing was left in the courtyard but four high walls, black and smoking, around a horrid mass of smouldering ruins still devouring each other like wild beasts in a circus.

When the pile had cooled, it was searched. Beneath a heap of stones and iron beams, twisted out of shape by the flames, was found a mass of whitened bones and disfigured corpses; with some thirty soldiers, most of whom were crippled, this was all that remained of the crack regiment of Munkholm.

When the site of the prison was searched, and they reached the fatal cell where the fire had broken out, and where Hans of Iceland had been imprisoned, they found the remains of a human body close beside an iron pan and a heap of broken chains. It was curious that among these ashes there were two skulls, although there was but one skeleton.

LI

Saladin. Bravo, Ibrahim! you are indeed the messenger of good fortune; I thank you for your joyful tidings.

The Mameluke. Well, is that all?

Saladin. What did you expect?

The Mameluke. Nothing more for the messenger of good fortune.

Lessing: *Nathan the Wise.*

PALE and worn, Count d'Ahlefeld strode up and down his apartment; in his hand he crushed a bundle of letters which he had just read, while he stamped his foot on the smooth marble floor and the gold-fringed rugs.

At the other end of the room, in an attitude of deep respect, stood Nychol Orugix in his infamous scarlet dress, felt hat in hand.

"You have done me good service, Musdœmon," hissed the chancellor.

The hangman looked up timidly: "Is your Grace pleased?"

"What do you want here?" said the chancellor, turning upon him suddenly.

The hangman, proud that he had won a glance from the chancellor, smiled hopefully.

"What do I want, your Grace? The post of executioner at Copenhagen, if your Grace will deign to bestow so great a favor on me in return for the good news I have brought you."

The chancellor called to the two halberdiers on guard at his door: "Seize this rascal; he annoys me by his impudence."

The guards led away the amazed and confounded Nychol, who ventured one word more: "My lord—"

"You are no longer hangman for the province of Throndhjem; I deprive you of your office!" cried the chancellor, slamming the door.

The chancellor returned to his letters, angrily read and re-read them, maddened by his dishonor; for these were the letters which once passed between the countess and Musdœmon. This was Elphega's handwriting. He found that Ulrica was not his daughter; that, it might be, the Frederic whom he mourned was not his son. The unhappy count was punished through that same pride which had caused all his crimes. He cared not now if vengeance evaded him; all his ambitious dreams vanished,—his past was blasted, his future dead. He had striven to destroy his enemies; he had only succeeded in losing his own reputation, his adviser, and even his marital and paternal rights.

But he must see once more the wretched woman who had betrayed him. He hastily crossed the spacious apartment, shaking the letters in his hand as if they were a thunderbolt. He threw open the door of Elphega's room; he entered—

The guilty wife had just unexpectedly learned from Colonel Vœthaün of her son Frederic's fearful death. The poor mother was insane.

CONCLUSION

What I said in jest, you took seriously.—*Old Spanish Romance*
(*King Alfonso to Bernard*).

FOR a fortnight the events which we have just related formed the sole topic of conversation in the town and province of Throndhjem, judged from the various standpoints of the various speakers. The people of the town, who had waited in vain to see seven successive executions, began to despair of ever having that pleasure; and purblind old women declared that, on the night of the lamentable fire at the barracks, they had seen Hans of Iceland fly up in the flames, laughing amid the blaze, as he dashed the burning roof of the building upon the Munkholm musketeers; when, after an absence which to his Ethel seemed an age, Ordener returned to the Lion of Schleswig tower, accompanied by General Levin de Knud and Chaplain Athanasius Munder.

Schumacker was walking in the garden, leaning on his daughter. The young couple found it hard not to rush into each other's arms; but they were forced to be content with a look. Schumacker affectionately grasped Ordener's hand, and greeted the two strangers in a friendly manner.

"Young man," said the aged captive, "may Heaven bless your return!"

"Sir," replied Ordener, "I have just arrived. Having seen my father at Bergen, I would now embrace my father at Munkholm."

"What do you mean?" asked the old man, in great surprise.

"That you must give me your daughter, noble sir."

"My daughter!" exclaimed the prisoner, turning to the confused and blushing Ethel.

"Yes, my lord, I love your Ethel. I have devoted my life to her; she is mine."

Schumacker's face clouded: "You are a brave and noble youth, my son. Although your father has done me much harm, I forgive him for your sake; and I should be glad to sanction this marriage. But there is an obstacle—"

"What is it, sir?" asked Ordener, anxiously.

"You love my daughter; but are you sure that she loves you?"

The two lovers cast at each other a rapid glance of mute amazement.

"Yes," continued the father. "I am sorry; for I love you, and would gladly call you son. But my daughter would never consent. She has recently confessed her aversion for you, and since your departure she is silent whenever I speak of you, and seems to avoid all thought of you as if you were odious to her. You must give up your love for her, Ordener. Never fear; love may be cured as well as hatred."

"My lord!" exclaimed the astonished Ordener.

"Father!" cried Ethel, clasping her hands.

"Do not be alarmed, my daughter," interrupted the old man; "I approve of this marriage, but you do not. I will never force your inclinations, Ethel. This last fortnight has wrought a great change in me; you are free to choose for yourself."

Athanasius Munder smiled. "She is not," he said.

"You are mistaken, dear father," added Ethel, taking courage; "I do not hate Ordener."

"What!" cried her father.

"I am —" resumed Ethel. She hesitated.

Ordener knelt at the old man's feet.

"She is my wife, father! Forgive me as my other father has forgiven me, and bless your children."

Schumacker, surprised in his turn, blessed the young couple.

"I have cursed so many people in my lifetime," said he, "that I now seize every opportunity for blessing. But explain."

All was made clear to him. He wept with emotion, gratitude, and love.

"I thought myself wise; I am old, and I did not understand the heart of a young girl!"

"And so I am Mrs. Ordener Guldenlew!" said Ethel, with child-like delight.

"Ordener Guldenlew," rejoined old Schumacker, "you are a better man than I, for in the day of my prosperity I would never have stooped to wed the penniless and disgraced daughter of an unfortunate prisoner."

The general took the old man's hand, and offered him a roll of parchment, saying: "Do not speak thus, Count. Here are your titles, which the king long since sent you by Dispolsen; his Majesty now adds a free pardon. Such is the dowry of your daughter, Countess Danneskiold."

"Pardon! freedom!" repeated the enraptured Ethel.

"Countess Danneskiold!" added her father.

"Yes, Count," continued the general; "your honors and estates are restored."

"To whom do I owe all this?" asked the happy Schumacker.

"To General Levin de Knud," answered Ordener.

"Levin de Knud! Did I not tell you, Governor, that Levin de Knud was the best of men? But why did he not bring me the good news himself? Where is he?"

Ordener pointed in surprise to the smiling, weeping general: "Here!"

The recognition of the two who had been comrades in the days of their youth and power was a touching one. Schumacker's heart swelled. His acquaintance with Hans had destroyed his hatred of men; his acquaintance with Ordener and Levin taught him to love them.

The gloomy wedding in the cell was soon celebrated by brilliant festivities. Life smiled upon the young couple who had smiled at death. Count d'Ahlefeld saw that they were happy; this was his most cruel punishment.

Athanasius Munder shared their joy. He obtained the pardon of his twelve convicts, and Ordener added that of his former companions in misfortune, Jonas and Norbith, who returned, free and happy, to inform the appeased miners that the king released them from the protectorate.

Schumacker did not long enjoy the union of Ethel and Ordener. Liberty and happiness were too much for him; he went to enjoy a different happiness and a different freedom. He died that same year, 1699, his children accepting this blow as a warning that there is no perfect bliss in this world. He was buried in Veer Church, upon an estate in Jutland belonging to his son-in-law, and his tomb preserves all the titles of which captivity deprived him. From the marriage of Ordener and Ethel sprang the race of the counts of Danneskiold.

THE LAST DAY OF A CONDEMNED

DEDICATION

TO THE QUEEN'S MOST GRACIOUS MAJESTY

Madam,—The personal favour which your Majesty has been so graciously pleased to confer on me, in allowing the present dedication,—thus implying a confidence in the probable nature of the work,—will not, I trust, be found to have been misused by me, should your Majesty hereafter honour the volume by perusal. In thus being the medium through which the pleadings of a class of society, so far removed from the sympathy of mankind, approach the throne of your Majesty, may I be permitted to take this opportunity of expressing what is responded to by every feeling heart in your Majesty's dominions,—a respectful appreciation of the mildness and clemency which have pervaded the administration of the laws during the present merciful reign.

With sincere prayers for the happiness of your Majesty,

I have the honour to be, Madam,

Your Majesty's

Most humble and faithful

Servant and subject,

P. Hesketh Fleetwood.

Rossall Hall, *Lancashire.*

PREFACE

"To be, or not to be—that is the question."

THAT is indeed the question we are about to consider,—BEING or DEATH; a short sentence, but of unequalled importance. Yet how little does the demise of a fellow-man dwell on the human mind, unless the ties of kindred, or any peculiarity of circumstance by which the event may happen to be encircled, impart to it adventitious interest.

A newspaper paragraph entitled "Awful and sudden death" may for a moment arrest our attention; but it is the "awful and sudden," not the actual transit, which attracts the fancy. Perchance, also, it may be printed in rather a larger type than the adjoining paragraph, or we may expect to find some exciting detail of the facts of the case; but the awful Reality, the earthly ending of the being, immortal though it is to be, elicits little sympathy, and the wearied eye turns to some other news.

The dying *speech* of the malefactor arrests our attention; the dead *speaker* of it is unregarded as a lump of clay. Who that amidst the excitement of a crowded court of justice has turned his thoughts within himself, and divesting the scene of all the panoply of pomp which surrounds him, has reflected on the moral effect to be the result of the sentence of death *if executed*, but has felt his sympathy rather awakened in favour of the culprit, and confessed to himself how inefficient the gibbet is when viewed (according to its intended purpose) as the roadside guidepost, by which other earthly travellers, who might be disposed to stray, should be warned of a pathway to be avoided.

Alas! the body on the gibbet is but like the scarecrow in the field of grain,—little heeded by its brethren in plumage, scarcely noticed by aught save the vacant gape of curiosity; it dangles for a time, and is remembered no more!

But let us take a more serious view of the question,—one which commands our deepest respect and our gravest veneration. Let us consider the question of the assumed right to take human life on the warranty, or, as is sometimes said, on the express command of Scripture.

It has been often urged that it is expressly commanded in the Old Testament that "he who sheddeth man's blood, by man *shall* his blood be shed;" and, consequently, that the punishment of death for murder is sanctioned by the high and holy God who inhabiteth eternity.

How cautious should we be, to ascertain that no fallacy exists in this our opinion! I grant that, according to our translation, the above isolated text, if taken alone, may be so construed; but what are the acts of the Creator recorded as following upon this text? What was his first judgment on the first of murderers, Cain? Not only did he not inflict death, but by a special providence protected him from its infliction by his fellow-man. Behold again the case of David, guilty of at least imagining the death of Uriah. Was David struck dead for the crime?

Whatever an isolated chapter (much less, then, a single verse) may amount to of itself, if we take the context of the same part of Genesis and behold the first murderer even especially guarded, by God's mark, from the effect of "every man's hand being against him;" and again if we search the New Testament, where we find no passage, under the new dispensation, that can be construed to call for the infliction of death for murder,—from these results I submit that the question must be left solely to mundane argument, to stand or fall by its own efficacy as a preventive of murder, and that the isolated phrase of Scripture should not be construed into a command as to what ought to be done, but rather as the probable result of human revenge, a feeling at variance with God's holy ordinance; for we read, "Vengeance is mine, saith the Lord,"—expressly and clearly withholding the power over human life from mere mortal judgment.

Let me here give a short extract from the "Morning Herald,"—a paper which has always so consistently and ably advocated the sacredness of human life:—

"On the motion of Mr. Ewart, some important returns connected with the subject of CAPITAL PUNISHMENTS have been made to the House of Commons, and ordered to be printed.

"*First Class.*—A return of the number of persons *sentenced to death* for MURDER in the year 1834, whose punishment was *commuted*,—specifying the counties in which their crimes occurred, and stating the number of *commitments* for murder in the same counties during the *same* year and in the *following* year, together with the *increase* or *diminution of commitments* for murder in the same counties in the year following the commutation of the sentences; similar returns for 1835, 1836, 1837, and 1838.

"*Second Class.*—A return of the number of EXECUTIONS which took place in England and Wales during the three years ending the 31st day of

December, 1836, and also during the three years ending the 31st day of December, 1839, together with the number of *commitments* in each of those periods respectively for offences *capital*, on the 2d day of January, 1834. Also, the total number of *convictions* for the same offences, together with the *centesimal proportions of convictions to commitments* in each of those periods respectively.

"The facts set forth upon the face of these returns furnish very strong evidence, indeed, to prove the utter *inutility of* CAPITAL PUNISHMENTS as a means of preventing or repressing crime.

"What are the facts?

"We find that in one county (Stafford) in the year 1834 the sentence of one convict for *murder* was *commuted*. In that year the commitments for murder were six, and in the following year the commitments for that crime were also six. Thus the commutation of the sentence in that instance was followed by neither a *diminution* nor an *increase* of commitments for murder.

"It is sufficient for the argument of the advocates of abolition of capital punishment to show that the suppression of the barbarous exhibitions of the scaffold would *not* necessarily cause an *increase* of heinous offences; for if the amount of crime were to remain the *same* under laws *non-capital* as under those which are *capital*, to prefer the latter to the former would evince a passion for the wanton and unavailing destruction of human life, unspeakably disgraceful to the Government or Legislature of any civilized country.

"In Derbyshire, in the year 1835, we find a similar result following a commutation of sentence for murder to that which followed a similar commutation in the county of Stafford in the preceding year; namely, the same number of *commitments for murder* in the year following the commutation as in that in which it occurred, — being two in each; thus, also, in this instance, there was neither increase nor diminution of the crime of murder in the year following that of the commutation, judging from the number of commitments.

"In Warwickshire, in the year 1835, the sentence of a convict for murder was commuted, the number of commitments for the crime in that year being five, whereas in the year following there was but one commitment. In this instance, then, we have not only *no increase* of the crime of murder, but an actual *diminution* amounting to four.

"In Westmoreland, in the year 1835, there was one commutation; and the commitments in the year following showed neither an *increase* nor *diminution*, being two in each.

"In Cheshire, in the year 1836, the sentences of *two* convicts for *murder* were *commuted*, the commitments for the crime in that year being two; the commitments for the year following were also two, showing *neither an increase nor diminution.*

"Here we have an instance where the sentences of *all* convicted were commuted, and no *increase* of the crime followed.

"In Devonshire, in the year 1836, there was one commutation of sentence for *murder*, the commitments being four. In the year following there were *no* commitments, making a *decrease* of four.

"In Lancashire, in the year 1836, the sentences of *four* convicts for *murder* were commuted, the number of commitments in the same year being seven. In the year following the number of commitments was one, making a *decrease* of six.

"In the county of Norfolk, in the year 1836, the sentences of *five* convicts for *murder* were commuted, the number of commitments for the same year being eight. In the following year the number of commitments for murder were but five, giving a *decrease* of three.

"In the counties of Norfolk, Nottingham, and Stafford, in the year 1837, there was one commutation of the sentence of murder for each respectively. The result was a fall in the committals of the following year from five to two in the first county,—giving a decrease of three; in the second county a fall from one to *none*; in the third county *neither* an increase nor diminution,—the number of committals having been three in each year.

"In the counties of Lincoln, Stafford, and Denbigh, in the year 1838, there was respectively *one* commutation of the sentence for *murder*. The result was that in the following year the commitments fell from two to one in the first county, from three to one in the second, and from one to *none* in the third, thus giving respectively a decrease of one-half, two-thirds, and of the whole. The last is more correctly called an extinction than a decrease.

"In Cheshire, Middlesex, Somersetshire, and Surrey, in the year 1838, there were, respectively, *two* commutations of the sentence for murder. The result was that in the first county the commitments, as between that year and the year following, fell from two to one; in the second county they fell from seven to three; in the third, from three to one; and in the fourth, from three to two; thus giving a diminution, respectively, of one-half, four-sevenths, two-thirds, and one-third.

"In Kent, in the year 1838, the sentences of *nine* convicts for murder were commuted, the commitments for that crime in the same year being seventeen. In the following year the commitments for murder were only two, showing a decrease of fifteen. In this last case, however, we cannot in fairness press the argument in favour of the *salutary* effect of discontinuing capital punishments to the extent that the arithmetical table would show. That year, if we recollect right, was the year of the extraordinary outbreak headed by the madman Courtenay or Thom. That event swelled the commitments for murder to an unprecedented height. The fall in the commitments from seventeen, in that year, to two in the year following, is not a fall under *equal* circumstances, and it would be illogical to make it an argument for more than this: that society received *no detriment* because the deluded followers of the frantic Courtenay *were sent to a penal settlement, instead of being strangled on the scaffold.*

"Looking to the table of EXECUTIONS, we find that in the *three* years ending the 31st of December, 1836, the number *executed* was 85, while during the *three* years ending the 31st of December, 1839, the number was only twenty-five. The *commitments* in the former period were 3,104, in the latter 2,989, showing a *decrease*, though a small one, in the number of *commitments*, while there is exhibited an *increase* in the number of *convictions*; namely, from 1,536 to 1,788, showing the *centesimal* proportion of convictions to commitments in the two periods, to be represented by the figures 49·48 and 59·48 respectively.

"These returns, as far as they go, are highly satisfactory as the testimony of experience to the *safe* policy of ABOLISHING CAPITAL PUNISHMENTS ALTOGETHER, and thus getting rid of the barbarous and brutalizing exhibitions of cold-blooded cruelty and deliberate slaughter which they present to the people."

Morning Herald, 1840.

From this statement of facts, and indeed from all that has taken place regarding crimes where capital punishment has been remitted, there can be little doubt that it is inexpedient; there can be none that it is unnecessary. But if any still persist that the Divine sanction is given by "He who sheddeth man's blood, by man shall his blood be shed," then the tyrant who engages in a war of aggression, the general who sanctions one effective shot being fired, should alike bear the penalty with the midnight assassin. Nay, does not the man who accidentally "sheds the blood" of him who is "made in the likeness of God," literally come within the pale of the command, if *command* it be?

The Chinese but seek to carry out this principle: they merely say, and with juster pretension to consistency, "we cannot remit it; there must be blood for blood."

Yet we would dispute their right to have *always* blood for blood; why then may we not question the right *ever* to have blood shed, under Bible sanction at least? God makes no mention of motives or comparative reasonings as to guilt; in this His supposed command there is no discretionary option to soften its asserted force. By whatever means or under whatever circumstances one man kills another, *blood is shed*; and if blood for blood should hold good, then under this reasoning the slayer must die. If it be argued, that *wilful* shedding of blood is meant, I point to the words of the text; they refer to "life for life," they give no exceptions: "Who then, oh man! made thee a judge to tell the signs of the times?"

Once grant an exception to execution, once admit the doctrine of reprieve, and the authority, as a command, in the Bible ceases altogether.

Those who argue in favour of executions say, "But as an earthly punishment, we *may* hang;" *may*, indeed! There are fifty things we *may* do that are better avoided. Why need we hang, when other punishments will suffice, and have been proved to have succeeded in other cases? A very few years back, and the advances we have recently made in the civilization of our laws would have been scouted as equally Utopian, as is now considered the attempt to abolish the punishment of death altogether. Let us reflect too that in a case of murder, the prisoner (from a feeling which imperceptibly affects the minds of all) is looked on with a degree of suspicious anxiety to convict that almost watches to make out a case against him sufficient to condemn. The very fact of his being put on his trial for murder prejudges him in our eyes; and a slight variation in reporting a conversation has marvellously increased many a poor man's danger of the gallows.

There is no recalling the erroneously condemned from the grave; a wrong judgment cannot there be reversed! Let us bear in mind, also, that the wisest judges may sometimes decide wrongfully. They were considered by myself and others to have erred in respect to the privileges of the House of Commons; why might they not commit a similar error in the case of a prisoner?

But enough; let errors in judgment speak for themselves. They contain matter for deep reflection and self-examination for us all.

If the average number of executions be reduced, even by one, I shall have the satisfaction of feeling at least that I have been an humble labourer in the great cause of mercy, which could not have a more zealous advocate, though it may have many more powerful and successful supporters.

Happy are we if, in all we do during the course of our career, we have not to answer for one death; for the bitter word, the cruel neglect, the light injurious observation, may be the cause of death, as well as the bludgeon or the steel.

I would here desire to make a few observations as to the medium through which I have introduced to the public my opinions in favour of the abolition of Capital Punishment, and the advantages to the cause obtained from its appearing in the form of a translation, the reflections being those of a foreigner who looked not to England when he penned his work. In all this there is a beneficial distraction of ideas created, for we look, as it were, at a foreign scene when we read the interesting paper of the narrative,—the sentiments conveyed, the idioms transcribed, are foreign, and the reader appropriates alone the portion he feels is applicable to the circumstances of his own country; in fact, he examines the context, not as he would an original treatise, but as one who would apply the problems found advantageous in one region to another. He cavils not at words or similes; his criticism is reserved for the object at which the translator aims,—no matter even if the phraseology be too flowery, the expressions too strong. There may be strange similes, strained amplifications; he studies but a translation, and cares comparatively little for them. True, he may have some curiosity awakened as to what the original author was in feeling and ideas; but these thoughts are light and evanescent compared with the anxiety, or more properly the curiosity, he has to ascertain what could be the translator's ideas in thus "wasting the midnight oil" by reducing into the phraseology of his vernacular (English) tongue, the varied thoughts, the acute observations, the (to English ears) novel ideas of that clever, eccentric, single-minded writer, Victor Hugo. "What was the aim of the copyist?" methinks I hear repeated by many; and as my object is one of serious importance to the realities of life, and to arrest the attention of the reader beyond the mere passing hour, I reply: The object for which I plead is the priceless value of human life. Well and truly may the reading public,—and happy for this my dear native land is it that its public is a reading one,—well may this public exclaim, "Who is he, or what his view, who has thus dared to scatter these additional leaves on the pathway of a nation's thoughts? Why has he done so, what motives urged him, what end did he seek?"

Such are the surmises that may flit across the reader's brain, and the translator humbly hopes that the lightning scowl, or the thunder of maledictive criticism, will be directed alone against the oaken plank of a hundred years' growth, and that this his nautilus bark will feel no breeze beyond the *aura populi*. Probably to the English public many of the observations in this translation will be original. Haply to the gay and frivolous the thoughts may appear exaggerated; but, alas! with too many they will come home to the heart. Numbers there are, who, steeped in misery before they were steeped in crime, had as little inclination to sin as their more fortunate fellow-men, but whose first transgressions were the offsprings of their misery, the necessitous urgings of their poverty. Yes, gentle reader,—for among the fair and young I hope to have many readers; readers whose hearts yet know how to feel,—ye would I address, and exclaim, for the startling fact is but too true, that though,—

> "we who in lavish lap have rolled
> And every year with new delight have told;
> We who recumbent on the lacquered barge
> Have dropped down life's gay stream of pleasant marge;
> We may extol life's calm untroubled sea,"

well may the miserable, the guilty answer,—

> "The storms of misery never burst on thee."

"You never felt poverty. You never were comparatively tempted to crime." "A noble," say they, and truly, "a noble is tried, is judged by his peers, as being those who alone are considered to know, to be able to appreciate his case. Let poverty have her peers also." "My poverty and not my will consented" is a phrase to which too little consideration is given when we discuss the question of crime and punishment; for though poverty cannot be pleaded by the criminal in justification of his offence (nor should such justification be permitted in the legal view), Society, whose interests are represented by the tribunal which adjudges, should be careful that any circumstances or defects in its conformation which may have had a tendency even to induce the criminality of the culprit, should go in mitigation of his punishment. It would be a startling observation in the present day, and one for which Society is not yet prepared, to hear the assertion made that *punishment* for crime is more often unjust than just; but after much reflection on the origin of crime, humanly speaking, I am constrained to come to this conclusion: that the criminality of individuals is more frequently traceable to the evils incidental to an imperfect social system than to the greater propensity towards crime, as affecting others, that exists in the heart of one person if compared with another. Had the judge or the prosecutor entered life under the same circumstances as the prisoner, been early initiated into the same habits, been taught to view society through the same distorted glass, and had their feelings blunted by the same cold blasts of adversity, who shall say what their respective positions might have been?

In the phrase "My poverty but not my will consented," let me not be understood to speak of poverty merely in the light of want of money; that is a very narrow view, and very confined as to what forms the real pains of poverty. Poverty is the want of means, intellectual and moral as well as pecuniary, to feed the being who is placed on the area of the world; with mind active as well as body, sustenance is necessary to its existence. If the poor man cannot obtain bread, he takes to gin to assuage cravings of the stomach. No less, if the mind cannot obtain light to guide it in the onward path, the visual organs become habituated to the dark and murky gloom of almost darkness; and through these confused gleamings, no wonder if the being fall into the pits and whirlpools which beset with danger the pathway of man, even when blessed with the clear light of day; how much more, therefore, when he has not light to discern good from evil, nor an intellectual poor-law to supply him with food, when a beggar by the way-side of knowledge! How strange it is that we can incarcerate the *bodies* of the poor because they are poor, objecting to let them be dependent on casual charity for bodily sustenance, and yet cannot be equally strict in legislating for the mind.

Surely if, as members of one common society, we contend it is necessary for the well-being of the community at large that each person should be provided with work to enable him to procure food, and that if persons be unable to obtain work, or purchase food, then that the State shall provide for them,—should we not equally be provident for the mental as well as we are for the corporeal wants of those who hold a less fortunate position in the scale of society; more particularly when we reflect on the effect mind has on matter, and that did we sufficiently provide for the former, each individual would probably find little difficulty in procuring a supply for his bodily wants.

The poverty of the mind, if relieved, will probably be a permanent good; whereas bodily relief is at best but temporary. How vast, too, is the effect of knowledge, on the creation of food. Knowledge teaches industry; knowledge and industry multiply an hundred fold the product of labour. Comfort and security are thus increased; idleness, and consequently crime, is diminished,—for a man of information is seldom idle, and one surrounded with comforts is rarely inclined to commit crimes against society.

Would not, therefore, the effects resulting from education be the best preventative of crime?—and, if so, heavy indeed is the responsibility of every man who puts an impediment in the way of a nation's enlightenment. Circumstanced as Great Britain now is, internally speaking, with her countless millions congregated or *hived* in large towns, ready to follow any leader of more daring or greater knowledge than themselves, comparatively indifferent as to the means for compassing any much desired end,—though actuated by no wish to work ill to others, even when excited beyond the unmanageableness of irrational physical force,—there is much to be feared from the effects of any combustion which might suddenly inflame a people thus charged to the full with every ingredient requisite for scenes of violence, whilst at the same time, through a strong line of prescribed demarcation, separated from the privileged classes; and it cannot but be mainly by the controlling power of knowledge that we can expect to see the masses endeavouring to be satisfied with their lot in life. Thus it is, as I have before asserted, that the poverty of opportunity for information, and consequently acquirement of knowledge, originates much of the present state of crime. Oh, that I could distinctly see my way through the halo which as yet obscures that glorious day, when ignorance shall be deplored as much as shame! With what satisfaction would the statesman then die and bequeath his country to the care of, not the fate of accident, as now, but the masses of its own population. Methinks the gleam which harbingers this bright morning, already, though faintly, begins to tinge the horizon, under the happy auspices of our beloved Queen; and to the credit of the liberal advisers of Her Majesty, a more liberal arrangement of schools has been established,—though it probably remains for ages yet unborn to develope fully the blessings of such a system. Well worthy, aye, brighter than a diadem of a thousand stars, is the advancement of a nation's happiness. May such thoughts have our beloved Queen's deep and considerate attention; and as her noble mind traces, on an ideal map, the future destinies of her people, and turns to times when another generation, with its train of guilt or happiness, shall arise, may she anticipate in time the benefits which will flow from a system of general education!

But if these things be now lightly accounted, the time may arrive when population shall be yet more dense, and the strong arm of numbers become yet more strong; for if no countervailing power intervene, force and numbers must prevail at last, and there must come a time when it will alone depend upon the respective powers of intellect or animal force being dominant, whether confidence in our stability shall be shaken, capital cease to be here expended, and commerce leave our shores,—whether, in fact, brute force or reason become the recognized sovereign of the people; whether the influence of intellect has been fostered, and nobler thoughts and more refined pleasures become the pastime of this great nation. Then, but not till then, will crime hide her head, and the race no longer be to the swift or the battle to the strong: a calm and steady breeze will temper the course of the swift to wrath, or the powerfully scientific lever of knowledge uproot violence out of the councils of the nation; for they will then appreciate law, knowing it is peculiarly the palladium of the defenceless, and confident in the strength of their cause, they will cast off the trammels of tradition, form unions of information, not restriction; and when the various classes of society shall have learned to know that each has his proper duties, each his proper limits, each is equally necessary to each, whose strength is a combination of the whole,—like the arch, sure to drop to pieces if the keystone were removed.

Oh, how the heart bleeds to reflect on the pains which are taken to render efficient the laws for punishing crime, and the little care to fortify the minds of the people to resist the first impress of crime. Train up the child in the way he should go, and he will not depart therefrom. If, therefore, we train it not up, it never has wherefrom to depart, but is cast forth, like a helmless, pilotless bark, on the waters of life; strange if it founder not, or at least if it become not damaged by striking on some of the shoals by which it is beset on every side. We talk of "penal laws" or a "penal settlement" as though the aim and intention of laws were to be *penal*, instead of being as they most decidedly are, or ought to be, *sanitary*. Wherefore do we, as we term it, *punish*, but to cure an evil which hurts and pains society? Just so we cauterize a wound, in order to heal the body, not for the sake of giving pain to the affected limb.

The very fact of the common acceptation of the word *penal*, as applied to our criminal system, is of itself a strong proof of the misunderstanding on which that system is founded, and on which we legislate. If we arrogate to ourselves a right to judge men for their criminality, instead of urging our only legitimate excuse for punishing, namely, "the giving over the offending member to that course of discipline we deem most likely to restrain a similar disposition to delinquency in another member of the frame-work of society," let us at least carry out this principle to the full extent; and then the man who cheats his neighbour of money by availing himself of his ignorance, and leads him to make an improvident bargain, will be deemed as guilty in the eye of the law as he who, throwing him off his guard, surreptitiously conveys his hand into the other's pocket.

But it is really absurd to talk of laws being framed to punish sin. It is to restrain others, as well as the culprit himself, from similar offences that pains and penalties are inflicted. If they fail of this end they become themselves improper; if the same end can be attained by a mild as by a severe sentence, the milder course should be adopted.

Perhaps there may be some who are only timid regarding the total abolition of capital punishment because they are fearful of a license being given which would render human life of less value in the sight of man. Can then the destruction of a second life increase the reverence for its sacredness? Surely, not! If we were, in imagination, to place ourselves in the chamber of the condemned, or by the fire-side of the mere spectator of an execution, we shall find the heart of the first generally in a morbid state, whilst the spectator commiserates the fate of the condemned more than he learns to reprobate the crime for which the guilty one suffered.

Punishment, when strained beyond what is necessary becomes revenge; punishment, also, should never exceed, but rather be milder than, public opinion. In the awful decision of death, more especially, we should be careful not to inflict a penalty which we cannot repay back to the sufferer if the condemnation should afterwards prove to have been erroneous. There can be no recall from the grave: in the beautiful words of our author, "THE DOOR OF THE TOMB OPENS NOT INWARDS!"

There are several points in "The Last Days of a Condemned" to which I would particularly invite the attention of the reader. In the first place, the story being left unfinished, and there being a doubt as to whether the condemned was executed or pardoned, takes from the feeling of horror without affecting our interest in his fate. It is as a veil cast over the last moments, — a film, an indistinctness that blends into harmony the last distorted features of the vision we are contemplating.

Next, I would mention the papers relating to chaplains. How touchingly does the author paint the pure and pastorly being who has dwelt in the homely cure, and amid the peaceful scenes of nature studied nature's God! the poor captive, crushed in worldly feeling, yearns for those "good and consoling words" that shall "heal the bruised reed, and quench the smoking flax." How beautiful to see the soul seeking for that hope which dieth not; and whether we cannot but feel a happy and holy wish that Heavenly Peace may rest on the poor condemned.

Pass we now to a beautiful scene of nature, — the final interview between the prisoner and his infant daughter, which few could read unmoved by its pathos. How happy for the parent who can enfold his child in his arms, — a happiness of which parents seldom know the value until the grave has closed over them, or they have left the homestead and parental hearth for the pathway of independent manhood. Agonizing must it be to a parent when absence has transferred much of the warmth of filial affection to strangers, to behold the child you have pictured, possibly for years, as anxious to welcome home from distant noxious climes the parent from whom it parted in the happy days of innocence, perhaps ere yet the mind was conscious of the father's parting blessing. How the pulse throbs and the heart beats when the vessel touches land, and the waving handkerchief is indistinctly discerned amidst hundreds of spectators; and if when disengaged from the crowd, and with the beloved object seated beside you as the carriage speeds you to your home, how scrutinizingly does the heart search each gaze, fearfully anxious lest it should be able to fathom the depth of a love it would hold fathomless! But oh! how bitter beyond expression must be a meeting such as is described by the author of "The Condemned:" not only want of recognition from the innocent little prattler, not only indifference towards him,—but *terror*! How infinitely more must this have reconciled him, and made him court death than all that myriads of arguments could have effected!

A widely contrasted scene is painted, wherein is described the departure of the convicts for the Galleys. What an interesting and painful study for the philanthropist or the moralist! In a few words we read the history of years, the downward path, the emulation in vice. The pride of the hardened sinner to show his superiority in crime, and the effort of the newer delinquent to hide his inexperience under a more hardened exterior, prove forcibly how equally emulative is man, whether the object be a sceptre or a public execution, that his fellows may admire him when he is gone, that his compeers shall not surpass him while he remains!

The deterioration of mind on all connected with a crowded gaol,—that university for crime—is shown, in a paper a few pages further, where even the song of a young girl, the outpouring of an unburthened heart, is tainted by the details of crime. The words are left in their original tongue; retained for the sake of showing the ability of the author, but not translated, as being little suited to give pleasure or effect any good. Alas! that the gaol should have power thus to efface even the charms of melody, and render discordant music's silvery tones. But even that sweetest of sounds, a female voice, becomes tainted by prison association: the rust of a gaol corrodes the heart, and eats into every thing; time cannot efface its mark, nor the brightest sun call forth one gleam from where its dimness has once affixed itself.

As it mars lovely woman's charms, so it renders disgustful the venerableness of age. From the song of the young girl we trace its earlier mildew; from the powerful paper narrating the history of the old convict (which is by far the most stirring and full of adventure of the whole) we learn its baleful effects on old age.

May a beneficent, rationally-grounded clemency be, in future, the means of redeeming "all such as have erred;" and may a widely-spread system of enlightened education happily train the children of adverse circumstances "in the way they should go."

P. Hesketh Fleetwood.

FIRST PAPER

Bicêtre Prison.

CONDEMNED to death!

These five weeks have I dwelt with this idea,—always alone with it, always frozen by its presence, always bent under its weight.

Formerly (for it seems to me rather years than weeks since I was free) I was a being like any other; every day, every hour, every minute had its idea. My mind, youthful and rich, was full of fancies, which it developed successively, without order or aim, but weaving inexhaustible arabesques on the poor and coarse web of life. Sometimes it was of youthful beauties, sometimes of unbounded possessions, then of battles gained, next of theatres full of sound and light, and then again the young beauties, and shadowy walks at night beneath spreading chestnut-trees. There was a perpetual revel in my imagination: I might think on what I chose,—I was free.

But now,—I am a Captive! Bodily in irons in a dungeon, and mentally imprisoned in one idea,—one horrible, one hideous, one unconquerable idea! I have only one thought, one conviction, one certitude,—

Condemned to death!

Whatever I do, that frightful thought is always here, like a spectre, beside me,—solitary and jealous, banishing all else, haunting me for ever, and shaking me with its two icy hands whenever I wish to turn my head away or to close my eyes. It glides into all forms in which my mind seeks to shun it; mixes itself, like a horrible chant, with all the words which are addressed to me; presses against me even to the odious gratings of my prison. It haunts me while awake, spies on my convulsive slumbers, and re-appears, a vivid incubus, in my dreams!

I have just started from a troubled sleep in which I was pursued by this thought, and I made an effort to say to myself, "Oh, it was but a dream!"

Well, even before my heavy eyes could read the fatal truth in the dreadful reality which surrounds me,—on the damp and reeking dungeon-walls, in the pale rays of my night-lamp, in the rough material of my prison-garb, on the sombre visage of the sentry, whose cap gleams through the grating of the door,—it seems to me that already a voice has murmured in my ear,—

"Condemned to death!"

SECOND PAPER

FIVE weeks have now elapsed since I was tried,—found guilty,—sentenced.

Let me endeavour to recall the circumstances which attended that fatal day.

It was a beautiful morning at the close of August. My trial had already lasted three days; my name and accusation had collected each morning a knot of spectators, who crowded the benches of the Court, as ravens surrounded a corpse. During three days all the assembly of judges, witnesses, lawyers, and officers had passed and repassed as a phantasmagoria before my troubled vision.

The two first nights, through uneasiness and terror, I had been unable to sleep; on the third I had slept, from fatigue and exhaustion. I had left the jury deliberating at midnight, and was taken back to the heap of straw in my prison, where I instantly fell into a profound sleep,—the sleep of forgetfulness. These were the first hours of repose I had obtained after long watchfulness.

I was buried in this oblivion when they sent to have me awakened, and my sound slumber was not broken by the heavy step and iron shoes of the jailor, by the clanking of his keys, or the rusty grating of the lock; to rouse me from my lethargy it required his harsh voice in my ear, his rough hand on my arm.

"Come," shouted he, "rise directly!"

I opened my eyes, and started up from my straw bed: it was already daylight.

At this moment, through the high and narrow window of my cell, I saw on the ceiling of the next corridor (the only firmament I was allowed to see) that yellow reflection by which eyes accustomed to the darkness of a prison recognize sunshine. And oh, how I love sunshine!

"It is a fine day!" said I to the jailor.

He remained a moment without answering me, as if uncertain whether it was worth while to expend a word; then, as if with an effort, he coolly murmured, "Very likely."

I remained motionless, my senses half sleeping, with smiling lips, and my eyes fixed on that soft golden reflection which reverberated on the ceiling.

"What a lovely day!" I repeated.

"Yes," answered the jailor; "*they are waiting for you.*"

These few words, like a web which stops the flight of an insect, flung me back into the reality of my position. I pictured to myself instantly, as in a flash of lightning, that sombre Court of Justice, the Bench of Judges, in their robes of sanguine hue, the three rows of stupid-looking witnesses, two gendarmes at the extremity of my bench; black robes waving, and the heads of the crowd clustering in the depth of the shadow, while I fancied that I felt upon me the fixed look of the twelve jurymen, who had sat up while I slept.

I rose: my teeth chattered, my hands trembled, my limbs were so weak that at the first step I had nearly fallen; however, I followed the jailor slowly.

Two gendarmes waited for me at the door-way of the cell; they replaced my fetters, to which I yielded mechanically, as in a dream.

We traversed an interior court, and the balmy air of morning reanimated me. I raised my head: the sky was cloudless, and the warm rays of the sun (partially intercepted by the tall chimneys) traced brilliant angles of light on the high and sombre walls of the prison. It was indeed a delicious day.

We ascended a winding staircase; we passed a corridor, then another, then a third, and then a low door was opened. A current of hot air, laden with noise, rushed from it; it was the breath of the crowd in the Court of Justice which I then entered.

On my appearance the hall resounded with the clank of arms and the hum of voices; benches were moved noisily; and while I crossed that long chamber between two masses of people who were walled in by soldiers, I painfully felt myself the centre of attraction to all those fixed and gaping looks.

At this moment I perceived that I was without fetters, but I could not recall where or when they had been removed.

At length I reached my place at the bar, and there was a deep silence. The instant that the tumult ceased in the crowd, it ceased also in my ideas: a sudden clearness of perception came to me, and I at once understood plainly, what until then I could not discover in my confused state of mind, that *the decisive moment was come*! I was brought there to hear my *sentence*!

Explain it who can: from the manner in which this idea came to my mind, it caused me no terror! The windows were open; the air, and the sounds of the City came freely through them; the room was as light as for a wedding; the cheerful rays of the sun traced here and there the luminous forms of the windows, sometimes lengthened on the flooring, sometimes spreading on a table, sometimes broken by the angles of the walls; and from the brilliant square of each window the rays fell through the air in dancing golden beams.

The Judges at the extreme of the hall bore a satisfied appearance, probably from the anticipation of their labours being soon completed. The face of the President, softly lighted by a reflected sunbeam, had a calm and amiable expression; and a young counsel conversed almost gaily with a handsome woman who was placed near him.

The Jury alone looked wan and exhausted, but this was apparently from the fatigue of having sat up all night. Nothing in their countenances indicated men who would pass sentence of death.

Opposite to me a window stood wide open. I heard laughter in the Market for Flowers beneath; and on the sill of the window a graceful plant, illumined by sunshine, played in the breeze.

How could any sinister idea be formed amongst so many soothing sensations? Surrounded by air and sunshine, I could think of nought save freedom. Hope shone within me, as the day shone around me; and I awaited my sentence with confidence, as one daily calculates on liberty and life.

In the meantime my counsel arrived; after taking his place he leaned towards me with a smile.

"I have hopes!" said he.

"Oh, surely!" I replied in the same light tone.

"Yes," returned he; "I know nothing as yet of the verdict, but they have doubtless acquitted you of premeditation, and then it will be only *hard labour for life!*"

"What do you mean, sir?" replied I, indignantly; "I would prefer death!"

Then the President, who had only waited for my counsel, desired me to rise. The soldiers carried arms; and, like an electric movement, all the assembly rose at the same instant. The Recorder, placed at a table below the Tribunal, read the verdict, which the Jury pronounced during my absence.

A sickly chill passed over my frame; I leaned against the wall to avoid falling.

"Counsel, have you anything to say why this sentence should not be passed?" demanded the President.

I felt that *I* had much to urge, but I had not the power,—my tongue was cleaving to my mouth.

My counsel then rose. His endeavour appeared to be, to mitigate the verdict of the Jury, and to substitute the punishment of hard labour for life,—by naming which he had rendered me so indignant! This indignation must again have been powerful within me to conquer the thousand emotions which distracted my thoughts. I wished to repeat aloud what I had already said to him, but my breath failed, and I could only grasp him by the arm, crying with convulsive strength, "No!"

The Attorney-General replied against my counsel's arguments, and I listened to him with a stupid satisfaction. The Judges then left the Court; soon returned, and the President read my sentence.

"*Condemned to death!*" cried the crowd; and as I was led away the assembly pressed on my steps with avidity, while I walked on, confused, and nearly in unconsciousness. A revolution had taken place within me. Until that sentence of Death I had felt myself breathe, palpitate, exist, like other beings. Now I felt clearly that a barrier existed between me and the world. Nothing appeared to me under the same aspect as hitherto. Those large and luminous windows, that fair sunshine, that pure sky,—all was pale and ghastly, the colour of a winding sheet. Those men, women, and children who pressed on my path seemed to me like phantoms.

At the foot of the stairs a black and dirty prison-cart was waiting; as I entered it, I looked by chance around.

"The Condemned Prisoner!" shouted the people, running towards the cart.

Through the cloud which seemed to me to interpose between me and all things, I distinguished two young girls who gazed at me with eager eyes.

"Well," said the youngest, clapping her hands, "*it will take place in six weeks.*"

THIRD PAPER

CONDEMNED to death!

Well, why not? I remember once reading, "All mankind are condemned to death, with indefinite respites." How then is my position altered?

Since my sentence was pronounced, how many are dead who calculated upon a long life! How many are gone before me, who, young, free, and in good health, had fully intended to be present at my execution! How many, between this and then, perhaps, who now walk and breathe in the fresh air any where they please, will die before me!

And then, what has life for me, that I should regret? In truth, only the dull twilight and black bread of a prison, a portion of meagre soup from the trough of the convicts; to be treated rudely,—I, who have been refined by education; to be brutalized by turnkeys without feeling; not to see a human being who thinks me worthy of a word, or whom I could address; incessantly to shudder at what I have done, and what may be done to me,— these are nearly the only advantages of which the executioner can deprive me!

Ah! still it is horrible.

FOURTH PAPER

THE black cart brought me here to this hideous Bicêtre Prison.

Seen from afar, the appearance of that edifice is rather majestic. It spreads to the horizon in front of a hill, and at a distance retains something of its ancient splendour, — the look of a Royal Palace. But as you approach it, the Palace changes to a ruin, and the dilapidated gables shock the sight. There is a mixture of poverty and disgrace soiling its royal façades; without glass or shutters to the windows, but massive crossed-bars of iron instead, against which is pressed, here and there, the ghastly face of a felon or a madman.

FIFTH PAPER

WHEN I arrived here the hand of force was laid on me, and numerous precautions were taken: neither knife nor fork was allowed for my repasts; and a strait-waistcoat—a species of sack made of sail-cloth—imprisoned my arms. I had sued to annul my sentence, so the jailors might have for six or seven weeks their responsibility; and it was requisite to keep me safe and healthful for the Guillotine!

For the first few days I was treated with a degree of attention which was horrible to me,—the civilities of a turnkey breathe of a scaffold. Luckily, at the end of some days, habit resumed its influence; they mixed me with the other prisoners in a general brutality, and made no more of those unusual distinctions of politeness which continually kept the executioner in my memory.

This was not the only amelioration. My youth, my docility, the cares of the Chaplain of the prison, and above all some words in Latin which I addressed to the keeper, who did not understand them, procured for me a walk once a week with the other prisoners, and removed the strait-waistcoat with which I was paralyzed. After considerable hesitation they have also given me pens, paper, ink, and a night-lamp. Every Sunday after Mass I am allowed to walk in the Prison-court at the hour of recreation; there I talk with the prisoners, which is inevitable. They make boon companions, these wretches. They tell me their adventures,—enough to horrify one; but I know they are proud of them. They also try to teach me their mystic idioms,—an odious phraseology grafted on the general language, like a hideous excrescence; yet sometimes it has a singular energy, a frightful picturesqueness. To be hung is called "marrying the widow," as though the rope of the gallows were the widow of all who had been executed! At every instant mysterious, fantastic words occur, base and hideous, derived one knows not whence; they resemble crawling reptiles. On hearing this language spoken, the effect is like the shaking of dusty rags before you.

These men at least pity me, and they alone do so. The jailors, the turnkeys,—and I am not angry with them,—gossip and laugh, and speak of me in my presence as of a mere animal.

SIXTH PAPER

I SAID to myself, "As I have the means of writing, why should I not do it? But of what shall I write? Placed between four walls of cold and bare stone, without freedom for my steps, without horizon for my eyes, my sole occupation mechanically to watch the progress of that square of light which the grating of my door marks on the sombre wall opposite, and, as I said before, ever alone with one idea,—an idea of crime, punishment, death,—can I have anything to *say*, I who have no more to *do* in this world; and what shall I find in this dry and empty brain which is worthy the trouble of being written?

"Why not? If all around me is monotonous and hueless, is there not within me a tempest, a struggle, a tragedy? This fixed idea which possesses me, does it not take every hour, every instant a new form, becoming more hideous as the time approaches? Why should I not try to describe for myself all the violent and unknown feelings I experience in my outcast situation? Certainly the material is plentiful; and, however shortened my life may be, there will still be sufficient in the anguish, the terrors, the tortures, which will fill it from this hour until my last, to exhaust my pen and ink! Besides, the only means to decrease my suffering in this anguish will be to observe it closely; and to describe it will give me an occupation. And then, what I write may not be without its use. This journal of my sufferings, hour by hour, minute by minute, torment after torment, if I have strength to carry it on to the moment when it will be *physically* impossible for me to continue,—this history necessarily unfinished, yet as complete as possible, of my sensations, may it not give a grand and deep lesson? Will not there be in this process of agonizing thought, in this ever increasing progress of pain, in this intellectual dissection of a condemned man, more than one lesson for those who condemned? Perhaps the perusal may render them less heedless, when throwing a human life into what they call 'the scale of justice.' Perhaps they have never reflected on the slow succession of tortures conveyed in the expeditious formula of a sentence of death. Have they ever paused on the important idea, that in the man whose days they shorten there is an immortal spirit which had calculated on life, a soul which is not prepared for death? No! they see nothing but the execution, and doubtless think that for the condemned there is nothing anterior or subsequent!"

These sheets shall undeceive them. Published, perchance, some day, they will call their attention a few moments to the suffering of the mind; for it is this which they do not consider. They triumph in the power of being able to destroy the body, almost without making it suffer. What an inferior consideration is this! What is mere physical pain compared to that of the mind? A day will come,—and perhaps these memoirs, the last revelations of a solitary wretch, will have contributed —

That is, unless after my death the wind carries away these sheets of paper into the muddy court, or unless they melt with rain when pasted to the broken windows of a turnkey.

SEVENTH PAPER

SUPPOSE that what I write might one day be useful to others,—might make the Judge pause in his decision, and might save the wretched (innocent or guilty) from the agony to which I am condemned,—why should *I* do it? What matters it? When my life has been taken, what will it be to me if they take the lives of others? Have I really thought of such folly?—to throw down the scaffold which I had fatally mounted!

What! sunshine, spring, fields full of flowers and birds, the clouds, trees, nature, liberty, life,—these are to be mine no more!

Ah, it is myself I must try to save! Is it really true that this cannot be, that I must die soon,—to-morrow, to-day perhaps; is it all thus? Oh, heavens! what a dreadful idea,—of destroying myself against the prison wall!

EIGHTH PAPER

LET me consider what time generally elapses between the condemnation and the execution of a prisoner.

Three days of delay, after sentence is pronounced, for the prisoner's final plea to annul it.

The plea forgotten for a week in a Court of Assize, before it is sent to the Minister; a fortnight forgotten at the Minister's, who does not even know that there are such papers, although he is supposed to transmit them, after examination, to the "Cour de Cassation."

Then classification, numbering, registering; the guillotine-list is loaded, and none must go before their turn! A fortnight more waiting; then the Court assembles, rejects twenty pleas together, and sends all back to the Minister, who sends them back to the Attorney-General, who sends them back to the executioner: this would take three more days.

On the morning of the fourth day the Deputies of the Attorney-General and Recorder prepare the order of execution; and the following morning, from day-break, is heard the noise of erecting the scaffold, and in the cross-streets a commotion of hoarse voices.

Altogether *six weeks*. The young girl's calculation was right! I have now been at least five weeks (perhaps six, for I dare not reckon) in this fatal prison; nay, I think I have been even three days more.

NINTH PAPER

I HAVE just made my will; what was the use of this?

I have to pay my expenses, and all I possess will scarcely suffice. A forced death is expensive.

I leave a mother, I leave a wife, I leave a child, —a little girl of three years old, gentle, delicate, with large black eyes and chesnut hair. She was two years and one month old when I saw her the last time.

Thus after my death there will be three women without son, without husband, without father, —three orphans in different degrees; three widows by act of law.

I admit that I am justly punished; but these innocent creatures, what have they done? No matter; they will be dishonoured, they will be ruined; and this is justice!

It is not so much on account of my poor old mother that I feel thus wretched; she is so advanced in years, she will not survive the blow; or if she still linger a short time, her feelings are so blunted that she will suffer but little.

Nor is it for my wife that I feel the most. She is already in miserable health, and weak in intellects; her reason will give way, in which case her spirit will not suffer while the mind slumbers as in death.

But my daughter, my child, my poor little Mary, who is laughing, playing, singing at this moment, and who dreams of no evil! Ah, it is the thought of her which unmans me!

TENTH PAPER

HERE is the description of my prison: eight feet square; four walls of granite, with a flagged pavement; on one side a kind of nook by way of alcove, in which is thrown a bundle of straw, where the prisoner is supposed to rest and sleep, dressed, winter, as in summer, in slight linen clothing. Over my head, instead of curtains, a thick canopy of cobwebs, hanging like tattered pennons. For the rest, no windows, not even a ventilator; and only one door, where iron hides the wood. I mistake; towards the top of the door there is a sort of window, or rather an opening of nine inches square, crossed by a grating, and which the turnkey can close at night. Outside, there is a long corridor lighted and aired by means of narrow ventilators high in the wall. It is divided into compartments of masonry, which communicate by a series of doors; each of these compartments serves as an antichamber to a dungeon, like mine. In these dungeons are confined felons condemned by the Governor of the Prison to hard labour. The three first cells are kept for prisoners under sentence of death, as being nearest to the goal, therefore most convenient for the jailor. These dungeons are the only remains of the ancient Bicêtre Castle, such as it was built in the fifteenth century by the Cardinal of Winchester, he who caused Jeanne of Arc to be burned. I overheard this description from some persons who came to my den yesterday, to gratify their curiosity, and who stared at me from a distance as at a wild beast in a menagerie. The turnkey received five francs for the exhibition.

I have omitted to say that night and day there is a sentry on guard outside the door of my cell; and I never raise my eyes towards the square grating without encountering his eyes, open, and fixed on me.

ELEVENTH PAPER

AS there is no appearance of daylight, what is to be done during the night? It occurred to me that I would arise and examine, by my lamp, the walls of my cell. They are covered with writings, with drawings, fantastic figures, and names which mix with and efface each other. It would appear that each prisoner had wished to leave behind him some trace here at least. Pencil, chalk, charcoal,—black, white, grey letters; sometimes deep carvings upon the stone. If my mind were at ease, I could take an interest in this strange book, which is developed page by page, to my eyes, on each stone of this dungeon. I should like to recompose these fragments of thought; to trace a character for each name; to give sense and life to these mutilated inscriptions,—these dismembered phrases.

Above where I sleep there are two flaming hearts, pierced with an arrow; and beneath is written "Amour pour la vie." Poor wretch! it was not a long engagement.

Beyond this, a three-sided cocked hat, with a small figure coarsely done beneath, and the words, "Vive l'Empereur!"

On the opposite wall is the name of "Papavoine." The capital P is worked in arabesques and embellished with care.

A verse of a popular drinking-song.

A Cap of Liberty, cut rather deeply into the stone, with the words beneath of "Bories, La Republique!"

Poor young man! he was one of the four subaltern officers of La Rochelle. How horrible is the idea of their (fancied) political necessity, to give the frightful reality of the guillotine for an opinion, a reverie, an abstraction!—And I! *I* have complained of its severity!—I who have really committed crime—

Ah, what have I seen! I can go no farther in my research! I have just discovered, drawn with chalk in the corner of the wall, that dreadful image, the representation of that scaffold, which even at this moment is perhaps being put up for my execution! The lamp had nearly fallen out of my trembling hands!

TWELFTH PAPER

I RETURNED precipitately to sit on my straw bed; my head sunk on my knees. After a time, my childish fear was dissipated, and a wild curiosity forced me to continue the examination of my walls.

Beside the name of Papavoine, I tore away an enormous cobweb, thick with dust, and filling the angle of the wall. Under this web there were four or five names perfectly legible, among others of which nothing remained but a smear on the wall,—Dautan, 1815. Poulain, 1818. Jean Martin, 1821. Castaing, 1823.

As I read these names, frightful recollections crowded on me. *Dautan* was the man who cut his brother in quarters, and who went at night to Paris and threw the head into a fountain, and the body into a sewer. *Poulain* assassinated his wife. *Jean Martin* shot his father with a pistol as the old man opened a window. And *Castaing* was the physician who poisoned his friend; and while attending the illness he had caused, instead of an antidote, gave him more poison. Then, next to these names, was Papavoine, the horrible madman who stabbed children to death in his phrenzy.

"These," I exclaimed, as a shudder passed over me, "these, then, have been my predecessors in this cell. Here, on the same pavement where I am, they conceived their last thoughts,—these fearful homicides! Within these walls, in this narrow square, their last steps turned and re-turned, like those of a caged wild-beast. They succeeded each other at short intervals; it seems that this dungeon does not remain empty. They have left the place warm,—and it is to me they have left it. In my turn I shall join them in the felons' cemetery of Clamart, where the grass grows so well!"

I am neither visionary nor superstitious, but it is probable these ideas caused in my brain a feverish excitement; for, whilst I thus wandered, all at once these five fatal names appeared as though written in flames on the dark wall; noises, louder and louder, burst on my ears; a dull red light filled my eyes, and it seemed to me that my cell became full of men,—strangers to me. Each bore his severed head in his left hand, and carried it by the mouth, for the hair had been removed; each raised his right hand at me, *except the parricide*.[5]

I shut my eyes in horror, and then I saw all even more distinctly than before!

Dream, vision, or reality, I should have gone mad if a sudden impression had not recalled me in time. I was near fainting, when I felt something cold crawling over my naked foot. It was the bloated spider, whom I had disturbed. This recalled my wandering senses. Those dreadful spectres, then, were only the fumes of an empty and convulsed brain. The sepulchre is a prison from whence none escape. The door of the tomb opens not inwards!

THIRTEENTH PAPER

I HAVE lately witnessed a hideous sight. As soon as it was day, the prison was full of noise, I heard heavy doors open and shut; the grating of locks and bolts; the clanking of bunches of keys; the stairs creaking from top to bottom with quick steps; and voices calling and answering from the opposite extremes of the long corridors. My neighbours in the dungeons, the felons at hard labour, were more gay than usual. All in the prison seemed laughing, singing, running, or dancing; I—alone silent in this uproar, alone motionless in this tumult—listened in astonishment.

A jailor passed; I ventured to call and ask him "if there were a Fête in the Prison."

"A Fête, if you choose to call it so," answered he; "this is the day that they fetter the galley-slaves who are to set off to-morrow for Toulon. Would you like to see them? It would amuse you."

For a solitary recluse, indeed, a spectacle of any kind was an event of interest, however odious it might be; and I accepted the "amusement."

The jailor, after taking the usual precautions to secure me, conducted me into a little empty cell, without a vestige of furniture, and only a grated window,—but still a real window, against which one could lean, and through which one could actually perceive the sky! "Here," said he, "you will see and hear all that happens. You will be 'alone in your box,' like the King!"

He then went out, closing on me locks, bolts, and bars.

The window looked into a square and rather wide court, on every side of which was a large six-storied stone edifice. Nothing could seem more wretched, naked, and miserable to the eye than this quadruple façade, pierced by a multitude of grated windows, against which were pressed a crowd of thin and wan faces, placed one above the other, like the stones of a wall; and all, as it were, framed in the intercrossings of iron bars. They were prisoners, spectators of the ceremony, until their turn came to be the actors.

All looked in silence into the still empty court; among these faded and dull countenances there shone, here and there, some eyes which gleamed like sparks of fire.

At twelve o'clock, a large gateway in the court was opened. A cart, escorted by soldiers, rolled heavily into the court, with a rattling of irons. It was the Convict-guard with the chains.

At the same instant, as if this sound awaked all the noise of the prison, the spectators of the windows, who had hitherto been silent and motionless, burst forth into cries of joy, songs, menaces, and imprecations, mixed with hoarse laughter. It was like witnessing a masque of Demons; each visage bore a grimace, every hand was thrust through the bars, their voices yelled, their eyes flashed, and I was startled to see so many gleams amidst these ashes. Meanwhile the galley-sergeants quietly began their work. One mounted on the cart, and threw to his comrades the fetters, the iron collars, and the linen clothing; while others stretched long chains to the end of the court and the Captain tried each link by striking it on the pavement,—all of which took place under the mocking raillery of the prisoners, and the loud laughter of the convicts for whom they were being prepared.

When all was ready, two or three low doors poured forth into the court a collection of hideous, yelling, ragged men; these were the galley-convicts.

Their entry caused increased pleasure at the windows. Some of them, being 'great names' among their comrades, were saluted with applause and acclamation, which they received with a sort of proud modesty. Several wore a kind of hat of prison straw, plaited by themselves, and formed into some fantastic shape; these men were always the most applauded.

One in particular excited transports of enthusiasm,—a youth of seventeen, with quite a girlish face. In his prison he had made himself a straw-dress, which enveloped him from head to foot; and he entered the court, jumping a summerset with the agility of a serpent. He was a mountebank condemned for theft, and there was a furious clapping of hands, and a volley of cheers, for him.

At length the names were called in alphabetical order, and they went to stand two and two, companions by similar initials; so that even if a convict had a friend, most likely their chains would divide them from suffering together.

Whilst they were exchanging their worn-out prison-garments for the thin and coarse clothing of the galleys, the weather, which had been hitherto uncertain, became suddenly cold and cloudy, and a heavy shower chilled their thin forms, and saturated their vesture.

A dull silence succeeded to their noisy bravadoes; they shivered, their teeth chattered, and their limbs shook in the wet clothes.

One convict only, an old man, retained a sort of gaiety. He exclaimed laughing, while wiping away the rain, and shaking his fist at the skies, "This was not in the playbill!"

When they had put on their miserable vestments, they were taken in bands of twenty or thirty to the corner of the court where the long chains were extended. At every interval of two feet in these long chains were fastened short transverse chains, and at the extremity of each of the latter was attached a square iron collar, which opened by means of a hinge in the centre and closed by an iron bolt, which is riveted, for the whole journey, on the convict's neck. The convicts were ordered to sit down in the mud on the inundated pavement; the iron collars were fitted on them, and two prison-blacksmiths, with portable anvils, riveted the hard, unheated metal with heavy iron hammers.

This was a frightful operation, and even the most hardy turned pale! Each stroke of the hammer, aimed on the anvil resting on their backs, makes the whole form yield; the failure of its aim, or the least movement of the head, might launch them into eternity.

When this operation was finished, the convicts rose simultaneously. The five gangs joined hands, so as to form an immense circle, and thus ran round and round in the court, with a rapidity that the eye could hardly follow. They sung some couplets, in their own idiom, to a melody which was sometimes plaintive, sometimes furious, often interrupted by hoarse cries and broken laughter, like delirious ravings, while the chains, clanking together in cadence, formed an accompaniment to a song more harsh than their own noise. A large trough was now brought in; the guards, striking the convicts to make them discontinue their dance, took them to the trough, in which was swimming I know not what sort of herbs in some smoking and dirty-looking liquid. Having partaken of it, they threw the remainder on the pavement, with their black bread, and began again to dance and sing. This is a liberty which is allowed them on the day they are fettered and the succeeding night.

I gazed on this strange spectacle with such eager and breathless attention, that I totally forgot my own misery. The deepest pity filled my heart, and their laughter made me weep.

Suddenly, in the midst of a profound reverie into which I had fallen, I observed the yelling circle had stopped, and was silent. Then every eye was turned to the window which I occupied. "The Condemned! the Condemned!" shouted they, pointing their fingers at me; and their bursts of laughter were redoubled.

I was thunderstruck. I know not where they knew me, or how I was recognized.

"Good day! good night!" cried they, with their mocking sneer. One of the youngest, condemned to the Galleys for life, turned his shining, leaden face on me, with a look of envy, saying, "He is lucky! he is to be *clipped*! Good bye, Comrade!"

I cannot describe what passed within me. I was indeed their "comrade!" The Scaffold is Sister to the Galleys. Nay, I was even lower than they were; the convicts had done me an honour. I shuddered: yes! their "comrade!" I remained at the window, motionless, as if paralyzed; but when I saw the five gangs advance, rushing towards me with phrases of disgusting cordiality; when I heard the horrible din of their chains, their clamours, their steps at the foot of my wall, it seemed to me that this knot of demons were scaling my cell! I uttered a shriek; I threw myself against the door violently, but there was no means of flight. I knocked, I called with mad fury. Then I thought I heard, still nearer, the horrid voices of the convicts. I thought I saw their hideous heads appearing on a level with the window; I uttered another shriek of anguish, and fainted.

FOURTEENTH PAPER

WHEN my consciousness returned it was night: I was lying on a truckle bed; a lamp which swung from the ceiling enabled me to see a line of beds similar to mine, and I therefore judged that I had been taken to the Infirmary. I remained a few moments awake, but without thought or recollection, totally engrossed by the happiness of being again in a bed. Certainly, in former days, this prison-hospital bed would have made me shrink with disgust; but I am no longer the same individual. The sheets were brown, and coarse to the touch, the blanket thin and ragged, and there was but one straw mattress.

No matter! I could stretch my limbs at their ease between these coarse sheets; and under this blanket, thin as it was, I felt the gradual decrease of that horrible chill in the marrow of my bones, to which I had lately been accustomed.—I slept again.

A loud noise awakened me at daylight. The noise came from without; my bed was beside the window, and I sat up to see from what it arose. The window looked into the large Court of the Bicêtre, which was full of people. Two lines of veterans had difficulty in keeping the crowd away from a narrow passage across the Court. Between this double rank of soldiers, five long wagons, loaded with men, were driven slowly jolting at each stone; it was the departure of the convicts.

These wagons were open, and each gang occupied one. The convicts, in consequence of their iron collars being attached to the centre chain, are obliged to sit back to back, their feet hanging over the sides of the wagon; the centre chain stretched the whole length of the cart, and on its unfastened end the Sergeant stood with his loaded musket. There was a continual clanking of the prisoners' chains, and at each plunge of the wagon their heads and pendant limbs were jolted violently. A quick penetrating rain chilled the air, and made their wet slight vesture cling to their shivering forms. Their long beards and short hair streamed with wet; their complexions were saturnine; they were shivering, and grinding their teeth with mingled rage and cold. But they had no power of moving: once riveted to that chain, each becomes a mere fraction of that hideous whole which is called the Gang. Intellect must abdicate,—the fetters condemn it to death; and the mere animal must not even hunger but at certain hours. Thus fixed, the greater part half clad, with bare heads, and no rest for their feet, they begin their journey of twenty-five days; the same sort of wagons, the same portion of dress being used in scorching July as in the cold rains of November. One would almost think that man wishes Heaven to take a part in his office of executioner.

Between the crowd and the convicts a horrible dialogue was maintained,—abuse on one side, bravadoes on the other, imprecations from both; but at a sign from the Captain I saw the sticks of the Guard raining indiscriminate blows into the wagon, on heads or shoulders, and all returned to that kind of external calm which is called "order." But their eyes were full of vengeance, and their powerless hands were clenched on their knees.

The five wagons, escorted by mounted gendarmes and guards on foot, passed slowly under the high arched door of the Bicêtre. The crowd followed them: all vanished like a phantasmagoria, and by degrees the sounds diminished of the heavy wheels, clanking fetters, and the yells of the multitude uttering maledictions on the journey of the convicts. And such was their happy beginning!

What a proposition my counsel made! The Galleys! I was right to prefer death; rather the Scaffold than what I had seen!

FIFTEENTH PAPER

UNFORTUNATELY I was not ill; therefore the next day I was obliged to leave the Infirmary to return to my dungeon.

Not ill? No truly, I am young, healthful, and strong; the blood flows freely in my veins; my limbs obey my will; I am robust in mind and body, constituted for a long life. Yes, all this is true; and yet, nevertheless, I have an illness, a fatal illness,—an illness given by the hand of man!

Since I came out of the Infirmary a vivid idea has occupied me,—a thought which affects me to madness; namely, that I might have escaped, had they left me there! Those Physicians, those Charity Sisters seemed to take an interest in me. "To die so young! and by such a death!" One would have imagined they pitied me by their pressing round my bed. Bah! it was curiosity! I have no chance now! My plea will be rejected, because all was legal; the witnesses gave correct evidence, the counsel pleaded well, the Judges decided carefully. I do not reckon upon it, unless—No! folly; there is no hope. The plea is a cord which holds you suspended over an abyss, and which you feel giving way at each instant until it breaks. It is as if the axe of the Guillotine took six weeks to fall.

If I could obtain my pardon!—my pardon! From whom, for what, and by what means? It is impossible that I should be pardoned. They say *an example is requisite.*

SIXTEENTH PAPER

DURING the few hours I passed at the Infirmary, I seated myself at a window in the sunshine (for the afternoon had become fine), and I enjoyed all the sun which the gratings of the window would allow me.

I sat thus, my heavy and fevered head within my hands, my elbows on my knees, my feet on the bar of the chair; for dejection had made me stoop, and sink within myself, as if I had neither bone nor muscular power.

The stifling air of the prison oppressed me more than ever; I still fancied the noise from the convicts' chains rung in my ears; I was almost overcome. I wished that some guardian spirit would take pity on me, and send even a little bird to sing there, opposite, on the edge of the roof.

I know not if it were a spirit of good or evil which granted my wish; but almost at the moment I uttered it, I heard beneath my window a voice,—not that of a bird, but far better,—the pure, fresh, *velvet* voice of a young girl of fifteen!

I raised my head with a start; I listened with avidity to the song she sung. It was a slow and plaintive air,—a sad yet beautiful melody. As I gathered the sense of the words, I cannot describe my pain and disappointment, while the following stanzas of prison-dialect marred the sweet music.[6]

I heard no more. I could listen to no more. The meaning, half-hidden, half-evident, of this horrible lament,—the struggle between the felon and the police; the thief he meets and despatches for his wife; his dreadful explanation to her: "I have sweated an oak" ("I have assassinated a man") the wife who goes to Versailles with a petition, and the King indignantly exclaiming that he "will make the guilty man dance where there is no floor!"—and all this sung to the sweetest air, and by the sweetest voice that ever soothed human ear! I was shocked, disgusted, overcome. It was a repulsive idea that all these monstrous words proceeded from a fresh rosy mouth: it was like the slime of a snail over a rosebud!

I cannot express what I felt; I was at once pained and gratified. The idiom of crime, a language at once sanguinary and grotesque, united to the voice of a young girl, that graceful transition from the voice of childhood to the voice of woman,—all these deformities of words delightfully sung, cadenced, rounded!

Ah, how infamous is a prison! It contains a venom which assails all within its pestilential reach. Everything withers there, even the song of a girl of fifteen!

If you find a bird within its courts, it has mud on its wing. If you gather a beauteous flower there, it exhales poison!

SEVENTEENTH PAPER

WHILST I was writing, my lamp faded, daylight appeared, and the clock of the chapel struck six.

What can be the meaning of what has since happened? The turnkey on duty came into my cell; he took off his cap, bowed to me, apologized for disturbing me, and making an effort to soften his rough voice, inquired what I wished to have for my breakfast—

A shudder has come over me. *Is it to take place to-day?*

EIGHTEENTH PAPER

I FEEL that it *is* for to-day!

The Governor of the prison himself came to visit me. He asked me how he could serve or accommodate me; he expressed a hope that I had no complaint to make respecting him or his subordinates; and he inquired with interest regarding my health, and how I had passed the night. On leaving me, he called me "Sir!"

Oh, it surely is for to-day!

NINETEENTH PAPER

THE Governor of the prison thinks I have no cause of complaint against him or his jailors. He is right, and it would be wrong of me to complain; they have done their duty, they have kept me safe; and then they have been complaisant at my arrival and departure. Ought I not to be satisfied?

This Governor, with his benign smile, his soft words, his eye which flatters and spies, his coarse heavy hands,—he is the incarnation of a prison!

Ah, hapless creature! what will become of me? What will they do with me?

TWENTIETH PAPER

NOW I am calm. All is finished—quite finished!

I am relieved from the dreadful anxiety into which I was thrown by the Governor's visit; for I confess I still felt hope. Now, thank Heaven! hope is gone.

Let me record what has happened.

At half-past six the door of my cell was opened; an old man with white hair entered, dressed in a brown great-coat. He unfastened it, and beneath I saw the black cassock and bands of a priest. He was not the usual Chaplain to the prison, and I thought this appeared ominous. He seated himself opposite to me, with a quiet smile; then shook his head, and raised his eyes to heaven. I understood him.

"My son!" said he, "are you prepared?"

I answered, in a low tone, "I am not prepared—but I am ready."

Then my sight became troubled; a chill damp pervaded my frame. I felt the veins on my temples swelling, and a confused murmur in my ears.

Whilst I vacillated on my chair as though asleep, the old man continued speaking,—at least, so it appeared to me, for I think I remember seeing his lips move, and his hand raised.

The door was opened again; the noise of the lock roused me from my reverie, and the Priest from his discourse. A person dressed in black entered, accompanied by the Governor of the prison, and bowed profoundly to me; he carried a roll of paper.

"Sir," said he, with a courteous smile, "I have the honour to bring you a message from the Attorney-General."

The first agitation was over; all my presence of mind returned, and I answered in a firm tone, "Read on, Sir."

He then read a long, technically-expressed paper, the purport of which was the rejection of my plea. "The execution will be to-day," added he; "we shall leave this for the Conciergerie Prison at half-past seven. My dear Sir, will you have the extreme goodness to accompany me at that hour?"

For some instants I had no longer listened to him; for while his eyes were fixed on the paper the Governor was occupied talking to the Priest; and I looked at the door which they had left half open!... Ah, hapless me! Four sentinels in the corridor. Again I was asked when I would be ready to go.

"When you please," I said; "at your own time."

"I shall have the honour of coming for you, then, in half an hour," said he, bowing; and all the party withdrew.

Oh, for some means of escaping! Good heavens! any means whatever! I *must* make my escape! I must! Immediately! By the doors, by the windows, by the roof! Even though in the struggle I should destroy myself!

Oh, rage! demons! malediction! It would take months to pierce this wall with efficient tools. And I have not one nail, nor one hour!

TWENTY-FIRST PAPER

Conciergerie Prison.

Here I am transferred, then. Let me record the details.

At half-past seven the messenger again presented himself at the threshold of my dungeon. "Sir," said he, "I wait for you."

Alas! and I saw that four others did the same! I rose, and advanced one step. It appeared to me I could not make a second. My head was so heavy, and my limbs so feeble; but I made an effort to conquer my weakness, and assumed an appearance of firmness.

Prior to leaving the cell, I gave it a final look; I had almost become attached to it. Besides, I left it empty and open, which gives so strange an appearance to a dungeon.

It will not be long untenanted. The turnkeys said they expected some one this evening,—a prisoner who was then being tried at the Court of Assizes.

At the turn of the corridor the Chaplain rejoined us; he had just breakfasted.

At the threshold of the gaol, the Governor took me by the hand; he had reinforced my escort by four veterans.

By the door of the Infirmary a dying old man exclaimed, "Good bye, we shall soon meet again!"

We arrived in the courtyard, where I could breathe again freely, and this refreshed me greatly; but we did not walk long in the open air. The carriage was stationed in the first court. It was the same which had brought me there,—a sort of oblong van, divided into two sections by a transverse grating of close wire. Each section had a door; one in the front, one in the back of the cart; the whole so dirty, so black, so dusty, that the hearse for paupers is a state carriage by comparison! Before I buried myself in this moving tomb, I cast a look round the yard,—one of those despairing looks which seem to ask a miracle. The court was already encumbered with spectators. Like the day when the convicts departed, there was a slight, chilling shower of the season; it is raining still, and doubtless there will be rain all the day,—

which will last when I am no more! We entered the van. The messenger and a gendarme, in the front compartment, the Priest, myself, and a gendarme in the other, with four mounted gendarmes around the carriage. As I entered it, an old grey-eyed woman who stood near exclaimed, "I like seeing this, even better than seeing the galley convicts!"

I can conceive this. It is a spectacle more easily taken in at one view. Nothing divides the attention; there is but one man, and on this isolated being there is as much misery heaped as on all the other convicts together. The van passed with a dull noise under the gateway, and the heavy doors of the Bicêtre were closed after us. I felt myself moving, but in stupor, like a man fallen into a lethargy, who can neither move nor cry out, and who fancies he feels that he is being buried alive. I listened vaguely to the peal of bells on the collars of the post-horses which drew the van, the iron wheels grating over various substances in the road, the clacking whips of the postillion, the galloping of the gendarmes round the carriage,—all seemed like a whirlwind which bore me away.

My mind was so stupefied with grief that I only conceived ideas as in a dream. I saw the blue towers of Nôtre Dame in the distance. "Those who will be on the tower with the flag will see my execution well," said I to myself, smiling stupidly.

I think it was at that moment that the Priest addressed me again; I patiently let him speak. I had already in my ears the noise of the wheels, the galloping horses, and the postillion's whip; therefore it was only one more incomprehensible noise. I listened in silence to that flow of monotonous words, which deadened my thoughts, like the murmur of a brook; and they passed before my torpid mind, always varied yet always the same, like the crooked elms we passed by the road-side. The short and jerking voice of the messenger in the front of the van suddenly aroused me.

"Well, Chaplain," said he, in almost a gay tone, "what news have you to-day?"

The Chaplain, who spoke to me without ceasing, and who was deafened by the carriage, made no answer.

"Well, well! how the van rattles; one can hardly hear oneself. What was I saying to you, Chaplain! Oh, aye!—do you know the great news of Paris to-day?"

I started as if he were speaking to me.

"No," said the priest, who had at last heard him, "I have not had time to read the papers this morning: I shall see them this evening. When I am occupied in this way all day, I order my servant to keep the papers, and I read them on my return."

"Bah!" replied the other, "it is impossible that you have not heard what I mean. The news of Paris—the news of this morning."

It was now my turn to speak; and I said, "I know what you mean."

The Messenger looked at me. "You? really! and pray what is your opinion about it?"

"You are inquisitive," said I.

"How so, sir?" replied he. "Every one should have a political opinion: I esteem you too much to suppose that you are without one. As to myself, I am quite in favour of re-establishing the National Guard. I was a serjeant in my company; and, faith! it was very agreeable to—"

I interrupted him by saying, "I did not think this was the subject in question."

"What did you suppose, then? You professed to know the news."

"I spoke of something else with which Paris is also occupied to-day."

The fool did not understand, and his curiosity was awakened.

"More news! Where the deuce could *you* learn news? What is it, my dear sir? Do you know what it is, Chaplain? Do let me hear all about it, I beg. I like news, you see, to relate to the President; it amuses him."

He looked from one to the other, and obtained no answer.

"Well," said he, "what are you thinking of?"

"I am thinking," said I, "that I shall be past thinking, this evening."

"Oh, that's it," returned he. "Come, come, you are too sad. Mr. Castaing conversed on the day of his execution."

Then, after a pause, he continued: "I accompanied Mr. Papavoine on his last day. He wore his otter-skin cap, and smoked his cigar. As for the young men of La Rochelle, they only spoke among themselves, but still they spoke. As for you, I really think you are too pensive, young man."

"Young man?" I repeated. "I am older than you; every quarter of an hour which passes makes me a year older."

He turned round, looked at me some minutes with stupid astonishment, and then began to titter.

"Come, you are joking; older than I am? why, I might be your grandfather."

"I have no wish to jest," I answered gravely. He opened his snuff-box.

"Here, my good sir, don't be angry. Take a pinch of snuff, and don't bear malice."

"Do not fear," said I; "I shall not have long to bear it against you."

At this moment the snuff-box which he extended to me came against the grating which separated us. A jolt caused it to strike rather violently, and it fell, wide open, under the feet of the gendarme.

"Curse the grating!" said the Messenger; then, turning to me, he added, "Now, am I not unlucky? I have lost all my snuff!"

"I lose more than you," said I.

As he tried to pick up his snuff, he muttered between his teeth, "More than I! that's very easily said. No more snuff until I reach Paris! It's terrible."

The Chaplain then addressed him with some words of consolation; and I know not if I were pre-occupied, but it seemed to me to be part of the exhortation of which the commencement had been addressed to me.

By degrees conversation increased between the Chaplain and the officer; and I became again lost in thought. The van was stopped for a minute before the toll-gate, and the inspector examined it. Had it contained a sheep or an ox which was going to be slaughtered, they would have required some money; but a human head pays no duty!

We passed through the gates, and the carriage trotted quickly through those old and crooked streets of the Faubourg St. Marceau and the city, which twist and cross each other like the many paths of an ant-hill. On the pavement of these narrow streets the rolling of the wheels became so noisy and rapid that I could hear no other sound, though I saw that people exclaimed, as the van passed, and bands of children followed its track. I fancied also I occasionally saw in the cross-streets ragged men displaying in their hands a bundle of printed papers, their mouths open as if vociferating something, while the passers stopped to purchase.

Half-past eight struck by the palace clock as we arrived in the court of the Conciergerie Prison. The sight of its wide staircase, its dark chapel, its sombre gates, made me shudder; and when the carriage stopped, I fancied the beatings of my heart stopped also.

But I collected my strength; the door was opened; with the rapidity of lightning I jumped from the moving prison, and passed between two lines of soldiers: already there was a crowd formed on my path.

TWENTY-SECOND PAPER

ALL my resolution abandoned me when I reached the low doors, private stairs, and interior corridors, which are only entered by the condemned. The Officer still accompanied me: the Priest had left me for a couple of hours — perchance to read the papers!

I was then taken to the Governor, into whose charge the Officer gave me. They made an exchange. The Director told him to wait a moment, as he had some "game" for him to take back in the Van to the Bicêtre. No doubt it was the man condemned to-day. He is to sleep to-night on the bundle of straw which I have not had time to wear out.

"Oh, very well," said the Officer to the Governor, "I will wait with pleasure; we can make out the two papers together, and it will be very convenient."

They then placed me in a small room adjoining the Governor's office, and left me, locked in, alone.

I know not of what I was thinking, or how long I had been there, when a sudden and loud burst of laughter in my ear dispersed my reverie.

I raised my eyes with a start. I was no longer alone in the cell; a man was beside me. He was about fifty-five years old, middle-sized, wrinkled, stooping, and bald: with a sinister cast in his grey eyes, and a bitter sneer on his countenance; he was dirty, half-clothed, ragged, disgusting.

We looked at each other steadfastly for some moments; he prolonging his bitter laugh, while I felt half astonished, half alarmed.

"Who are you?" said I to him at last.

"That is a funny question," said he. "I am a *friauche*."

"A friauche?" said I; "what does that mean?"

This question redoubled his merriment.

"Why," cried he, in the midst of a shout of laughter, "it means that they will play the same game with my head in six weeks hence, as they will with thine in six hours! Ha! ha! ha! thou seem'st to understand now!"

And truly I was pale, and my hair stood on end. This, then, was the other condemned prisoner, the one just sentenced, whom they expected at the Bicêtre; the heir of my cell.

He continued: "Never mind! Here's *my* history. I am son of a famous thief; it is a pity that they gave him one day a hempen cravat; it was during the 'reign of the Gallows by the grace of Heaven.' At six years of age I had neither father nor mother; in summer I turned summersets in the dust on the high-road, that carriage-travellers might throw me money; in winter I walked with naked feet in the mud, in ragged clothes, and blowing on my purple hands to excite pity. At nine years old I began to use my fingers; at times I emptied a pocket or a reticule; at ten years old I was a pilferer: then I made acquaintances, and at seventeen I became a thief. I broke into a shop, I robbed the till; I was taken and sent to the Galleys. What a hard life that was! Sleeping on bare boards, drinking plain water, eating black bread, dragging a stupid fetter which was of no use; sun-strokes and whip-strokes: and then all the heads are kept shaved, and I had such fine chesnut hair! Never mind! I served my time; fifteen years. That wears one famously!

"I was two-and-thirty years old; one fine morning they gave me a map of the road, a passport, and sixty-six francs, which I had amassed in my fifteen years at the Galleys, working sixteen hours a-day, thirty days a-month, twelve months a-year. Never mind! I wished to be an honest man with my sixty-six francs; and I had finer sentiments under my rags than you might find beneath the cassock of a priest. But deuce take the passport! It was yellow, and they had written upon it *'Freed convict.'* I was obliged to show this at every village, and to present it every week to the mayors of the towns through which I was ordered to pass. A fine recommendation! a galley-convict! I frightened all the folk, and little children ran away, and people locked their doors. No one would give me work; I expended the last of my sixty-six francs,—and then—one must live. I showed my arms, fit for labour; the people shut their doors. I offered my day's work for fifteen sous, for ten sous, for five sous! and no one would have me. What could be done? One day, being hungry, I knocked my elbow through a baker's window; I seized on a loaf, and the baker seized on me. I did not eat the loaf, yet I was condemned to the Galleys for life, with three letters branded on my shoulder; I'll show them to you if you like. They call that sort of justice *the relapse.* So here I was, a returned horse. I was brought back to Toulon,— this time among the Green-caps (galley-slaves for life); so now I decided to escape. I had *only* three walls to pierce, two chains to break, and I had one nail! I escaped. They fired the signal gun; for we convicts are, like the Cardinals of Rome, dressed in red, and they fire cannons when we depart! Their powder went to the sparrows! This time, no yellow passport, but then no money either. I met some comrades in the neighbourhood who had also served their time or broken their chains. Their captain proposed to me to join the band. They killed on the highways. I acceded, and I began to kill to live. Sometimes we attacked a Diligence, sometimes it was a post-chaise, sometimes a grazier on horseback. We took the money, we let the horses go, and buried the bodies under a tree, taking care that their feet did not appear; and then we danced on the graves, so that the ground might not seem fresh broken.

"I grew old this way, hiding in the bushes, sleeping in the air, hunted from wood to wood, but at least free and my own master. Everything has an end, and this like the rest: the gendarmes one night caught us at our tricks; my comrades escaped; but I, the oldest, remained under the claw of these cats in cocked hats. They brought me here. I had already mounted all the steps of the justice-ladder, except one. Whether I had now taken a handkerchief or a life was all the same for me. There was but one 'relapse' to give me, — the executioner. My business has been short: faith, I began to grow old and good for nothing. My father *married the widow* (was hanged); I am going to retire to the Abbey of Mont-à-Regret (the Guillotine); that's all, comrade!"

I remained stupefied during the recital. He laughed louder than at the beginning, and tried to take my hand. I drew back in horror.

"Friend," cried he, "you don't seem game. Don't be foolish on the scaffold: d'ye see? There is one bad moment to pass on the board, but that's so soon done. I should like to be there to show you the step! Faith, I've a great mind not to plead, if they will finish me with you to-day. The same Priest will serve us both. You see I'm a good fellow, eh? I say, shall we be friends?"

Again he advanced a step nearer to me.

"Sir," I answered, repulsing him, "I decline it."

Fresh bursts of laughter at my answer.

"Ha, ha, ha! Sir, you must be a Marquis."

I interrupted him, "My friend, I require reflection: leave me in peace."

The gravity of my tone rendered him instantly thoughtful. He shook his grey and nearly bald head, while he murmured between his teeth, "I understand now, — the Priest!"

After a few minutes' silence, he said to me, almost timidly, —

"Sir, you are a Marquis; that is all very well; but you have on such a nice great-coat, which will not be of much use to you. The Executioner will take it. Give it to me, and I will sell it for tobacco."

I took off my great-coat, and gave it to him. He began to clap his hands with childish joy; then looking at my shirt-sleeves, and seeing that I shivered, he added, "You are cold, Sir; put on this; it rains, and you will be wet through; besides, you ought to go decently on the wagon!"

While saying this, he took off his coarse, grey woollen jacket, and put my arms into it, which I allowed him to do unconsciously. I then leaned against the wall, and I cannot describe the effect this man had on me. He was examining the coat which I had given him, and uttered each moment an exclamation of delight. "The pockets are quite new! The collar is not in the least worn! It will bring me at least fifteen francs. What luck! I shall have tobacco during all my six weeks."

The door opened again. They were come to conduct me to the room where the condemned finally await their execution; and the guard was also come to take the other prisoner to the Bicêtre. He placed himself, laughingly, amongst them, and said to the gendarmes, —

"I say, don't make a mistake! We have changed skins, the gentleman and I; but don't take me in his place. That won't suit me at all, now that I can have tobacco for six weeks!"

TWENTY-THIRD PAPER

THAT old scoundrel! he took my great-coat from me, for I did not give it to him; and then he left me this rag, his odious jacket. For whom shall I be taken?

It was not from indifference, or from charity, that I let him take it. No; but because he was stronger than I! If I had refused, he would have beaten me with those great coarse hands. Charity, indeed! I was full of bad feeling; I should like to have strangled him with my own hands, the old thief!—to have trampled him under my feet.

I feel my heart full of rage and bitterness, and my nature turned to gall: the approach of violent death renders one wicked.

TWENTY-FOURTH PAPER

THEY brought me into an empty cell. I asked for a table, a chair, and writing materials. When all these were brought, I asked for a bed. The turnkey eyed me with astonishment, and seemed mentally to say, "What will be the use of it?" However they made up a chaff bed in the corner. But at the same time a gendarme came to install himself in what was called my chamber. Are they afraid that I would strangle myself with the mattress?

TWENTY-FIFTH PAPER

IT is ten o'clock.

Oh, my poor little girl! In six hours more thy Father will be dead,—something to be dragged about the tables of lecturing rooms; a head to be cast by one party, a trunk to be dissected by another; then all to be thrown together into a bier, and despatched to the felons' burial-ground. This is what they are going to do with thy Father; yet none of them hate me, all pity me, and all could save me! They are going to kill me, Mary, to kill me in cold blood,—a ceremonial for the general good. Poor little girl! thy Father, who loved thee so well, thy Father who kissed thy little white neck, who passed his hands so fondly through the ringlets of thy silken hair, who danced thee on his knee, and every evening joined thy two little hands to pray to God!

Who will do all this for thee in future? Who now will love thee? My darling child, what wilt thou do for my presents, pretty play things, and kisses? Ah, unfortunate Orphan! What wilt thou do for food and raiment?

If the Jury had seen thee, my pretty little Mary, they would have understood it was wrong to kill the Father of a child three years old.

And when she grows up, what will become of her? Her Father will be one of the disgraces of Paris. She will blush for me and at hearing my name; she will be despised, rejected, reviled, on account of him who loved her with all the tenderness of his heart. Oh, my little Mary, whom I so idolized! can it be true that thou wilt encounter shame and horror through me?

Oh! can it be true that I shall die before the close of day? Those distant shouts which I hear, that mass of animated spectators who are already hastening to the Quays, those gendarmes preparing in their barracks,—is it all for me? Yes, I—myself am going to die?—this actual self which is here, which lives, moves, breathes,—this self which I touch and can feel!

TWENTY-SIXTH PAPER

IF I even knew how *it* is built, and in what way one dies upon it; but it is horrible, I do not know this.

The very name of it is frightful, and I cannot understand how I have hitherto been able to write and utter it. The idea I attach to this hateful name is vague, undefined, and therefore more sinister. I construct and demolish in my mind continually its hideous scaffolding.

I dare not ask a question about it; yet it is dreadful not to know what it is, and how to act. I fancy there is a sort of hollow, and that you are laid on your face, and—

Ah, my hair will be white before my head falls!

TWENTY-SEVENTH PAPER

I HAD a glimpse of *it* once. I was passing by the Grêve in a carriage, about eleven o'clock, one morning, when a crowd impeded our progress. I looked out of the window; a dense throng of men, women, and children filled the place and the neighbouring streets. Above the crowd I saw a kind of frame of red wood, which three men were building. I turned away my head with disgust. Close to the carriage there was a woman who said to a child, "Now, look! the axe slides badly; they are going to grease the slide with a candle-end."

They are probably doing the same now. Eleven o'clock has just struck. No doubt they are greasing the slide.

Oh, unhappy creature! this time I shall not turn away my head.

TWENTY-EIGHTH PAPER

OH for a pardon! My reprieve! Perhaps I shall be pardoned. The King has no dislike to me. I wish to see my lawyer! He was right, and I should prefer the galleys. Five years of the galleys,—nay, twenty years, or even the galleys for life. Yes, and to be branded with letters! But it would let me have a reprieve of my life! A galley-slave can move, come and go, and see the sunshine.

Oh! I must see my lawyer; he shall discover some new plea to urge in mitigation of my sentence.

The Priest and the Condemned Man.

Photo-Etching.—From drawing by J. F. Raffaelli.

How can I thus write when every point of his eloquence has already failed, and been unanswerably refuted!

TWENTY-NINTH PAPER

THE Priest returned. He has white hair, a very gentle look, a good and respectable countenance, and is a charitable man. This morning I saw him empty his purse into the hands of the prisoners. Whence is it then that his voice causes no emotion, and he does not ever seem affected by his own theme? Whence is it that he has as yet said nothing which has won on my intellect or my heart?

This morning I was bewildered; I scarcely heard what he said; his words seemed to me useless, and I remained indifferent; they glided away like those drops of rain off the window-panes of my cell.

Nevertheless, when he came just now to my room, his appearance did me good. Amongst all mankind he is the only one who is still a brother for me, I reflected; and I felt an ardent thirst for good and consoling words.

When he was seated on the chair, and I on the bed, he said to me, —

"My son, —"

This word opened my heart. He continued:

"My son, do you believe in God?"

"Oh, yes, Father!" I answered him.

"Do you believe in the holy Catholic, Apostolic, and Roman Church?"

"Willingly," said I.

"My son," returned he, "you have an air of doubt."

Then he began to speak. He spoke a long time; he uttered a quantity of words. Then, when he had finished, he rose, and looked at me for the first time since the beginning of his discourse, and said "Well?"

I protest I had listened to him with avidity at first, then with attention, then with consideration.

I also rose and said, "Sir, leave me for a time, I beg of you."

He asked, "When shall I return."

"I will let you know, Sir."

Then he withdrew in silence, but shaking his head as though inwardly exclaiming, "An Unbeliever."

No! low as I have fallen, I am *not* an unbeliever. God is my witness that I believe in Him. But how did that old man address me? Nothing to be felt, nothing to affect me, nothing to draw forth tears, nothing which sprung from his heart to enter into mine,—nothing which was addressed from himself to myself.

On the contrary, there was something vague, inaccentuated, applicable to any case and to none in particular: emphatic where it should have been profound, flat where it ought to have been simple; a species of sentimental sermon and theological elegy. Now and then a quotation in Latin; here and there the names of Saint Augustine and Saint Gregory, and others of the Calendar. And throughout he had the air of reciting a lesson which he had already twenty times repeated; seeming to go over a theme almost obliterated in his memory from being so long known; but not one look in his eyes, not one accent in his voice, to indicate that *he* was interested!

And how could it be otherwise? This Priest is the head Chaplain of the Prison; his calling is to console and exhort,—that is, he lives by it. Condemned felons are the spring of his eloquence; he receives their confession, and prays with them, because he keeps his place by it. He has advanced in years in conducting men to death from his youth, he has grown accustomed to that which makes others shudder. The dungeon and scaffold are every-day matters with him.

He receives notice the preceding evening that he will have to attend some one the following day, at a certain hour. He asks, "Is it for the Galleys or an execution?" and he asks no more respecting them, but comes next day as a matter of course.

Oh that they would bring me, instead of this man, some young curate, some aged Priest, taken by chance from the nearest parish! Let them find him at his devotional studies, and, without warning, say to him, "There is a man who is going to die, and it is reserved for you to console him. You must be there when they bind his hands; you must take a place in the fatal cart, with your crucifix, and conceal the executioner from him. You must pass with him through that horrible crowd which is thirsting for his execution; you must embrace him at the foot of the scaffold, and you must remain there until his soul has flown!"

When they have said this, let them bring him hither, agitated, palpitating, all shuddering from head to foot. Let me throw myself into his arms; then kneel at his feet, and he will weep, and we will weep together; and he will be eloquent, and I shall be consoled, and my heart will unburthen itself into his heart,—and I shall receive the blessed hope of Redemption, and he will take my Soul!

THIRTIETH PAPER

BUT that old man, what is he to me? What am I to him? Another individual of an unhappy class, a shadow of which he has seen so many; another unit to add to his list of executions.

I have been wrong, perhaps, not to attend to him more; it is he who is good, while I am the reverse. Alas! it was not my fault. The thought of my violent death has spoiled and hardened all within me.

They have just brought me food, as if I could possibly wish for it! I even tried to eat, but the first mouthful fell untasted from my lips.

THIRTY-FIRST PAPER

SINCE then a strange circumstance happened. They came to relieve my good old gendarme, with whom, ungrateful egotist that I am, I did not even shake hands. Another took his place; a man with a low forehead, heavy features, and stupid countenance. Beyond this I paid no attention, but seated myself at the table, my forehead resting on my hands, and my mind troubled by thought. A light touch on my shoulder made me look round. It was the new gendarme, with whom I was alone, and who addressed me pretty nearly in these terms:—

"Criminal, have you a kind heart?"

"No!" answered I, impatiently. The abruptness of my answer seemed to disconcert him. Nevertheless, he began again, hesitatingly,—

"People are not wicked for the pleasure of being so?"

"Why not?" answered I. "If you have nothing but that to say to me, leave me in peace. What is your aim?"

"I beg your pardon, Criminal," he returned; "I will only say two words, which are these: If you could cause the happiness of a poor man, and that it cost you nothing, would you not do so?"

I answered gravely, "Surely, you cannot allude to me as having power to confer happiness?"

He lowered his voice and assumed a mysterious air, which ill-suited with his idiotic countenance.

"Yes, Criminal, yes,—happiness! fortune!" whispered he; "all this can come to me through you. Listen here, I am a poor gendarme; the service is heavy, the pay is light; my horse is my own, and ruins me. So I put into the lottery as a counterbalance. Hitherto I have only missed by not having the right numbers. I am always very near them. If I buy seventy-six, number seventy-seven comes up a prize. Have a little patience, if you please; I have almost done. Well, here is a lucky opportunity for me. It appears, Criminal, begging your pardon, that you are to be executed to-day. It is a certain fact that the dead who are destroyed that way see the lottery before it is drawn on earth. Promise that your spirit shall appear to me to-morrow evening, to give me three numbers,—three good ones, eh? What trouble will it be to you? and I am not afraid of ghosts. Be easy on that point. Here's my address: Popincourt Barracks, staircase A, No. 26, at the end of the corridor. You will know me again, won't you? Come even to-night, if it suits you better."

I would have disdained to reply to such an imbecile, if a mad hope had not crossed my mind. In my desperate position there are moments when one fancies that a chain may be broken by a hair.

"Listen," said I to him, acting my part as well as a dying wretch could. "I can indeed render thee richer than the King. I can make thee gain millions, on one condition."

He opened his stupid eyes.

"What, what? I will do anything to please you, Criminal."

"Then instead of three numbers I promise to tell you four. Change coats with me."

"Oh, is that all?" cried he, undoing the first hooks of his uniform cheerfully.

I rose from my chair; I watched all his movements with a beating heart. I already fancied the doors opening before the uniform of a gendarme; and then the prison—the street—the town—left far behind me! But suddenly he turned round with indecision, and asked,—

"I say,—it is not to go out of this?"

I saw that all was lost; nevertheless, I tried one last effort, useless as it was foolish.

"Yes, it is," said I to him; "but as thy fortune will be made—"

He interrupted me.

"Oh, law, no! on account of my numbers! To make them good, you must be dead, you know!"

I sat down again, silent, and more desponding, from all the hope that I had conceived.

THIRTY-SECOND PAPER

I SHUT my eyes, covered them with my hands, and sought to forget the present in the past. In a rapid reverie, the recollections of childhood and youth came back one by one, soft, calm, smiling, like islands of flowers on the black gulf of confused thoughts which whirled through my brain.

I was again a child,—a laughing, healthy schoolboy, playing, running, shouting with my brothers, in the broad green walks of the old garden where my first years were passed.

And then, four years later, behold me there again, still a child, but a passionate dreamer. And there is a young girl in the garden,—a little Spaniard, with large eyes and long hair, her dark polished skin, her rosy lips and cheeks, the Andalusian of fourteen, named *Pepa*. Our mothers had told us to "go and run together;" we had come forth to walk. They had told us to play; but we had talked instead. Only the year before, we used to play and quarrel and dispute together. I tyrannized over Pepita for the best apple in the orchard; I beat her for a bird's nest. She cried; I scolded her, and we went to complain of each other to our mothers. But now—she was leaning on my arm, and I felt proud and softened. We walked slowly, and we spoke low. I gathered for her some flowers, and our hands trembled on meeting. She spoke to me of the birds, of the sky above us, of the crimson sun-set behind the trees; or else of her schoolfellows, her gown and ribbons. We talked in innocence, but we both blushed. The child had grown into a young girl. After we had walked for some time, I made her sit down on a bank; she was smiling. I was serious.

"Sit down there," said she, "there is still daylight; let us read something. Have you a book?"

I happened to have a favourite volume with me. I drew near her, and opened it by chance. She leaned her shoulder against mine, and we began to read the same page. Before turning the leaf, she was always obliged to wait for me. My mind was less quick than hers. "Have you finished?" she would ask, when I had only just commenced. Then our heads leaned together, our hair mixed, our breath gradually mingled, and at last our lips met.

When we again thought of continuing our reading it was starlight. I shall remember that evening all my life!

Oh, heavens! All *my* life!

THIRTY-THIRD PAPER

THE clock had just struck some hour,—I do not know which. I do not hear the strokes plainly. I seem to have the peal of an organ in my ears. It is the confusion of my last thoughts. At this final day, when I look back over the events of life, I recall my crime with horror; but I wish to have still longer to repent of it. I felt more remorse after my condemnation; since then it seems as if there were no space but for thoughts of death. But now, oh, how I wish to repent me thoroughly! When I had lingered for a minute on what had passed in my life, and then came back to the thought of its approaching termination, I shuddered as at something new. My happy childhood, my fair youth,—a golden web with its end stained. If any read my history, after so many years of innocence and happiness, they will not believe in this execrable year, which began by a crime, and will close with an execution. It would appear impossible.

And nevertheless, oh,—imperfection of human laws and human nature!—I was not ill-disposed.

THIRTY-FOURTH PAPER

OH! to die in a few hours, and to think that a year ago, on the same day, I was innocent and at liberty, enjoying autumnal walks, wandering beneath the trees! To think that in this same moment there are, in the houses around me, men coming and going, laughing and talking, reading newspapers, thinking of business; shopkeepers selling their wares, young girls preparing their ball-dresses for the evening; mothers playing with their children!

THIRTY-FIFTH PAPER

I REMEMBER once, when a child, going alone to see the belfry of Nôtre Dame.

I was already giddy from having ascended the dark winding staircase, from having crossed the slight open gallery which unites the two towers, and from having seen Paris beneath my feet; and I entered the cage of stone and woodwork where the great bell is hung. I advanced with trembling steps over the ill-joined planks, examining at a distance that bell, so famous amongst the children and common people in Paris; and it was not without terror that I observed the slated pent-houses, which surrounded the belfry with inclined planes, were just on a level with my feet. Through the openings I saw, in a bird's-eye view, the street beneath, and the passengers diminished to the size of ants.

Suddenly the enormous bell resounded; its deep vibration shook the air, making the heavy tower rock, and the flooring start from the beams. The noise had nearly upset me. I tottered, ready to fall, and seemed on the point of slipping over the pent-houses. In an agony of terror I lay down on the planks, pressing them closely with both my arms, — speechless, breathless, with this formidable sound in my ears, while beneath my eyes was the precipice, a profound abyss, where so many quiet and envied passengers were walking.

Well, it appears to me as if I were again in that belfry; my senses seem again giddy and dazzled; the booming of that bell seems to press on my brain, and around me I no longer see that tranquil and even life which I had quitted (where other men walk still) except from a distance, and beyond a terrible abyss.

THIRTY-SIXTH PAPER

IT is a quarter past one o'clock.

The following are my sensations at present: a violent pain in my head, my frame chilled, my forehead burning. Every time that I rise, or bend forward, it seems to me that there is a fluid floating in my head, which makes my brain beat violently against the bone.

I have convulsive startings, and from time to time my pen falls from my hand as if by a galvanic shock. My eyes ache and burn, and I suffer greatly in all my limbs.

In two hours and three-quarters hence, *all will be cured*.

THIRTY-SEVENTH PAPER

THEY say that it is nothing,—that one does not suffer; that it is an easy death. Ah! then, what do they call this agony of six weeks,—this summing-up in one day? What, then, is the anguish of this irreparable day, which is passing so slowly and yet so fast? What is this ladder of tortures which terminates in the scaffold? Are they not the same convulsions whether life is taken away drop by drop, or intellect extinguished thought by thought?

THIRTY-EIGHTH PAPER

IT is singular that my mind so often reverts to the King. Whatever I do, there is a voice within me which says,—

"There is, in this same town, at this same hour, and not far from hence, in another Palace, a man who also has guards to all his gates; a man alone, like thee, in the crowd,—with this difference, that he is as high as thou art low. His entire life is glory, grandeur, delight. All around him is love, respect, veneration; the loudest voices become low in speaking to him, and the proudest heads are bent. At this moment he is holding a Council of Ministers, where all coincide with his opinions; or else he thinks of the Chase to-morrow, or the Ball for this evening, feeling certain that the Fête will come, and leaving to others the trouble of his pleasures.

Well, this man is of flesh and blood like thee! And in order that at this instant the scaffold should fall, and thou be restored to life, liberty, fortune, family, it would only be requisite for him to write his name at the foot of a piece of paper; or even that his carriage should meet thy fatal cart! And he is good, too, and perhaps would be glad to do it; and yet it will not be done!

THIRTY-NINTH PAPER

WELL then, let me have courage with death,—let me handle this horrid idea, let me face it boldly. I will ask what it is, know what it demands, turn it in every sense, fathom the enigma, and look before-hand into the tomb.

I have speculated upon Death and Eternity until my mind seems bewildered by its own horrible fantasies. My ideas wander. Oh, for a Priest,—a Priest who could instruct me! I must have a Priest, and a crucifix to embrace.

Alas! here is the same Priest again!

FORTIETH PAPER

AFTER a time, I begged of him to let me sleep. I threw myself on the bed. I had a fulness of blood in my head which made me sleep,—my last sleep on earth. I had a horrible dream, from which I awoke in terror, shuddering and in agony.

The Chaplain was seated at the foot of my bed, reading prayers.

"Have I slept long?" I inquired of him.

"My son," said he, "you have slept an hour. They have brought your child, who is waiting in the next room; I would not allow them to awaken you."

"Oh," cried I, "my darling child! Let them bring in my idolized child!"

FORTY-FIRST PAPER

MY child looked rosy and happy, and her large eyes were bright. Oh, she is so pretty! I drew her towards me; I raised her in my arms, and placing her on my knees, kissed her dear hair. I asked, "Why is her Mother not with her?" And I learnt that she was very ill, and my poor old mother also.

Mary looked at me with astonishment. Caressed, embraced, devoured with kisses, she submitted quietly; but, from time to time, cast an uneasy look towards her Nurse, who was crying in the corner.

At length I was able to speak.

"Mary," I exclaimed. "My own little Mary!" and I pressed her violently against my breast, which was heaving with sobs. She uttered a little cry, and then said, "Oh, you hurt me, Sir."

"*Sir!*" It is nearly a year since she has seen me, poor child! She has forgotten me, face, words, voice; and then who could know me with this beard, this dress, and this pallor?

What! already effaced from that memory, — the only one where I wished to survive! What! already, no longer a Father, am I condemned to hear no more that word, so soft in the language of children that it cannot remain in the language of men, "Papa"?

And yet to have heard it from that sweet mouth, once more, — only once more, — that is all that I would have asked in payment for the forty years of life they will take from me.

"Listen, Mary," said I to her, joining her two little hands in mine. "Do you not know me?"

She looked at me with her bright beautiful eyes and answered, —

"Oh, no indeed."

"Look at me well," I repeated. "What! dost thou not know who I am?"

"Yes, Sir," she answered. "You are a gentleman."

Alas! while loving one being on earth, loving with all your deep affection, having that being before you, who sees and looks at you, speaks and answers you, and yet knows you not! You wish for consolation but from this one being, who is the only one that does not know that you require it because you are going to die!

"Mary," I continued, "hast thou a papa?"

"Yes, Sir," said the child.

"Well, then, dearest, where is he?"

She raised her large eyes in astonishment:—

"Ah, then you don't know, Sir? Papa is dead."

Here she began to cry: I nearly let the little angel fall.

"Dead!" I exclaimed: "Mary, knowest thou what it is to be dead?"

"Yes, Sir," she answered. "He is in earth and in Heaven;" and she continued of her own accord, "I pray to God for him morning and evening at mamma's knees."

I kissed her on her forehead.

"Mary, say to me thy prayer."

"I could not, Sir; a prayer you do not say in the middle of the day. Come to-night to my house, and you shall hear me say it."

This was enough. I interrupted her.

"Darling Mary, it is *I* who am thy papa."

"You!" returned she.

I added, "Wouldst thou like me for thy papa?"

The child turned away. "No, Sir; my papa was much prettier."

I covered her with kisses and tears. She tried to escape from my arms, crying,—

"Sir, you hurt me with your beard."

Then I replaced her on my knees, devouring her with my eyes, and continued,—

"Mary, canst thou read?"

"Yes," she answered, "I can read very well. Mamma makes me read my letters."

"Well, then, read a little to me," said I, pointing to a printed paper which she held crumpled in one of her dimpled hands.

She shook her pretty head, saying,—

"Oh, dear me! I can only read fables."

"But try, my darling: come, open your paper."

She unfolded the paper, and began to spell with her finger, "S E N— sen,—T E N C E—tence,—*Sentence*." I snatched it from her hands. It was my own sentence of death she was reading to me!

Her nurse had bought the paper for a penny. To me it had cost more.

No words can convey what I felt; my violence had alarmed the child, who was ready to cry.

Suddenly she said to me,—

"Do give me back my paper; I want to play with it!"

I restored her to her nurse.

"Take her hence!" and I fell back in my chair, gloomy, desolate, in despair! Now they may come: I care for nothing more; the last fibre of my heart is broken.

FORTY-SECOND PAPER

THE Priest is kind; so is the jailor: tears came in their eyes when I sent away my child.

It is done. Now I must fortify myself, and think firmly of the Executioner, the cart, the gendarmes, the crowd in the street and the windows.

I have still an hour to familiarize myself with these ideas. All the people will laugh and clap their hands, and applaud; yet among those men, now free, unknown to jailors, and who run with joy to an execution,—in that throng there is more than one man destined to follow me sooner or later, on the scaffold.

More than one who is here to-day on my account, will come hereafter on his own.

FORTY-THIRD PAPER

MY little Mary. She is gone away to play; she will look at the crowd from the coach-window, and already she thinks no more of the "Gentleman." Perhaps I may still have time to write a few pages for her, so that she may read them hereafter, and weep, in fifteen years hence, the sorrows of to-day. Yes, she shall know my history from myself, and why the name I leave her is tarnished.

FORTY-FOURTH PAPER

MY HISTORY

[Note. The pages which immediately followed this have not been found. Perhaps, as the next chapter seems to indicate, the Condemned had not time to write his history, as it was so late when he thought of it.]

FORTY-FIFTH PAPER

From a Chamber of the Town Hall.

The Town Hall. Yes, I am here; the execrable journey is over. The place of execution is before me, and beneath the window, a horrible throng, laughing and yelling, while they await my appearance. My efforts at composure were vain: when above the heads of the crowd I saw the frightful scaffold, my heart failed. I expressed a wish to make my last declaration; so they brought me in here, and have sent for some law-officer to receive it. I am now waiting for him; so there is thus much gained. Here is what occurred, on my removal from the Conciergerie.

At three o'clock they came to tell me it was time. I trembled as if I had thought of any thing else during the last six hours, six weeks, six months. It produced on me the effect of something quite unexpected. They made me cross corridors, and descend stairs, they pushed me through a low door into a sombre room, narrow, arched, and scarcely lighted by a day of rain and fog. A chair was in the centre, on which I seated myself at their desire. Some persons were standing near the door; and beside the Priest and gendarmes, there were three men. The first of these, the tallest and oldest, was stout, with a red countenance. This was HE.

This was the Executioner,—the servant of the Guillotine; the others were his own servants. When I was seated, these walked quietly behind me; then suddenly I felt the cold of steel in my hair, and heard the grating action of scissors. My hair, cut carelessly, fell in heavy locks on my shoulders, and the executioner removed them gently with his coarse hand.

The parties in the room spoke in subdued tones. There was a heavy dull sound from without, which I fancied at first was caused by the river; but a shout of laughter soon proved to me it came from the crowd.

A young man near the window, who was writing with a pencil, in his pocket-book, asked one of the turnkeys, what was the name of the present operation? He was answered "The Toilet of the Condemned." From this I gathered that he was preparing the Report for to-morrow's newspaper. One of the servants then removed my waistcoat, and the other one taking my hands, placed them behind me, and I felt the knots of a cord rolled slowly round my wrists; at the same time the other took off my cravat. My linen,—the only remains of former times,—being of the finest quality, caused him a sort of hesitation for a moment; but at length he began to cut off the collar.

At this dreadful precaution, and the sensation of the steel touching my neck, a tremor passed over me, and a stifled groan escaped; the man's hand trembled.

"Sir," said he, "I beg your pardon; I fear I've hurt you."

The people shouted louder in the street. The tall red-faced man offered a handkerchief, steeped in vinegar, for me to inhale.

"Thank you," said I to him, in the firmest tone I could summon, "it is needless; I am recovered."

Then one of the men stooped down and fastened a small cord to my ankles, which restricted my steps; and this was again tied to the cord around my wrists; finally, the tall man threw my jacket over my shoulders, and tied the sleeves in front. All was now completed.

Then the Priest drew near with his Crucifix.

"Come, my son," said he.

The men raised me by my arms; and I walked, but my steps were weak and tottering. At this moment the folding doors were thrown open. A furious clamour, a chill breeze, and a strong white light reached me in the shade. From the extreme of the dark chamber I saw through the rain a thousand yelling heads of the expectant mass. On the right of the doorway, a range of mounted gendarmes; in front, a detachment of soldiers; on the left, the back of the cart, with a ladder. A hideous picture, with the appropriate frame of a prison-door.

It was for this dread moment that I had reserved my courage. I advanced a few steps, and appeared on the threshold.

"There he is! there he is!" bellowed the crowd. "He's come out at last!" and the nearest to me clapped their hands. Much as a king might be loved, there could not be more greeting for him.

The tall man first ascended the cart.

"Good morning, *Mr. Sampson!*" cried the children hanging by the lamp-posts. One of his servants next followed. "Bravo, *Tuesday!*" cried out the children, as the two placed themselves on the front seat.

It was now my turn, and I mounted with a firm step.

"He goes well to it!" said a woman beside the gendarmes.

This atrocious commendation gave me courage. The Priest took his seat beside me. They had placed me on the hindmost seat, my back towards the horse. I shuddered at this last attention. There is a mixture of humanity in it.

I wished to look around me,—gendarmes before and behind: then crowd! crowd! crowd! A sea of heads in the street. The officer gave the word, and the procession moved on, as if pushed forward by a yell from the populace.

"Hats off! hats off!" cried a thousand voices together, as if for the King. Then I laughed horribly also myself, and said to the Priest, "Their hats—my head."

We passed a street which was full of public-houses, in which the windows were filled with spectators, seeming to enjoy their good places, particularly the women.

There were also people letting out tables, chairs, and carts; and these dealers in human life shouted out, "Who wishes for places?"

A strange rage seized me against these wretches, and I longed to shout out to them, "Do you wish for mine?"

The procession still advanced. At each step the crowd in the rear dispersed; and I saw, with my wandering eyes, that they collected again farther on, to have another view. I know not how it was, that, notwithstanding the fog and the small white rain which crossed the air like gossamer, nothing which passed around escaped me; every detail brought its torture: words fail to convey my emotions. My great dread was lest I should faint. Last vanity! Then I endeavoured to confuse myself into being blind and deaf to all, except to the Priest, whose words I scarcely heard amidst the tumult. I took the Crucifix and kissed it.

"Have mercy on me," said I. "O my God!"

And I strove to engross myself with this thought.

But every shake of the cart disturbed me; and then I became excessively chilled, as the rain had penetrated my clothes, and my head was bare.

"Are you trembling with cold, my son?" demanded the Priest.

"Yes," answered I. "Alas! not only from cold."

At the turn to the Bridge, the women expressed pity at my being so young. We approached the fatal Quay. My hearing and sight seemed about to fail me. All those voices, all those heads at the windows, at doors, at shop fronts, on lamp-posts; these thirsting and cruel spectators; this crowd where all knew me, and I knew none; this road paved and walled with human visages,—I was confounded, stupefied, senseless. There is something insupportable in the weight of so many looks being fixed upon one. I could scarcely maintain my place on the seat, and lent no further attention to the Priest. In the tumult which surrounded me, I no longer distinguished exclamations of pity from those of satisfaction, or the sounds of laughter from those of complaint. All formed together a noise in my ears like sounding brass.

My eyes read mechanically the signs over the shops.

Once I felt a painful curiosity to look round on *that* which we were approaching.

It was the last mental bravado, and the body would not aid it; for my neck remained paralyzed, and I could not turn it.

And the cart went on, on. The shops passed away; the signs succeeded each other,—written, painted, gilt; and the populace laughed while they tramped through the mud; and I yielded my mind, as persons do in sleeping. Suddenly this series of shops ended as we turned into the square; the voice of the mob became still more loud, yelling, and joyous; the cart stopped suddenly, and I had nearly fallen on my face. The Priest held me up.

"Courage!" murmured he.

They next brought a ladder to the back of the cart. I leaned on the arm of the Priest and descended. I made one step, and turned round to advance another, but I had not the power; beyond the lamp I saw something startling....

Oh, it was the Reality!

I stopped as if staggered by a blow.

"I have a last declaration to make," cried I, feebly.

And then they brought me up here.

I asked them to let me write my last wishes; and they unbound my hands; but the cord is here, ready to be replaced.

FORTY-SIXTH PAPER

A JUDGE, a Commissioner, a Magistrate,—I know not what was his rank,—has just been here.

I intreated him to procure my pardon; I begged it with clasped hands, and dragging myself on my knees at his feet.

He asked, with a fatal smile, if that were all I had to say to him?

"My pardon, my pardon!" I repeated. "Oh, for mercy's sake, five minutes more! Who knows, my pardon may come. It is so horrible at my age to die in this manner. Reprieves have frequently arrived even at the last moment! And to whom would they show mercy, Sir, if not to me?"

That detestable Executioner! He came in to tell the Judge that the execution was ordered for a certain hour, which hour was at hand, and that he was answerable for the event.

"Oh, for mercy's sake! five minutes to wait for my pardon," cried I, "or I will defend myself."

The Judge and the Executioner went out. I am alone,—at least with only two gendarmes present.

That horrible throng, with its hyena cry! Who knows but that I shall escape from it, that I shall be saved? If my pardon,—it is impossible but that they will pardon me! Hark! I hear some one coming upstairs!

FOUR O'CLOCK.

PREFACE OF M. VICTOR HUGO, TO THE RECENT EDITIONS OF "LE DERNIER JOUR D'UN CONDAMNÉ"

PREFACE

IN the earlier editions of this work, published at first without the name of the author, the following lines formed the sole introduction to the subject:—

"There are two ways of accounting for the existence of the ensuing work. Either there really has been found a roll of papers on which were inscribed, exactly as they came, the last thoughts of a condemned prisoner; or else there has been an author, a dreamer, occupied in observing nature for the advantage of society, who, having been seized with those forcible ideas, could not rest until he had given them the tangible form of a volume."

At the time when this book was first published, I did not deem fit to give publicity to the full extent of my thoughts; I preferred waiting to see whether the work would be fully understood, and I find such has been its fate.

I may now, therefore, unmask the political and social ideas which I wished to render popular under this harmless literary guise. I avow openly, that "The Last Day of a Condemned" is only a pleading, direct or indirect, for *the abolition of punishment by death*. My design herein (and what I would wish posterity to see in my work, if its attention should ever be given to so slight a production) is, not to make out the special defence of any particular criminal, such defence being transitory as it is easy: I would plead generally and permanently for *all* accused persons, present and future; it is the great point of Human Right stated and pleaded before society at large,—that highest judicial court; it is the sombre and fatal question which breathes obscurely in the depths of each capital offence, under the triple envelopes of pathos in which legal eloquence wraps them; it is the question of life and death, I say, laid bare, denuded of the sonorous twistings of the bar, revealed in daylight, and placed where it should be seen, in its true and hideous position,—not in the law courts, but on the scaffold,—not among the judges, but with the Executioner!

This is what I have desired to effect. If futurity should award me the glory of having succeeded,—which I dare not hope,—I desire no other crown.

I proclaim and repeat it, then, in the name of all accused persons, innocent or guilty, before all courts, juries, or judges. And in order that my pleading should be as universal as my cause, I have been careful, while writing "The Last Day of a Condemned," to omit any thing of a special, individual, contingent, relative, or modifiable nature, as also any episode, anecdote, known event, or real name,—keeping to the limit (if "limit" it may be termed!) of pleading the cause of *any* condemned prisoner whatever, executed at any time, for any offence; happy if, with no other aid than my thoughts, I have mined sufficiently into my subject to make a heart bleed, under the *æs triplex* of a magistrate! happy if I could render merciful those who consider themselves just! happy if I penetrate sufficiently deep within the Judge to reach the man.

When this book first appeared, some people thought it was worth while to dispute the authorship. Some asserted that it was taken from an English work, and others that it was borrowed from an American author. What a singular mania there is for seeking the origin of matters at a great distance,—trying to trace from the source of the Nile the streamlet which flows through our village! In this work there is no English, American, or Chinese assistance. I formed the idea of "The Last Day of a Condemned" where you all might form it,—where perhaps you may all have formed it (for who is there that has not reflected and had reveries of "the last day of a condemned"?)—there, on the public walk, the place of execution!

It was there, while passing casually during an execution, that this forcible idea occurred to me; and, since then, after those funereal Thursdays of the Court of Cassation, which send forth through Paris the intelligence of an approaching execution, the hoarse voices of the assembling spectators, as they hurried past my windows, filled my mind with the prolonged misery of the person about to suffer, which I pictured to myself, from hour to hour, according to what I conceived was its actual progress. It was a torture which commenced from daybreak, and lasted, like that of the miserable being who was tortured at the same moment, until *four o'clock*. Then only, when once the *ponens caput expiravit* was announced by the heavy toll of the clock, I breathed again freely, and regained comparative peace of mind. One day at length—I think it was after the execution of Ulbach—I commenced writing this work; and since then I have felt relieved. When one of those public crimes called *legal executions* is committed, my conscience now acquits me of participation therein. This, however, is not sufficient; it is well to be freed from self-accusation, but it would be still better to endeavour to save human life. I do not know any aim more elevated, more holy, than that of seeking the abolition of capital punishment; with sincere devotion I join the wishes and efforts of those philanthropic men of all nations who have laboured, of late years, to throw down the patibulary tree,—the only tree which revolution fails to uproot! It is with pleasure that I take my turn to give my feeble stroke, after the all-powerful blow which, seventy years ago, Beccaria gave to the ancient gibbet, which had been standing during so many centuries of Christianity.

I have just said that the scaffold is the only edifice which revolutions do not demolish. It is rare indeed that revolutions are temperate in spilling blood; and although they are sent to prune, to lop, to reform society, the punishment of death is a branch which they have never removed! I own, however, if any revolution ever appeared to me capable and worthy of abolishing capital punishment, it was the Revolution of July, 1830. It seemed, indeed, as if it belonged to the merciful popular rising of modern times to erase the barbarous enactments of Louis the Eleventh, of Richelieu, and of Robespierre, and to inscribe at the head of the code, "the inviolability of human life!" 1830 was worthy of breaking the axe of 1793.

At one time we really hoped for it. In August, 1830, there seemed so much generosity afloat, such a spirit of gentleness and civilization in the multitude, that we almost fancied the punishment of death was abolished, by a tacit and unanimous consent, with the rest of the evils which had oppressed us. For some weeks confiding and credulous, we had faith in the inviolability of life, for the future, as in the inviolability of liberty.

In effect, two months had scarcely passed, when an attempt was made to resolve into a legal reality the sublime Utopia of Cæsar Bonesana. Unfortunately, this attempt was awkward, imperfect, almost hypocritical, and made in a different spirit from the general interest.

It was in the month of October, 1830, as may be remembered, that the question of capital punishment was brought before the Chamber of Deputies, and discussed with much talent, energy, and apparent feeling. During two days there was a continued succession of impressive eloquence on this momentous subject; and what was the subject?—to abolish the punishment of death? Yes and No! Here is the truth.

Four "gentlemen,"—four persons well known in society,[7]—had attempted in the higher range of politics one of those daring strokes which Bacon calls crimes, and which Machiavel calls *enterprises*. Well! crime or enterprise,—the law, brutal for all, would punish it by death; and the four unfortunates were prisoners, legal captives guarded by three hundred tri-coloured cockades at Vincennes. What was now to be done? You understand the impossibility of sending to the place of execution, in a common cart, ignobly bound with coarse ropes, seated back to back with that functionary who must not be named,—four men of our own rank,—four "gentlemen"!

If there were even a mahogany Guillotine!

Well, to settle the matter, they need only *abolish the punishment of death*; and thereupon the Chamber set to work!

Only yesterday they had treated this abolition as Utopian,—as a theory, a dream, a poetic folly. This was not the first time that an endeavour had been made to draw their attention to the cart, the coarse ropes, and the fatal machine. How strange it is that these hideous details acquired such sudden force in their minds!

Alas! it was not on account of the general good that they sought to abolish capital punishment, but for their own sakes,—as Deputies, who might become Ministers. And thus an alloy of egotism alters and destroys the fairest social combinations. It is the dark vein in statuary marble, which, crossing everywhere, comes forth at each moment unexpectedly under the chisel!

It is surely unnecessary for me to declare that I was not among those who desired the death of the Ministers. When once they were imprisoned, the indignant anger I had felt at their attempt changed with me, as with every one else, into profound pity. I reflected on the prejudices of education of some among them; on the ill-developed head of their chief (fanatic and obstinate relapse of the conspiracies of 1804), whitened before its time, in the damp cells of state prisons; on the fatal necessity of their common position; on the impossibility of their placing a drag on that rapid slope down which monarchy rushed blindly on the 8th of August, 1829; on the influence of personal intercourse with Royalty over them, which I had hitherto under-rated: and finally I reflected, above all, on the dignity which one among them spread, like a purple mantle, over their misfortunes! I was among those who sincerely wished their lives saved, and would have readily lent my aid to that effect.

If a scaffold had been raised for them in Paris, I feel quite certain (and if it be an illusion, I would preserve it) that there would have been an insurrection to pull it down; and I should have been one of the rioters.

Here I must add that, in each social crisis, of all scaffolds, the political one is the most abominable, the most fatal, the most mischievous, the most necessary to extirpate.

In revolutionary times, beware of the first execution. It excites the sanguinary passions of the mob.

I therefore agreed thoroughly with those who wished to spare the four Ministers, both as a matter of feeling and of political reasoning. But I should have liked better that the Chamber had chosen another occasion for proposing the abolition of capital punishment. If they had suggested this desirable change not with reference to those four Ministers, fallen from a Palace to a Prison, but in the instance of the first highwayman,—in the case of one of those wretches to whom you neither give word nor look, and from whom you shrink as they pass: miserable beings, who, during their ragged infancy, ran barefoot in the mud of the crossings; shivering in winter near the quays, or seeking to warm themselves outside the ventilator from the kitchens of the hotels where you dine; scratching out, here and there, a crust of bread from the heaps of filth, and wiping it before eating; scraping in the gutter all day, with a rusty nail, in the hopes of finding a farthing; having no other amusement than the gratuitous sight of the King's fête, and the public executions,—that other gratuitous sight,—poor devils! whom hunger forces on theft, and theft to all the rest; children disinherited by their step-mother, the world; who are adopted by the House of Correction in their twelfth year,—by the Galleys at eighteen,—and by the Guillotine at forty! unfortunate beings whom, by means of a school and a workshop, you might have rendered good, moral, useful; and with whom you now know not what to do,—flinging them away like a useless burthen, sometimes into the red ant-heaps of Toulon, sometimes into the silent cemetery of Clamart; cutting off life after taking away liberty.

If it had been in the instance of one of these outcasts that you had proposed to abolish the punishment of death, oh, then your councils would have indeed been noble, great, holy, majestic! It has ever belonged to those who are truly great and truly powerful, to protect the lowly and weak. How grand would be a Council of Bramins advocating the cause of the Paria! And with us the cause of the Paria is the cause of the people. In abolishing the penalty of death for sake of the people, and without waiting until you were personally interested in the question, you would have done more than a political work,—you would have conferred a social benefit.

Instead of this, you have not yet even completed a political act, while seeking to abolish it not for the abolition's sake, but to save four unfortunate Ministers detected in political delinquency. What has happened? As you were not sincere, the people were distrustful; when they suspected the cause of your change, they became angry at the question altogether, and, strange to say, they declared in favour of that condign punishment, the weight of which presses entirely on themselves.

Immediately after the famous discussion in the Chamber, orders were given to respite, indefinitely, all executions. This was apparently a great step gained; the opponents of punishment by death were rendered happy; but the illusion was of short duration. The lives of the Ministers were spared, and the fortress of Ham was selected as a medium, between death and liberty. These different arrangements once completed, all fear was banished from the minds of the ruling statesmen; and along with fear humanity was also banished. There was no farther question of abolishing capital punishment; and, when they no longer wished to prove to the contrary, Utopia became again Utopia!

There were yet in the prisons some unfortunate condemned wretches, who, having been allowed during five or six months to walk about the prison-yards and breathe the fresh air, felt tranquil for the future, sure of life, mistaking their reprieve for pardon.

There had indeed been a reprieve of six months for these hapless captives, whose sufferings were thus gratuitously aggravated, by making them cling again to life: then, without reason, without necessity, without well knowing why, the respites were all revoked, and all these human beings were launched into eternity.

Let me add, that never were executions accompanied by more atrocious circumstances than since that revocation of the reprieve of July. Never have the "anecdotes" been more revolting, or more effectual to prove the execration of capital punishment. I will cite here two or three examples of the horrors which have attended recent executions. I must shock the nerves of the wives of king's counsel. *A wife is sometimes a conscience!*

In the South, towards the close of last September, the following circumstance occurred: I think it was at Pamiers. The officers went to a man in prison, whom they found quietly playing at cards, and gave him notice that he was to die in two hours. The wretched creature was horror-struck; for during the six months he had been forgotten, he had no longer thought on death; he was confessed, bound, his hair cut off, he was placed in the fatal cart, and taken to the place of execution. The Executioner took him from the Priest; laid him down and bound him on the Guillotine, and then let loose the axe. The heavy triangle of iron slowly detached itself, falling by jerks down the slides, until, horrible to relate, it wounded the man, without killing him! The poor creature uttered a frightful cry. The disconcerted Executioner hauled up the axe, and let it slide down again. A second time, the neck of the malefactor was wounded, without being severed. Again he shrieked, the crowd joining him. The Executioner raised the axe a third time, but no better effect attended the third stroke. Let me abridge these fearful details. Five times the axe was raised and let fall, and after the fifth stroke, the condemned was still shrieking for mercy. The indignant populace commenced throwing missiles at the Executioner, who hid himself beneath the Guillotine, and crept away behind the gendarmes' horses: but I have not yet finished. The hapless culprit, seeing he was left alone on the scaffold, raised himself on the plank, and there standing, frightful, streaming with blood, he demanded with feeble cries that some one would unbind him! The populace, full of pity, were on the point of forcing the gendarmes to help the hapless wretch, who had five times undergone his sentence. At this moment the servant of the Executioner, a youth under twenty, mounted on the scaffold, told the sufferer to turn round, that he might unbind him: then taking advantage of the posture of the dying man, who had yielded himself without any mistrust, sprang on him, and slowly cut through the neck with a knife! All this happened; all this was seen.

According to law, a judge was obliged to be present at this execution; by a sign he could have stopped all. Why was he leaning back in his carriage then, this man, while they massacred another man? What was he doing, this punisher of assassins, while they thus assassinated, in open day, his fellow-creature? And the Judge was not tried for this; nor the Executioner was not tried for it; and no tribunal inquired into this monstrous violation of all law on one of God's creatures.

In the seventeenth century, that epoch of barbarity in the criminal code, under Richelieu, under Christophe Fouquet, Monsieur de Chalais was put to death at Nantes by an awkward soldier, who, instead of a sword-stroke, gave him thirty-four strokes of a cooper's adze.[8] But at least it was considered execrable by the parliament of Paris, there was an inquest and a trial; and, although Richelieu and Fouquet did not suffer, the soldier was punished,—an injustice doubtless, but in which there was some show of justice.

In the modern instance, nothing was done. The fact took place after July, in times of civilization and march of intellect, a year after the celebrated lamentation of the Chamber on the penalty of death. The circumstance attracted no attention; the Paris papers published it as an anecdote, and no one cared about it. It was only known that the Guillotine had been put out of order by a dismissed servant of the Executioner, who, to revenge himself, had taken this method of action.

Another instance. At Dijon, only three months ago, they brought to the scaffold a woman (a woman!). This time again the axe of the Guillotine failed of its effect, and the head was not quite detached. Then the Executioner's servants pulled the feet of the woman; and, amidst the yells of the populace, thus finished the law!

At Paris, we have come back to the time of secret executions; since July they no longer dare to decapitate in the town, for they are afraid. Here is what they do. They took lately from the Bicêtre prison a man, under sentence of death, named Desandrieux, I think; they put him into a sort of panier on two wheels, closed on every side, bolted and padlocked; then with a gendarme in front, and another at the back, without noise or crowd, they proceeded to the deserted barrier of St. James. It was eight in the morning when they arrived, with but little light. There was a newly erected Guillotine, and for spectators, some dozens of little boys, grouped on the heaps of stones around the unexpected machine. Quickly they withdrew the man from the basket; and without giving him time to breathe, they furtively, secretly, shamefully deprived him of life! And that is called a public and solemn act of high justice! Infamous derision! How then do the lawgivers understand the word civilization? To what point have we attained? Justice reduced to stratagems and frauds! The law reduced to expedient! Monstrous! A man condemned to death, it would seem, was greatly to be feared, since they put an end to him in this traitorous fashion!

Let us be just, however; the execution was not quite secret. In the morning people hawked and sold, as usual, the sentence of death through the streets. It appears there are people who live by such sales. The crime of a hapless fellow-creature, its punishment, his torture, his agony, forms their stock in trade—a paper that they sell for a penny. Can one conceive anything more hideous than this coin, *verdigrised* in blood?

Here are enough of facts; here are too many. Is not all this horrible? What can be alleged in favour of punishment by death?

I put this question seriously. I ask it that it may be answered; I ask it of Legislators, and not of literary gossips. I know there are people who take "the excellence of punishment by death" for a text of paradoxes, like any other theme; there are others who only advocate capital punishment because they hate so-and-so who attack it. It is for them almost a literary question, a question of persons, and proper names; these are the envious, who do not find more fault with good lawyers than with good artists. The Joseph Grippas are no more wanting to the Filangieri than the Torregiani to the Michael Angelos, and the Scuderies to the Corneilles.

It is not to these that I address myself, but to men of law, properly so called,—to logicians, to reasoners; to those who love the penalty of death for its beauty, its goodness, its grace!

Let them give their reasons.

Those who judge and condemn say that "punishment by death is necessary,—first, because it is requisite to remove from the social community a member which has already injured it, and might injure it again."

If this be all, perpetual imprisonment would suffice. What is the use of inflicting death? You argue that a prisoner may escape from gaol,—keep watch more strictly! If you do not believe in the solidity of iron bars, how do you venture to have menageries? Let there be no executioner where the jailer can be sufficient.

They continue, "But society must avenge itself, society must punish."

Neither one nor the other; *vengeance* is an individual act, and *punishment* belongs to God. Society is between the two; punishment is above its power, retaliation beneath it. Society should not punish, to avenge itself; it should correct, to ameliorate others!

Their third and last reason remains, the theory of example. "We must make examples. By the sight of the fate inflicted on criminals, we must shock those who might otherwise be tempted to imitate them!"

Well, in the first place, I deny the power of the example. I deny that the sight of executions produces the desired effect. Far from edifying the common people, it demoralizes and ruins their feeling, injuring every virtue; proofs of this abound and would encumber my argument if I chose to cite them. I will allude to only one fact, amongst a thousand, because it is of recent occurrence. It happened only ten days back from the present moment when I am writing; namely, on the 5th of March, the last day of the Carnival. At St. Pol, immediately after the execution of an incendiary named Louis Camus, *a group of Masqueraders came and danced round the still reeking scaffold*!

Make, then, your fine examples! Shrove Tuesday will turn them into jest!

If, notwithstanding all experience, you still hold to the theory of example, then give us back the Sixteenth Century; be in reality formidable. Restore to us a variety of suffering; restore us Farinacci; restore us the sworn torturers; restore us the gibbet, the wheel, the block, the rack, the thumb-screw, the live-burial vault, the burning cauldron; restore us in the streets of Paris, as the most open shop among the rest, the hideous stall of the Executioner, constantly full of human flesh; give us back Montfaucon, its caves of bones, its beams, its crooks, its chains, its rows of skeletons; give us back, in its permanence and power, that gigantic outhouse of the Paris Executioner! This indeed would be wholesale example; this would be "punishment by death," well understood; this would be a system of execution in some proportion,—which, while it is horrible, is also terrible!

But do you seriously suppose you are making an example, when you take the life of a poor wretch, in the most deserted part of the exterior Boulevards, at eight o'clock in the morning?

Do not you see then, that your public executions are done in private? That fear is with the execution, and not among the multitude? One is sometimes tempted to believe, that the advocates for capital punishment have not thoroughly considered in what it consists. But place in the scales, against any crime whatever, this exorbitant right, which society arrogates to itself, of taking away that which it did not bestow: that most irreparable of evils!

The alternatives are these: First, the man you destroy is without family, relations, or friends, in the world. In this case, he has received neither education nor instruction; no care has been bestowed either on his mind or heart; then, by what right would you kill this miserable orphan? You punish him because his infancy trailed on the ground, without stem, or support: you make him pay the penalty of the isolated position in which you left him! you make a crime of his misfortune! No one taught him to know what he was doing; this man lived in ignorance: the fault was in his destiny, not himself. You destroy one who is innocent.

Or, Secondly,—the man has a family; and then do you think the fatal stroke wounds him alone?—that his father, his mother, or his children will not suffer by it? In killing him, you vitally injure all his family: and thus again you punish the innocent.

Blind and ill-directed penalty; which, on whatever side it turns, strikes the innocent!

Imprison for life this culprit who has a family: in his cell he can still work for those who belong to him. But how can he help them from the depth of the tomb? And can you reflect without shuddering, on what will become of those young children, from whom you take away their father, their support? Do you not feel that they must fall into a career of vice?

In the Colonies, when a slave is condemned to public execution, there are a thousand francs of indemnity paid to the proprietor of the man! What, you compensate a master, and you do not indemnify a family! In this country, do you not take the man from those who possess him? Is he not, by a much more sacred tie than master and slave, the property of his father, the wealth of his wife, the fortune of his children?

I have already proved your law guilty of assassination; I have now convicted it of robbery!

And then another consideration. Do you consider the soul of this man? Do you know in what state it is, that you dismiss it so hastily?

This may be called "sentimental reasoning," by some disdainful logicians, who draw their arguments only from their minds. I often prefer the reasonings of the heart; and certainly the two should always go together. Reason is on our side, feeling is on our side, and experience is on our side. In those States where punishment by death is abolished, the mass of capital crime has yearly a progressive decrease. Let this fact have its weight.

I do not advocate, however, a sudden and complete abolition of the penalty of death, such as was so heedlessly attempted in the Chamber of Deputies. On the contrary, I desire every precaution, every experiment, every suggestion of prudence: besides, in addition to this gradual change, I would have the whole penal code examined, and reformed; and time is a great ingredient requisite to make such a work complete. But independently of a partial abolition of death in cases of forgery, incendiarism, minor thefts, et cætera, I would wish that, from the present time, in all the greater offences, the Judge should be obliged to propose the following question to the Jury: "Has the accused acted from Passion, or Interest?" And in case the Jury decide "the accused acted from Passion," then there should be no sentence of death.

Let not the opposite party deceive themselves; this question of the penalty of death gains ground every day. Before long, the world will unanimously solve it on the side of mercy. During the past century, punishments have become gradually milder: the rack has disappeared, the wheel has disappeared; and now the Guillotine is shaken. This mistaken punishment will leave France; and may it go to some barbarous people,— not to Turkey, which is becoming civilized, not to the savages, for they will not have it;[9] but let it descend some steps of the ladder of civilization, and take refuge in Spain, or Russia!

In the early ages, the social edifice rested on three columns, Superstition, Tyranny, Cruelty. A long time ago a voice exclaimed, "Superstition has departed!" Lately another voice has cried, "Tyranny has departed!" It is now full time that a third voice shall be raised to say, "The Executioner has departed!"

Thus the barbarous usages of the olden times fall one by one; thus Providence completes modern regeneration.

To those who regret Superstition, we say, "God remains for us!" To those who regret Tyranny, we say, "Our Country remains!" But to those who could regret the Executioner we can say nothing.

Let it not be supposed that social order will depart with the scaffold; the social building will not fall from wanting this hideous keystone. Civilization is nothing but a series of transformations. For what then do I ask your aid? The civilization of penal laws. The gentle laws of Christ will penetrate at last into the Code, and shine through its enactments. We shall look on crime as a disease, and its physicians shall displace the judges, its hospitals displace the Galleys. Liberty and health shall be alike. We shall pour balm and oil where we formerly applied iron and fire; evil will be treated in charity, instead of in anger. This change will be simple and sublime.

The Cross shall displace the Gibbet.

FOOTNOTES:

[1] The Gypsy form of marriage.

[2] There were grave differences between Denmark and Sweden, because Count d'Ahlefeld insisted, during the negotiation of a treaty between the two States, that the Danish king should be addressed as *rex Gothorum*, which apparently attributed to him supremacy over Gothland, a Swedish province; while the Swedes persisted in styling him *rex Gotorum*, a vague title, equivalent to the ancient name of Danish sovereigns, — King of the Goths. It is probably to this "h" — the cause not of a war, but of long and threatening negotiations — that Schumacker alluded.

[3] Certain chroniclers assert that in 1525 a bishop of Borglum made himself notorious by his depredations. He is said to have kept pirates in his pay, who infested the coast of Norway.

[4] According to popular superstition, Nistheim was the hell reserved for those who died of disease or old age.

[5] This forcible passage scarcely requires the explanation that in France a parricide has the right hand taken off, prior to execution, and all criminals about to be guillotined have their hair removed, lest the axe might be impeded, and cause extra suffering.

[6] The translator having a detestation of "slang idiom" in any language has declined the task of rendering this prison-song into English; not from any actual indecorum being in its clever though coarse composition, but from a doubt of any advantage to be obtained by familiarizing the reading public with the idiom of a Gaol, and which was doubtless invented for the concealment and furtherance of immoral or criminal purposes.

It has become a sort of fashion of the hour to descend from the utmost refinement of sentiment, or the most elevated speculation of philosophy, to grovel and almost revel in the phraseology hitherto confined to the obscure haunts of crime. In order to render justice to M. Victor Hugo's versatile powers, his skilful imitation of a low ballad shall be given here, in the original, the translator only disliking to be the means of interrupting the refined illusion arising from the author's elegant conception of the "Condemned." The general meaning of the song is given afterwards in the text.

SONG OF THE YOUNG GIRL OF THE PRISON.

I.

C'est dans la rue du Mail, Lirlonfa malurette,
Où j'ai été coltigé, Maluré,
Par trois coquins du railles, lirlonfa malurette,
Sur mes sique' ont foncé, lirlonfa maluré.

II.

Ils m'ont mis la tartouve, lirlonfa malurette,
Grand Meudon est aboulé, lirlonfa maluré;
Dans mon trimin rencontre, lirlonfa malurette,
Un peigre du quartier, lirlonfa maluré.

III.

Va-t'en dire à ma largue, lirlonfa malurette,
Que je suis enfourraillé, lirlonfa maluré.
Ma largue tout en colère, lirlonfa malurette,
M'dit: Qu' as-tu donc morfillé? lirlonfa maluré.

IV.

J'ai fait suer un chêne, lirlonfa malurette,
Son auberg j'ai enganté, lirlonfa maluré.
Son auberg et sa toquante, lirlonfa malurette,
Et ses attach 's de cés, lirlonfa maluré.

V.

Ma largu' part pour Versailles, lirlonfa malurette,
Aux pieds d' sa Majesté, lirlonfa maluré.
Elle lu fonce un babillard, lirlonfa malurette,
Pour m' fair' defourrailler, lirlonfa maluré.

VI.

Ah! si j'en défourraille, lirlonfa malurette,
Ma largue j'entiferai, lirlonfa maluré.
J'li ferai porter fontange, lirlonfa malurette,
Et souliers galuchés, lirlonfa maluré.

VII.

Mais grand dabe qui s'fâche lirlonfa malurette,
Dit: par mon caloquet, lirlonfa maluré,
J'li ferai danser une danse, lirlonfa malurette,
Où il n'y a pas de plancher, lirlonfa maluré.

[7] The Ministers, who were afterwards imprisoned in the fortress of Ham.

[8] La Porte says twenty-two strokes, but Aubery says thirty-four. Monsieur de Chalais shrieked until the twentieth.

[9] The Parliament of Otaheite have just abolished capital punishment.